+|2|

D0787782

MURDER IN THE CLOISTER

Also by Tania Bayard

The Christine de Pizan mysteries

IN THE PRESENCE OF EVIL *
IN THE SHADOW OF THE ENEMY *
IN THE COMPANY OF FOOLS *

Non-fiction

A MEDIEVAL HOME COMPANION
SWEET HERBS AND SUNDRY FLOWERS

* *available from Severn House*

MURDER
IN THE
CLOISTER

Tania Bayard

SEVERN
HOUSE

First world edition published in Great Britain and the USA in 2021
by Severn House, an imprint of Canongate Books Ltd,
14 High Street, Edinburgh EH1 1TE.

Trade paperback edition first published in Great Britain and the USA in 2021
by Severn House, an imprint of Canongate Books Ltd.

severnhouse.com

British Library Cataloguing-in-Publication Data
A CIP catalogue record for this title is available from the British Library.

ISBN-13: 978-0-7278-8945-4 (cased)
ISBN-13: 978-1-78029-757-6 (trade paper)
ISBN-13: 978-1-4483-0495-0 (e-book)

All Severn House titles are printed on acid-free paper.

Typeset by Palimpsest Book Production Ltd.,
Falkirk, Stirlingshire, Scotland.
Printed and bound in Great Britain by
TJ Books Limited, Padstow, Cornwall.

PROLOGUE

The Royal Priory of Saint-Louis at Poissy. Late March, 1399

Matins and Lauds (early morning, before daylight)

This office is observed so that the first motions of the soul and mind may be dedicated to God, and so that we admit nothing else into our minds before we have rejoiced in the thought of God.

Saint Basil, fourth century

The young nun was nearly alone in the dark dormitory. One other sister, who'd been ill, lay snoring at the far end of the cavernous room, but the sound was so far away it hardly reached her. Everyone else, shaken out of sleep by Sister Claude, had gone to the church to chant matins and lauds. She'd been excused because she'd just returned from a journey, and the prioress, seeing how tired she was, had given her permission to stay in bed. She'd intended to tell the prioress something, but she'd fallen asleep before she could say it. It would have to wait until morning.

Lumps in the flocking of her mattress dug into her back, and the unfinished wool of her blanket scratched her face, but in spite of the discomfort she fell into a deep, dreamless sleep. Then, all of a sudden, she was awake. She lay in the darkness, breathing air so cold it stung her nostrils, and tried to think what had disturbed her. She reached for an embroidered tapestry that was used as a bed cover during the day and curled up under it, pressing her hands against her stomach. The bed shook as her body was racked by sobs.

After a while, the weeping subsided, and she lay quietly in darkness so complete it seemed to weigh on her, pressing her down into the hard mattress, drawing her into an abyss. She felt as though she were enclosed in a coffin, wanting to scream but unable to make a sound.

Then she saw a light. It floated through the gloom, emitting a faint crackling sound. She sat up and stared through the darkness as it came close, then moved away. She rose and followed it out of the dormitory into a passageway beside the church. She could hear the other sisters chanting in the choir, and she thought she should join them, but the light beckoned, drawing her away, out into the cloister, across a lawn wet with rain, and under the branches of a huge pine tree whose water-laden branches grazed her cheeks. The light stopped. She saw a small dog. She reached out for it, but an unseen hand pulled it away. Then there were two figures, and the dog was circling them. She reached for the dog again and caught its collar. The collar broke. She felt a sharp pain in her chest. She cried out and fell to the ground.

Prime (first morning light)

After morning prayers let it not be lawful to return to sleep; but when matins are finished let prime be said forthwith. Then let all employ themselves in reading until the third hour.

Saint Aurelian, sixth century

After matins and lauds, none of the sisters returned to the dormitory for more sleep because they'd been summoned to the chapter house to confess their faults and receive their penances. Silence reigned in the dormitory as the first morning light came through the windows and revealed row upon row of empty beds.

Terce (mid-morning)

The Holy Ghost descended on the disciples at the third hour.

Saint Cyprian, third century

At nine, the sisters filed back into the choir for terce. Only then did they notice that someone was missing. They looked at the prioress, but she turned away. The chantress raised her hand to gain the attention of those sisters whose attention had wandered.

Sext (midday)

The Lord was crucified at the sixth hour.

Saint Cyprian, third century

After the office of sext, they assembled for mass. Then they gathered for the midday meal. The prioress remained in her own residence, so they were not able to question her about the missing sister.

Nones (mid-afternoon)

At the ninth hour Christ washed away our sins with His blood.

Saint Cyprian, third century

At nones, the sisters filed into the choir again. The prioress and the infirmaress were not with them.

Vespers (sunset)

The Eucharist was delivered to the apostles by the Lord the Savior in the evening.

Saint Cassian, fourth century

After vespers, the sisters were called to the chapter house, where the prioress told them that one of the novices had unexpectedly died. They were not to mourn, but to rejoice, because Sister Thérèse was now with the Blessed Mother in Heaven.

Compline (before going to bed)

With what hope will you come to the season of night; with what dreams will you expect to converse, if you have not walled yourself round with prayers to keep you safe?

Saint Chrysostom, fourth century

Each sister prayed fervently for protection throughout the night, for who could say that she might not be taken without warning, like Sister Thérèse.

ONE

Paris, the first week of April, 1399

> *Since my youth and earlier occupations were behind me, I
> returned to what most suited me – a life of solitude and
> tranquility.*
>
> Christine de Pizan, *L'advision Christine*, 1405

I t rained every day. Sometimes the water poured down so heavily
the trees bent under the sudden weight of it. At other times,
the drops fell lightly for days, and the sound of the incessant
dripping nearly drove people mad. The gloom that enveloped Paris
invaded Christine's house, where Francesca was preoccupied with
the rain, peering out first thing every morning to see if it had
stopped and then muttering imprecations as she slammed the door
against the never-ending stream of water. She told everyone to
watch out for ants. 'If you see one, don't step on it!' she cried.
'Stepping on ants causes rain.'

Francesca was even more downcast because she missed two of
her grandchildren: Jean, Christine's older son, now fifteen, who'd
gone to England as a companion for a rich man's child, and Marie,
Christine's eighteen-year-old daughter, who'd become a Dominican
nun at the Royal Priory of Saint-Louis at Poissy. Christine felt their
absence deeply, too, but she kept her feelings to herself. She told
her mother she should be happy: Jean was living in luxury in a
wealthy man's home, and Marie was doing exactly what she'd
always wanted to do.

Francesca was not comforted. 'The house is so lonely without
them,' she muttered to herself early one morning as she tried to
push parsley seeds into the wet soil of the little garden she tended
behind the house. '*Maledizione!*' she cried as the seeds stuck to her
finger. 'Nothing goes right, now that those two are gone.'

The hired girl, Georgette, stood at the kitchen door, very pregnant and reluctant to go outside where she might slip in the mud and fall. 'At least Jean and Marie are alive, not like my poor brother,' she said, referring to her brother Colin, who'd died in the disastrous crusade against the infidels at Nicopolis three years earlier.

'I am so sorry, Georgette.' Francesca said as she made her way through the muck to the door and put her arms around the girl. 'I miss Colin, too. I wish he had not volunteered to go on that foolish campaign.'

Georgette, who had married her beau, Robin, one of the palace guards, and was now expecting their first child, covered her face with her hands and started to cry. 'He wanted to take care of the horses. Poor Colin. I wish I'd been nicer to him. He had some nonsensical ways, but he meant well.'

'You must not be sad. You have Robin, and soon there will be a little one to care for.' Francesca wiped her muddy hands on her apron. 'Come with me. I know what will cheer you.'

Georgette followed Francesca into the kitchen and watched her light a taper in the flames of the fireplace and hold it in front of one of the copper pots hanging on the wall. As the reflection of the taper's flame flickered over the surface of the pot, Francesca stared at it as if in a trance. She grasped Georgette's arm. 'Do you see it?' she asked. 'There! In the flames! It is Colin's face! I often see my husband this way. You can do the same with your brother.'

Georgette stared at the reflection. 'I think I see him. Hold the taper closer.'

'You two will be accused of necromancy!' Christine cried as she stormed into the kitchen, followed by her son, Thomas, her niece, Lisabetta, and the family's two dogs, Goblin and Berith. 'Do you know what happens to necromancers?'

'*I* do,' Thomas said. 'They get burned at the stake for trying to call up the dead. Sometimes, just before they die, they cry out and say they're sorry, but nobody believes them.'

'How do you know that?' Christine asked.

'I've seen them.' At fourteen, Thomas knew where to look for all the hangings, burnings, and other gruesome punishments that took place at the city's street crossings and open spaces.

Georgette started to cry again. 'Don't talk about those things. I don't want to think of people dying. I just want to see Colin again!'

'Don't feel so sorry for yourself,' Thomas said. 'You've lost a brother. The king has lost his mind. Don't you think that's worse?'

'I don't know,' Georgette wailed. Lisabetta, who was eleven, put her arms around her and started to cry, too.

'That's not an apt comparison, Thomas,' Christine said. She took the taper from her mother's hand. 'Don't you have anything better to do, Mama?'

Francesca sighed and sat down on the bench by the table. 'It is the rain, *Cristina*. Will it never stop?'

Christine didn't mind the rain. It gave her an excuse to stay at home. She earned her living as a scribe, often working at the court, but now that she had a little money, she'd gained enough confidence to think she might be able to support herself and her family with her own writing. At home, she had to listen to her mother holding forth about her outrageous superstitions, Georgette weeping for her brother, Thomas telling silly jokes and Lisabetta worrying that her father, who'd gone to Italy to settle some family affairs, was never going to come back. But any of that was better than the turmoil at the court, where the king had gone mad, his uncles battled for power, and the queen was always in tears. At home, she could at least go to her room, close the door, and concentrate on her writing.

'The rain will stop someday, Mama. In the meantime, I'm going to make the most of the opportunity to stay here.'

'I am glad when you do not go to the court. There is evil there. But if you are going to stay at home, you might help with the housework.'

'You know I hate housework. I'm too old to start fussing around in the kitchen and trying to sew straight seams.'

'So what are you going to do?'

'I'm going to finish the poem I started yesterday.'

'I don't think so,' Thomas said. He'd gone to the front door to see if it was still raining, and he'd come running back followed by a messenger who bowed to Christine and said, 'The king requests your presence at the palace immediately.'

TWO

*Oh Fortune . . . the force of your gale threw him to the ground
so violently that he lay there from that time on, his feathers
and his whole body ripped apart.*

Christine de Pizan, *L'advision Christine*, 1405

Christine was used to being summoned to the palace. In the past, when Georgette's brother, Colin, had been the messenger, Francesca had always warned her not to go. 'The palace is infested with sorcerers and magicians,' she'd say. 'They claim they can cure the king, but they are really putting spells on him.' Colin loved this kind of talk and encouraged Francesca to tell him more. But now Francesca was silent. She sat on the bench and stared at the solemn young man dressed in a green tunic with black sleeves – the king's livery – as he stood waiting for Christine, who'd gone upstairs to put on a suitable gown, a starched linen headdress, and a cloak to keep off the rain.

Thomas and Lisabetta sat at the table and stared, too. Georgette began chopping onions, keeping her head lowered and muttering, 'Who needs clothes like that? Colin was fine without them.' Then she broke down and wept. The messenger didn't move a muscle. 'I wonder what he'd do if I pinched him,' Thomas whispered to Lisabetta. The messenger stood straighter than before, but the corners of his mouth twitched.

Christine came back carrying a scarf to put over her headdress. 'You will not need that,' the messenger said. 'The king has sent a covered carriage for you.'

Thomas let out a whoop, Lisabetta giggled, and Francesca gasped, but Christine and the messenger were out the door before anyone could speak. Standing in the street was a four-wheeled carriage decorated with broom flowers and white stags, the king's devices. The magnificent vehicle, the roof and sides of which were covered with densely woven woolen cloth to keep the rain off its passengers, was drawn by two large brown horses who pawed the ground and shifted uneasily as the messenger helped Christine into her seat. She rode away, oblivious to the fact that her mother, Georgette, Thomas, Lisabetta, Goblin, and Berith were standing in the rain in front of her house watching her go.

The messenger stood at the front of the carriage and looked at her shyly. She smiled, hoping that would encourage him to say something. She missed Colin and his incessant chatter. He drew a deep breath. 'I know who you are, *Madame*. My late grandfather worked for the old king, and he told me about your father.'

'How did he know my father?'

'My grandfather was a footman, and he was often with the king when his doctors visited him. My grandfather told me that, of all the physicians, your father was the best.'

Christine was not surprised. Her father had been summoned from Italy to the court of Charles the Fifth in Paris because of his impressive reputation. She and her family had lived at the royal palace, the Hôtel Saint-Pol, when she was a child, and she knew how much the old king had relied on Thomas de Pizan for medical as well as astrological advice.

'Your father was a great man,' the messenger said.

'As was the old king,' Christine said. She looked away, because any further discussion might lead to indiscreet talk about Charles the Fifth's son. She sat back in her seat, listened to the sound of the horses' hooves sloshing through the puddles that filled the street, and thought of King Charles the Sixth, who'd gone mad seven years earlier. It had happened suddenly, and no one knew why. Nor did anyone know what to do about it. To Christine, Charles seemed like a bird that had been attacked by a violent wind and so brutally dismembered that he could never be put back together again. He had brief periods of relief, but even then he was withdrawn and dejected, never seeming to completely understand what was going on around him. After the terrible defeat and slaughter of the French crusaders at Nicopolis, he'd fallen into an especially severe state of madness, and although at the moment he was somewhat recovered, it was obvious that he would never be well again.

She heard a clamor in the street and peered out through an opening in the carriage cover to see a group of Cistercian monks carrying a piece of cloth up the rue Saint-Antoine, the street that led to the palace. She'd heard about those monks. They claimed the cloth they carried was the shroud of Christ, capable of curing the king of his madness. The king had not yet touched the shroud, but ordinary people were convinced of its miraculous powers, and they followed the monks around, begging to be allowed to lay their hands on it. Christine knew that a piece of cloth – she doubted it was a real shroud – would not help the king any more than the potion of crushed pearls two Augustinian monks had tried the year before, or the magical book a sorcerer had carried all the way from Guienne to Paris before that. Even one of the king's own doctors had tried sorcery. All these charlatans had been brutally punished – burned at the stake or decapitated, their heads stuck on lances and displayed around the city. *Those Cistercian monks will meet a similar fate*, she said to herself.

The carriage stopped in front of the queen's residence. 'I thought it was the king who summoned me,' Christine said to the messenger as he helped her down.

'It was indeed the king. But he is with the queen, so you will have your audience here.' He took off his cloak and held it over her head as they hurried through the rain to the entrance.

'The king and queen are waiting for you,' the burly *portier* said as he opened the door. She went into the entrance hall, removed her cloak, and stepped into a great gallery where the heavy tapestries on the walls brought back disturbing memories: many years earlier, she'd discovered a body behind one of them. She hurried past, crossed several courtyards, went through a doorway decorated with a frieze of dragons and centaurs, and climbed a winding staircase. She walked slowly when she came to the long hallway that led to the queen's apartments because she was apprehensive about what she was going to find there. Before entering, she stopped to peer in through the open door.

Queen Isabeau, wearing a simple white housecoat, sat on her day bed, her unbound black hair swirling around her face as she tried to calm the king, who sat beside her, crying and shaking. Christine had known the king since the days when she and her family had lived at the palace, and she was horrified to see what madness had done to him. His once thick blond hair was now thin and dirty, and his beard was a patchwork of stubble and bare skin. Emaciated and slovenly dressed in an embroidered houppelande that had once been elegant but was now torn and ragged, he looked more like a beggar than a king.

She looked around for the queen's ladies-in-waiting, but none of them were in attendance. Missing, too, were the queen's fools, her minstrel, and her two mutes. Without the ladies in their richly embroidered gowns and big jeweled headdresses, the fools and their ceaseless banter, the minstrel and her lute, the room was colorless, silent, and sad. The only member of the queen's entourage present was her white greyhound. The dog sat at the king's feet, looking up at him quizzically.

Christine went in and sank to her knees before the king. He stared at her and began to bite his fingernails. She felt a shiver go down her spine.

'Sire, do you not remember me? We played together when we were children.'

Charles looked at his hand, which was bleeding where he'd bitten his nails down to the quick, and wept. 'I don't recall. But if you knew me as a child, tell me what I was like.'

She wanted to tell him he'd been healthy and strong, good at hunting, jousting, and war games, a kind and loving little boy everyone thought would grow up to be a great king. But before she could say anything, the queen spoke.

'This is Christine, Sire, Thomas de Pizan's daughter. We asked her to come here.' She took her husband's hand and stroked it.

The king slumped against his wife and gazed at Christine. 'Yes, yes, I remember now. Tell her to rise. Get on with what you have to ask her.'

Isabeau had a letter in her hand. She held it up and said to Christine, 'The prioress of the priory at Poissy has written, asking for you.'

'Is it my daughter?'

The queen shook her head. 'This has nothing to do with your daughter. She is safe and well. The prioress wants you to go to her and copy a manuscript.'

'But many people copy manuscripts for the sisters!'

'Then you will be one of them. And since your daughter is at the priory, no one will think your presence odd.'

Christine didn't know what to say. She could think of no reason why the prioress would need her to come and copy a manuscript. *Does it perhaps have something to do with the king's daughter?* she asked herself. She'd always wondered about the child, who'd been promised to the priory from the moment she was born – a sacrifice, it seemed, a wild hope that in exchange God might give the king back his sanity. The promise had been fulfilled in the summer of 1397, when the princess, not yet five years old, had been brought to Poissy and given over to the nuns. The king had received nothing in return. Instead, his condition had worsened. Christine remembered that summer with sadness, for, against her wishes, her own daughter had entered the priory at that time. Unlike the king's daughter, who had not had any say in the matter, Marie had chosen the cloistered life on her own.

The queen was waiting for her to speak. Christine was torn. She was anxious to see her daughter, but she was not sure she wanted to go to Poissy, which was half a day's ride from Paris, just at the moment when she'd begun to concentrate on her writing.

The king suddenly sat up straight, clenching his hands together to keep them still. The greyhound sprang up and pawed at his leg. Charles smiled, looking more like the person he'd been before he'd fallen ill, and stroked the dog's head gently. Then he spoke, much to Christine's surprise, because she wasn't sure he'd been following the conversation.

'You will not go alone,' he said. 'Brother Michel from the Abbey of Saint-Denis will go with you. I know he is a friend of yours.' The greyhound lay down on the floor and rolled over on to his back. The king bent down and rubbed his stomach. Then, still bending over the dog, he looked up at Christine and spoke again. 'Brother Michel will be helpful because he knows the friars who live at the priory and serve the sisters. And to keep you safe, you will have Henri Le Picart, who is eager to offer his help.'

Christine started to remonstrate. She disliked and mistrusted Henri Le Picart, who seemed to turn up every time she became involved in events at the court. The disagreeable little man had no respect for women and he always seemed to be contradicting and mocking her. He'd been a friend of her father's, but her mother detested him as much as she did.

'Henri is a fine man. It will be good to have him by your side,' the queen said.

'I think Brother Michel would be able to protect me,' Christine said.

The king stopped petting the greyhound. The dog rolled over and nuzzled his leg, trying to get his attention again. Charles pushed him away, got up from the bed, and stood before Christine. The smell of his unwashed body sickened her. 'It is my command,' he said.

'Then I will do as you ask,' she said meekly.

'So it is settled,' Isabeau said. 'I will send a message to the prioress to let her know you are coming. Will you go tomorrow?'

'If you wish,' Christine said, wondering what she was going to tell her mother. She curtsied and left the room. As she walked slowly down the long corridor away from the queen's apartments, her head bowed in thought, she heard footsteps behind her. She turned to find the queen's dwarf, Alips.

'I heard,' Alips said.

Christine had to smile. Alips was so small she could hide behind the furniture and listen to conversations no one was meant to hear. She made no secret of this; even the queen knew, and she didn't seem to mind, for she was fond of the dwarf, who was privy to her deepest thoughts.

Alips stood on her toes and pulled Christine's face down close to hers. 'There's more to this than they're telling you,' she whispered. 'Something is wrong at Poissy, and they're willing to do what the prioress asks because they're concerned for their daughter.'

'Doesn't the princess have someone to look after her?' Christine asked.

'One of the nuns is her constant companion. But that doesn't mean she's free from danger.'

'What danger?' Christine asked.

'I don't know.'

'Does anyone else know about this?'

'I don't think so. I heard only the king and queen talking about it. Unfortunately, they whispered, so I didn't hear everything. All I can tell you is they're afraid of something. It must be serious if they're sending Brother Michel and Henri Le Picart with you. You'd better be careful.'

Christine thought of her mother. Francesca would never believe her daughter was going to the priory just to copy a manuscript. She always told Christine she should be afraid when the queen sent for her.

She may be right this time, Christine thought.

THREE

I have a daughter who, as everyone says, is beautiful and gentle, young, intelligent, and gracious. She is a nun in a rich, sumptuous, and delightful royal abbey.

Christine de Pizan, *Le Livre du Dit de Poissy*, 1400

'That's ridiculous, Mama. What place could be safer than a priory?' Christine threw down the carrot she was peeling and glared at her mother.

'I have a feeling about it. You are putting yourself in danger if you go there.'

'You always have those feelings. I suppose you had a dream about it, too.'

Francesca fiddled with the strings of her apron. 'I did.'

Christine sighed. 'I don't want to hear it.'

Her mother took off her apron and sat down on the bench by the table. 'It has to do with Marie. She was crying.'

Christine clasped her hands together and prepared for what she knew was coming. When Marie had entered the priory of Poissy two years earlier, Francesca had pleaded with her not to let it happen. 'A woman cannot be happy unless she is married, with children,' she'd said. But Christine had informed her that Marie had the right to make up her own mind. Then Francesca had resorted to warnings that Marie would be especially unhappy because the priory of Poissy was reserved for daughters of the nobility, and she wouldn't fit in. It was true that most of the nuns were from noble families. The king had made an exception for Marie because of the family's association with the court. 'The king has made a mistake,' Francesca had wailed. 'Everyone will come to regret it.' But none of her objections had any effect: Marie had entered the priory, without all the ceremony that would have been accorded the daughter of a noble family, but with a determination that Christine had to admire.

'Why was she crying?'

'She is unhappy. Why else would she be crying?'

'Then you should be glad I'm going. I'll be able to find out what's wrong.'

'It is such a long journey, *Cristina*.'

'It's not so far. I'll be there in half a day.' Christine smiled. She suddenly realized that she was glad to have this opportunity to go to Poissy. She hadn't seen her daughter since she'd left, and she missed her.

Francesca sniffed and got up from the bench. She put on her apron again and strode out into the garden. Christine watched as she gathered up several pots of violets, came back into the kitchen, and set them on the table. The flowers had been beaten down by the rain, and Christine wondered out loud whether they would survive.

Francesca wiped her muddy hands on her apron. 'Of course they will survive, now that I have brought them in. Do not pick one. It is bad luck to pick a single violet.'

'Where did you learn that?'

'I do not remember. But I am sure it is true.'

Christine went to the door and looked out. Goblin and Berith were racing around in the mud, trying to follow the rivulets that flowed through the garden beds. Little Goblin's white coat had turned dirty brown, and black Berith had been transformed into a big brown bear.

'You planted lettuce seeds yesterday, Mama. What happened to them?'

Francesca shook her head. 'All washed away. Now I will have to do it all over again. But what does it matter? Perhaps you will not be here to eat it if you go on this dangerous journey.'

'It's not dangerous. And I'll have Brother Michel and Henri Le Picart for company.'

'I suppose Michel will be helpful, but Henri Le Picart?' She threw up her hands. 'I do not trust him.'

The dogs came in, shaking themselves and spraying water and mud everywhere.

'Besides, you have to go through a forest. Who knows what will be lurking there!'

'There might be a sorcerer. One was arrested in a forest last year,' said Thomas, who'd just come in.

'That sorcerer is dead. He was burned at the stake,' Christine said.

'I know. I saw it. They burned all his books of magic, too. They made a splendid fire.'

'That's enough, Thomas!' Christine cried. 'And besides, he was practicing sorcery in a forest in Brie, not Poissy.'

'There's a forest near Poissy, too. Another sorcerer could be in there.'

Francesca reached up to an overhead rack and pulled down a dried plant that was shedding its dusty leaves. She handed it to Christine, who coughed and asked, 'What is it?'

'Artemisia. Take it with you to ward off sorcerers.'

Christine sneezed and brushed her mother's hand away. 'You know I don't believe in things like that.'

'Take me,' Thomas cried. 'I'll protect you better than any old plant.'

'You weren't invited,' Christine said. 'Where would you stay?'

'With me,' said a voice from the other side of the kitchen. A man with a little black beard and a black cape with a long hood and an ermine collar stood at the door. When Christine saw who it was, she stamped her foot.

'Why are you here now?' she asked. 'We don't leave until tomorrow.'

'I wanted to see how your preparations are coming along,' Henri Le Picart said. 'I hear your son would like to come with you. I'm bringing a little palfrey for you, and I can just as easily bring a larger horse for Thomas.'

Thomas jumped up and down with excitement.

'No one said you could go,' Francesca said.

'Oh, let him,' Henri said. 'He'll be safe with me.'

Francesca turned away, mumbling to herself. 'I have never liked the man.'

Henri heard, and he laughed. 'I'm just as acceptable as Christine's other friends.'

'You aren't my friend,' Christine said.

'Who are your friends, then?'

'*Prostituti e reprobi*,' Francesca muttered.

'I heard that, Mama. First of all, you know Marion isn't a prostitute anymore. And second, the reprobates, as you call them, are Marion's friends, not mine, and they haven't done you any harm.'

Francesca stomped up the stairs.

'Admirable woman,' Henri said. 'Even though she doesn't like me.'

'I don't like you either,' Christine said. 'It was not my idea to have you accompany me to Poissy. But since you are determined to do so, why don't you go away so I can prepare for the trip?'

'Gladly. Just be ready first thing tomorrow morning. You, too,

Thomas.' Henri turned and left. Christine went upstairs to gather together her clothes, pack her writing materials, and fume.

FOUR

The church, built in the most pleasing manner, is in the town of Poissy, six leagues from Paris.

Christine de Pizan, *Le Livre du Dit de Poissy*, 1400

V ery early the next morning, Henri arrived on a big black destrier, leading a dun-colored rouncey for Thomas and a brown palfrey for Christine. Thomas helped Christine on to the palfrey, then mounted the rouncey, eager to get started. Christine, who liked horses and had been an excellent rider all her life, patted the palfrey's neck and whispered into its ear, 'Go slowly. If we stay behind, I won't have to talk to that man.'

'We'll meet Brother Michel on the rue Saint-Antoine,' Henri said. He bowed to Francesca, who ignored him, and waved to Georgette, who stood by the door looking heavy and uncomfortable. 'That girl will be a mother before you return,' he said to Christine. She turned the palfrey's head and started down the street. Goblin and Berith ran after her, barking and nipping at the horse's heels.

For a change, the day was sunny, and the streets, glistening with rain from the night before, were coming alive. Women swept water from their doorsteps, vendors hawked pork pies and cheese pasties, and horsemen urged their mounts through crowds of early morning shoppers. Brother Michel, on a large brown mule, was waiting for them on the rue Saint-Antoine, pretending he didn't see several old crones who were watching him and smiling because they believed they'd have good luck after seeing a black monk so early in the morning. Henri spurred his horse and raced past Christine, and Michel followed, his mule going nearly as fast as the horse, his black cloak flying out behind him. People cursed as they tried to escape from the mud splashing up from the animals' hooves.

Henri led them down the rue du roi de Sicile and on to the rue de la Verrerie, where the glassmakers were just opening their shops. He sped past the church of Saint-Merry, across the rue Saint-Martin, and on down to Les Halles. At the crossing of the rue Saint-Honoré and the rue de l'Arbre-Sec, he laughed when he saw a fresh corpse swinging on a gallows. Thomas laughed with him, and Christine was sorry she'd let this man get anywhere near her son.

They turned on to the rue Saint-Honoré, went down to the Porte Saint-Honoré, and passed through a gate in the city wall. Suddenly, they were in a different world – a world of wide meadows and small farmhouses, their roofs glistening in the aftermath of the rain. Tall grasses grazed the legs of the horses, and ground-nesting birds shot up into the air, screeching calls of alarm.

They crossed the Seine with its many islands and islets where the plumes of reeds swayed gently in the breeze. A lone fisherman sat on the riverbank under a silvery willow tree, watching his rod. Then they rode through a small forest, and the Seine, which went around the forest rather than through it, met them on the other side, and they crossed it a second time.

For a while, the clouds stayed away and allowed the sun to shine. The grass sparkled, and in its depths, spring flowers appeared. But it wasn't long before the rain fell again, first gently, then in torrents. Christine pulled her wool cloak over her head, and the thick fabric kept her dry. Twice more they crossed the Seine, which followed a more circuitous route than theirs. Each time, the river seemed to have risen higher than before, and she wondered how long it would be before it overflowed its banks.

She was glad when they came to another forest and the shelter of the new leaves of trees growing so close together that much of the rain never reached the ground. 'This is the forest of Saint-Germain-en-Laye,' Henri said.

'I've never seen such big trees,' Thomas said. 'What are they?'

'Oak, beech, hornbeam, and chestnut.'

Thomas looked around, hardly able to contain his excitement.

Henri laughed. 'Are you expecting to see the sorcerer?'

Thomas blushed. 'Do you think I'm stupid? The sorcerer burned in Paris last year was caught in another forest, in Brie.'

Henri chuckled. 'Someone could be hiding among these trees, too. The sorcerer had an assistant who was never caught.'

Christine shuddered.

Michel said, 'That's enough, Henri.'

'The sorcerer's name was Jean of Bar,' Henri continued. 'The assistant knows all about Jean's practices. I do, too, because Jean's confession was written down, and I've read it.'

Thomas's eyes widened.

'It's chilling,' Henri said, looking at Christine.

She shook her head.

'Your mother doesn't want me to tell you, Thomas. She doesn't like things like that.'

'I certainly don't,' Christine said, remembering the signs of sorcery that had been left around the Hôtel Saint-Pol several years earlier.

The forest seemed to draw close around them as dense fog rolled out from under the trees and swirled around their horses' feet. Over their heads, the leaves drooped under the weight of the rain.

Henri took hold of the bridle of Thomas's horse and drew him close to his own mount. 'Never mind your mother. She doesn't have to listen if she doesn't want to.'

Thomas leaned in close.

'This Jean of Bar was a man of many talents. He had demon friends, and he could call them whenever he wanted. He even imprisoned one of them in a crystal stone.'

'Did you see it?' Thomas asked.

'No. But you might have been able to. I've heard that sorcerers get little boys to invoke demons by polishing their fingernails and using them as mirrors.'

Thomas started to laugh. 'That's ridiculous. And anyway, I'm not a little boy anymore.'

'That is so,' Henri said. 'You are man enough now to find a sorcerer in this wood.'

Christine rode close to Thomas, took hold of his horse's bridle, and pulled him away. She glared at Henri, and Henri glared back, then broke out laughing.

By now they'd passed through the forest, and they looked over rolling fields to see the village of Poissy rising out of the mist.

'Where is the river?' Thomas asked Michel. 'I thought we'd have to cross it again, but I don't see it.'

'It curves around the forest, and now it's on the other side of the village. The priory is very close to it, but you can't tell from here.'

Seen from afar, Poissy appeared to be a collection of small houses and churches, dominated by one huge church with a tall spire.

Henri called out, 'That's the priory church. Isn't it a beauty?'

'Have you been here before?' Thomas asked.

'Many times.'

Christine had to admit that the church was magnificent. She'd seen it when her daughter had entered the priory as a novice, and she'd marveled at its flying buttresses, gables, turrets, pinnacles, and walls that seemed to be made of nothing but glass.

'It has so many windows!' Thomas cried.

'Wait until you see them up close. I've made a study of them. I want to learn how the glassmakers achieved those colors.'

'But how can you study them when they are all so high?'

'Passageways, Thomas. Passageways. The high parts of the church are riddled with them. You can stand in them and admire the glass to your heart's content.'

'I'd like to do that,' Thomas said.

'Perhaps you'll get a chance.'

Christine said, 'Don't listen to Henri. Men can go into only one place in the church, the transept, where people from the town attend mass. The rest of the church and the parts of the priory where the nuns live are strictly forbidden to men.'

'Does that mean that I won't be able to go in and see my sister?'

'Probably not. Will you be disappointed?'

'I guess I shouldn't be. You told me that was what would happen when she went away.' Thomas rode in silence for a while. Then he asked, 'Why does a community of nuns need such a big church?'

'Those nuns are as rich as Croesus,' Henri said. 'If you think the church is grand, wait until you see the rest of the priory.'

Christine said, 'You won't see it, Thomas. I just told you: men aren't allowed in.'

'It's like a small city, walled in and quiet as a tomb,' Henri went on.

Christine thought of her daughter, living in the silence imposed on the nuns. The idea of silence appealed to her.

Henri broke into her thoughts. 'It isn't as peaceful as it looks.'

'You just said it was as quiet as a tomb.'

Henri spurred his horse so that it wheeled around. 'So I did. But things change.' Then he charged toward the village, waving his arms and shouting to Thomas to follow. Thomas, excited, complied, and Christine blanched at the thought that he seemed to be falling under the spell of a man she disliked and distrusted. Several years earlier, she'd watched as Georgette's brother, Colin, had been beguiled by Henri and had helped him with his alchemical experiments. It had never been clear to her whether Henri was actually trying to make gold, and the exasperating little man had never been willing to tell her. She'd always suspected him of nefarious motives, and the fact that he was trying to interest Thomas in sorcery angered her. She watched with dread as the two of them rode toward the village.

Brother Michel brought his mule to her side. 'I know what you're thinking,' he said. 'I know you've never liked the man, but you are wrong to suspect him of evil.'

'What else can one think?' Christine asked. 'He seems to be involved in everything, and one ever knows what he is really doing. Now he's trying to get Thomas to think about sorcerers!' She was so exasperated that she dug her heels into her palfrey, and he lunged forward, nearly unseating her.

They crossed the fields, arrived at the walls of the village, and entered through one of the gates. The quiet countryside was suddenly replaced by noise and confusion, for the town of Poissy had a lively cattle market, and they were in the midst of it. Throngs of sheep, pigs, bulls, and cows milled around, and men rushed after them, holding their cloaks over their heads to ward off the rain and slipping in mud as they tried to keep order. After the long ride from Paris, the bellowing and shouting and the odor of dung and wet hay made Christine's head reel. She breathed a sigh of relief when they arrived at the priory, where she hoped to find peace and quiet in spite of what Henri had said.

FIVE

The prioress of this place is my indomitable, gracious lady, the king's aunt, Marie of Bourbon, who embodies everything good and casts out all vice.

Christine de Pizan, *Le Livre du Dit de Poissy*, 1400

Christine had met the prioress of Poissy when she was a child living with her family at the palace in Paris. Queen Jeanne of Bourbon, the wife of King Charles the Fifth, had died, and her sister, Marie of Bourbon, thirty-one years old and then just a nun at the priory of Poissy, had attended the funeral. She'd been a formidable presence, tall and imposing with a rather large nose and dark, hooded eyes, austere in the white wool habit, black mantle and black veil of the Dominican order. Now she was fifty-two and the prioress of Poissy. *She's probably even more intimidating than she was twenty-one years ago*, Christine said to herself.

The priory, surrounded by a high wall and entered through a huge wooden door flanked by two large round towers, resembled a fortress. Brother Michel rang a bell next to the door, and they waited, standing close to the wall in a vain attempt to escape the raindrops. Then, miraculously, the rain stopped.

An ancient man, the *portier*, appeared, smiling and bowing and adjusting his tunic. Out of the corner of her eye, Christine noticed something in a high window of one of the towers. She looked up to see a boy leaning out, watching them. The *portier* called to him, 'Come down and hold their horses, Jacques.' The boy, who appeared to be about eight years old, disappeared for a moment, then reappeared at the old man's side. 'My grandson,' the *portier* said. Jacques, dressed in a bright yellow tunic and green leggings, stepped forward, took the reins of the horses and the mule in one hand, and with the other hand patted the animals' soft noses.

'They'll be safe with him,' the *portier* said as he led his visitors through a wide courtyard to the entrance to the church. They heard singing.

'You may enter here and listen, but that is as far as you gentlemen may go,' the *portier* told Henri and Thomas. 'You, I suppose, will be with the friars who live here,' he said to Michel. Then he bowed to Christine. 'The prioress is expecting you.'

They went into the church. The sun had come out, and light flowed in through the huge colored glass windows, throwing shifting patterns of blue, red, yellow, and green on to the stones of the floor. Christine stopped, as if in a trance. The great space in which they stood, the transept, was filled with the sound of women's voices, clear and crisp, chanting, sometimes in unison, sometimes singly, on and on, with no beginning and no end, encompassing everything in an endless flow. Stunned by the exquisite colored light and the sound of the glorious singing, Christine imagined for a moment that she'd been transported to heaven. Then a cloud passed over the sun, and the light dimmed.

She felt a tug on her sleeve. 'Where are the nuns?' Thomas asked.

'You will never see them,' she said.

'But they have to be here somewhere! I hear them singing.'

Christine took his arm and led him to the center of the transept. On one side they could look into the choir with the high altar and a ring of chapels. On the other side was a latticework grille that blocked their view into the nave of the church. 'That's where the sisters are,' Christine said. 'Their choir is in the nave, behind the grille.'

Thomas went to the grille and put his ear close to it. 'In there?' he asked in a whisper.

'They're meant to be heard, not seen.'

Thomas took his mother's hand and led her to the center of the transept. 'You can hear them best from here,' he said. 'I wish they would go on forever.'

'They will,' Christine said. 'Many years ago a great king gave them this church so they would chant praises of God for him and his family endlessly.'

'Which king?'

'He was called Philip the Fair. His heart is buried in a tomb under the place where they are singing.'

'I know about him. He was the grandson of Saint Louis.'

'That's right. Philip revered his grandfather, who was born here, in a castle that stood on this spot before the church was built.'

'Some say that Louis was born where the high altar is now,' Henri said. 'It's probably just a myth.'

'I want to believe it,' Thomas said. 'It's a beautiful story.'

'So it is,' said a voice behind them, and they turned to find a nun who seemed to be looking down at them over her prominent nose. Thomas stepped back, looking frightened, until he realized that she was smiling at him. Christine had thought Marie of Bourbon forbidding when she'd first met her, but now, watching Thomas smile timidly back at her, she found her motherly, in spite of her austere countenance.

'Welcome, Christine,' the prioress said. 'It was good of you to agree to come.'

'I am happy to be here,' Christine said. 'This is my son, Thomas. And this is Brother Michel from the Abbey of Saint-Denis.'

Michel and Mother Marie broke out laughing. 'We need no introduction,' the prioress said. 'We've known each other for years.' Then she looked at Henri. 'How nice to see you again, Henri. Have you changed your mind about my ability to run this establishment?'

'Under the present circumstances, I reserve judgment,' Henri said.

He knows there's a problem here, Christine thought. *He doubts a woman, even this formidable woman, can solve it.* She was embarrassed for the prioress, but only for a moment, because the woman looked down at Henri from her greater height and said, 'Your arrogance will be your undoing one day, Henri Le Picart.'

Henri stepped back and said, 'We'll see about that.'

There's a game going on here that I don't understand, Christine said to herself. As usual, she had no idea what Henri was up to. She regretted that she would have to let Thomas stay with him.

The prioress put her finger to her lips. 'Listen to the chant,' she said. 'There is nothing like it to quiet troubled spirits.' They all stood quietly, letting the otherworldly music wash over them. For a moment, Christine thought even Henri was caught up in the spell. But then he yawned. The prioress glared at him. He whispered to Christine, 'Meet us later at the priory gate.' He took Thomas's arm and dragged him away.

Michel said to Christine, 'I will leave you, too. I will be with the friars. They have their own quarters. If you need me, someone will find me there.'

The prioress said, 'As much as I would like to stay here and listen, we must go, too.' She led Christine out into the courtyard and through a cemetery behind the choir to her residence, which was separate from the cloistered space in which the other nuns lived. Christine noticed that she avoided going through the refectory, which was on the other side of the church and would have been a more direct route to her chambers. *She doesn't want anyone to know I'm here*, she thought.

In the prioress's residence, they went into a study and found another nun sitting at a desk covered with papers. 'This is Sister Richarde, our treasuress,' Mother Marie said. 'Richarde, I would like you to meet Christine. She is the daughter of *Maître* Thomas de Pizan, the renowned physician and astrologer, and the widow of *Maître* Étienne de Castel, who served as secretary to our present king.'

Sister Richarde, a tall, lean woman with a hooked nose, scrutinized Christine through narrowed eyes, nodded, arranged her papers into a neat pile, and quietly left the room. 'No one is more competent to handle our business affairs, in spite of what Henri Le Picart thinks of women,' the prioress said.

Christine reflected on what those business affairs might be. The wealth of the priory, which had been established for a very large community of noblewomen, was well known. The women brought with them riches from their prosperous families, and the priory also garnered income from its vast landholdings in Poissy and the surrounding area.

The prioress was smiling at her. 'I know what you're thinking. But we need our wealth; there are more than one hundred twenty sisters here. Our expenses are enormous.'

Christine thought of the huge complex that made up the priory – not just the cloistered area where the sisters lived, but also the accommodations for the friars who attended to their spiritual requirements and for the lay sisters and commoners who cared for their daily needs.

'In many ways we have to operate as a business enterprise, just to keep ourselves going,' the prioress continued. 'I'm sure you passed through the cattle market on your way here. Many of the animals you saw there came from our farms. That is just one example of the way we make our living.' She looked down at the papers the treasuress had left on her desk. 'Sister Richarde has been reviewing our accounts. They take up a great deal of our time, and we always have to remind ourselves that our chief function is to sing the divine office perpetually, to offer prayers to God for the royal family, and for all of France.'

Christine thought of the extraordinary singing she'd heard, and knew that what the prioress said of their devotion to their mission was true. Nevertheless, as she glanced around Mother Marie's quarters, she couldn't help being amazed that the prioress lived in such luxurious surroundings. There were tapestries as elegant as any she'd seen on the walls of the royal palace, a large window of colored glass, shelves with books in jeweled bindings, cabinets on which were displayed silver platters and crystal goblets, and even a small reliquary glittering with rubies and emeralds resting on a cushion on a table. When the prioress saw her looking at the reliquary, she laid her hand on it and caressed it gently. 'This is a gift from the king. It was brought here yesterday, and I could not resist the temptation to keep it for a while so I might enjoy it before I take it to our treasury. Come closer so you can see it better.'

Christine admired the reliquary, which was exquisite. She hoped she would be invited to look at the equally exquisite books.

'Our treasury contains many treasures like this,' the prioress said.

'Offerings our sisters have brought with them, as well as gifts from their families and from the king.'

Christine had heard about the treasury, which contained hundreds of priceless objects – gold tabernacles, crystal crosses, reliquaries studded with emeralds, diamonds, and rubies, and a gilded bust containing a relic of Saint Louis.

The prioress went to a large cupboard, took out a platter of cheese tarts, poured some wine into a goblet, and set everything on a table before a large fireplace. 'Please help yourself. You have had a long journey, and I'm sure you're hungry.'

While Christine ate, the prioress sat at her desk, looking through the papers Sister Richarde had left there. She glanced at Christine from time to time, and when she saw that the food was gone, she put the papers back the way Sister Richarde had left them and began to speak.

'I know you are wondering why I have asked to come here. You, of all people, would suspect it has little to do with my need for a copyist.'

Christine smiled. 'I am well aware that you have many copyists to provide all the manuscripts you need for your choir.'

'We do. What we do *not* have is a woman capable of solving a mystery – something that threatens the existence of the priory.'

Christine clenched her hands together and tried to compose her face so it wouldn't register what she felt. She didn't succeed.

The prioress said, 'I'm sure you imagined you might be coming to a place untouched by any of the world's problems.'

Christine thought of the light-filled church and the beautiful singing. She had indeed dreamed of a place where she could escape for a while from the horrors of the king's illness and the difficulties of supporting her family. She had even hoped she might find time to work on her writing.

'You were mistaken,' the prioress continued. 'We have a real problem here.' She rose from her seat and went to stand by one of the tapestries on the wall. A choir of angels looked down on her. 'I know that in the past you have helped the king and his brother. Now I need you to help me.'

Christine swallowed hard and said, 'I wonder whether what happens at the priory is any of my business.'

'Of course it is your business. You have a daughter here.'

Where is Marie now? Christine wondered. *When will I see her?*

'Marie is safe. I will have her come to you soon.'

Christine breathed a sigh of relief. But she knew the prioress had led her into a trap. How could she not agree to help, when her own daughter's safety might be involved?

The prioress was smiling at her, triumphantly, Christine thought. She said, 'This concerns more than the priory. It concerns all of France.' She spread her arms wide, as though she would enclose the entire country within them. 'I am sure you know the king's daughter is here. I am concerned that she may be in danger.'

Christine shifted on the bench, folded her hands together in her lap, and said, 'Perhaps you'd better tell me what has happened.'

The prioress turned and looked at the angels in the tapestry. They hovered above the Virgin and Child, who were seated on a golden throne. She reached up, touched the Child's foot gently with the tip of her finger, and said, 'One of our sisters has died. Her name was Thérèse.' She turned and faced Christine. 'I told everyone her weak heart gave out. But that is not true. She was murdered.'

Christine caught her breath. *Such things don't happen in a priory!*

'We have our problems, just like other people,' the prioress said. 'But this is a tragedy.'

'What happened?'

'Thérèse had gone home to attend her sister's funeral in Archères, not far from here. The night she returned, she said she had something important to tell me, but she was exhausted, and I told her it could wait until morning. I took her to the dormitory and put her to bed, with instructions to ignore the summons to get up in the middle of the night for matins and lauds. She fell asleep instantly, and I assumed she was still sleeping when she didn't appear for prime the next morning. But then I happened to go into the cloister, and I found her lying under a big pine tree that grows there. She was dead. Stabbed in the chest.'

The prioress went to her desk, picked up a small ivory statue of the Madonna, and gazed at it sadly.

'I called Sister Geneviève, our infirmaress, and we were able to carry Thérèse to the infirmary without being seen. Geneviève said it would be best not to let anyone know she had been murdered. I agreed. All the sisters knew she was frail, and we decided to tell them that her weak heart had finally given out. Otherwise, everyone would have been terribly frightened, and some of the more excitable sisters might have panicked.

'Thérèse's habit was covered with blood, so we removed it and dressed her in a clean one. Then we called the doctor. Our regular doctor was ill, and his temporary replacement was young and very shy, not a man accustomed to treating nuns. Geneviève assumed a fierce demeanor and told him in no uncertain terms that there was no need to examine the body because it was obvious that her weak heart had failed. He didn't insist.'

'What about Thérèse's family?' Christine asked.

'We had a service for her in the church and buried her quietly in our cemetery. Her father and one of her brothers came, but they asked no questions. I was surprised that her mother was not with them, but they told me she was ill, and I accepted this because Thérèse often had to go home to visit members of her family who were sick.'

The prioress stood up, went to a chest, opened the lid, and took out a folded cloth. She sat down beside Christine and opened it. In her hand lay a small dog collar made of a narrow piece of leather. It was broken, as though it had snapped when someone pulled on it.

'I found this in the cloister, beside Thérèse's body,' she said.

'But how could a dog have gotten into the cloister?'

'That is the question.'

'Have you told anyone else about this?'

'No. Only you. This is why I have called you here. I want you to find out who killed Sister Thérèse, and why.'

SIX

Your daughter, because of divine inspiration and pure desire, and in spite of yourself, has given herself to the church and to God and is with the noble community of ladies at Poissy . . .

Christine de Pizan, *L'advision Christine*, 1405

Before Christine could say anything, there was a knock on the door, and one of the sisters entered with a message that Reverend Mother was wanted elsewhere. 'I am sorry, I must leave you,' the prioress said to Christine. 'But you will have company. I have given your daughter permission to come to you. You may tell her why you are here; I trust her to keep the knowledge to herself.'

She went to a cupboard and took out a manuscript. 'This *Life of Saint Dominic*, the founder of our order, was loaned to me by another prioress. I will tell the other sisters you are here to copy it.' She laid it on her desk and turned a few pages. 'It has lovely illustrations.'

I wish I could get to work on it right away, Christine thought as she looked at the beautiful manuscript.

'Of course, you will not have much time for this,' the prioress said. 'But you will at least be comfortable while you are here. I have had one of my guest rooms prepared for you. The bed there is not as hard as those on which the sisters sleep.' With that, she left.

Christine sat at the desk and wondered how she could ever do what the prioress asked of her. There were one hundred twenty nuns at the priory, and Michel had told her there were more than a dozen friars who acted as their priests and confessors. In addition, there would be lay brothers, doctors, gardeners, cooks, bakers, laundresses, carters, carpenters, coopers, and countless domestic servants. Any one of these people could have murdered Sister Thérèse. The prioress had given her an impossible task, and she sat with her head in her hands, feeling despair. She was awakened from her reverie when the door opened and she heard soft footsteps. She raised her head and was delighted to see her daughter, Marie, standing before her with her arms outstretched.

Christine had not wanted her daughter, a lively, intelligent child who'd grown into a beautiful young woman, to become a nun. She'd felt that life as a nun would be too restrictive for her. Her mother had wept and pleaded with the girl not to do it, and even her sons, especially Thomas, had tried to dissuade their sister. But Marie had resisted all their arguments. She said she felt a true calling, and she was utterly determined to follow it. Now, as Christine saw her standing before her in the white wool habit of a Dominican nun, still wearing the white veil of a novice, she almost wept. She'd always envisioned her daughter in fine silks and furs. But the look on Marie's face belied these feelings: she was happy. Christine rose to embrace her.

Marie gently pushed her mother down on the bench and sat beside

her. 'I'm glad to see you,' she said. 'But tell me quickly why you
are here. Has something happened at home?'

'No, no. Everyone is fine. Your grandmother sends her love.'

'And the others?'

'Didn't I write? Jean is in England. He's a companion for the
Earl of Salisbury's son. Lisabetta is growing to be a fine young
lady. Georgette has married her beau, Robin, and now she's quite
pregnant.'

'And Thomas?'

'Thomas is here with me.'

'Surely not at the priory! We're not allowed to have male visitors.'
Marie stood and faced her mother. 'You had better tell me what is
going on. Something is wrong – I know it!'

'Nothing is amiss in our family. The prioress has asked me to
help her find out about something that has happened here.'

'Does it have something to do with Sister Thérèse?'

Christine hadn't expected Marie to know there was anything
unusual about the death. 'Do you suspect something?' she asked.

'She was frail. We all knew that. But why would she have gone
into the cloister in the middle of the night?'

'Are the other sisters asking that question, too?'

'Mother Marie is trying to make her death seem natural. She
wouldn't want everyone to be frightened. Most of the sisters accept
her explanation, but some of them have questions.'

'And you?'

'You know me, Mama. I've never been able to accept things that
don't seem right.'

Christine smiled. 'I know only too well.' She got up from the
bench, walked to the desk, and picked up the cloth with the dog's
collar. 'Mother Marie says I may tell you everything. She trusts you
to keep it to yourself.' She opened the cloth and showed her daughter
the collar. 'She found this in the cloister next to Thérèse's body.'

Marie let out a little cry. 'Did a dog attack her?'

'Oh, no. But there was a dog there.'

'How strange! Why?'

'That's what the prioress wants me to find out.'

Marie covered her face with her hands. Her shoulders were
shaking.

'I'm sorry,' Christine said. 'I know you came here to live a life
of peace and quiet, and now I've come and upset all that.'

Marie uncovered her face. She was laughing. 'That's exactly right, Mama. You have a habit of upsetting everything. I thought it would be a relief to get away from you.'

'Well, is it? A relief, I mean?'

'I made the right decision. There is no need to discuss it further.' She got up from the bench. 'I have to go soon. Tell me what you're going to do.'

'I'm not sure. This is such a big place and there are so many people. I don't know anyone, and I don't know where to start.'

'You said Thomas is with you. Where is he staying?'

'He's here because Henri Le Picart brought him. Henri will have to be responsible for finding him a place to stay.'

'Henri? What has he to do with this?'

'The king and queen had a letter from your prioress requesting my presence here. They decided I needed to travel with people to protect me, so they gave the job to Brother Michel and Henri. Henri took it upon himself to invite Thomas to come along.'

'I can imagine how you feel about that. Does Henri know what this is all about?'

'I'm sure he does. But he keeps it to himself.'

'Henri likes you, Mama.'

'Don't start that. I despise the man.'

'Is Thomas with him now?'

'Where else would he be? He can't come into the priory.'

'I'm glad Brother Michel is with you. He will know everyone here.'

Christine gazed at her daughter for a while, then said, 'Perhaps you could help me.'

Marie stood up. 'We sisters are expected to spend our days chanting the divine office. There is little time for anything else. And besides, we aren't allowed to talk to anyone. It's very unusual for me to be here with you now.'

'Is it a particular feast day today?' Christine asked.

'Not here. But I know that some other places observe the feast of Saint Mary of Egypt today. I will pray to her.'

'Why to her especially?'

'Because she was a prostitute, and when I think of her, I think of your friend Marion.'

Christine smiled. She missed Marion, who claimed she was no longer a prostitute – although no one was really sure – and made her living selling her embroidery to wealthy people, including the queen. Marion had helped her solve murders in the past, and she wished she were here to help her now.

'You'd better go about your business,' she said. 'In a little while, I will come into the church and listen to the singing again.'

'You have heard us?'

'When we first arrived. As you know, I had my doubts about your becoming a nun. But after listening to the chant, I can't think of anything better you could do with your life.'

Marie hugged her mother and started out the door. But before she left, she turned and said, 'I'm glad Mother Prioress let you tell me what is going on.' She stepped back inside and whispered, 'Don't tell anyone, Mama, but I do get a little bored sometimes, singing all day.'

SEVEN

[Marie de Bourbon] called Humility her dear companion and never ceased to ask to perform the vilest duties. She was often seen going down to the door to give alms to lepers who were hideous to look at.

L'Année Dominicaine, 1678

C hristine sat for a while at the prioress's desk, wondering what to do. She'd been given an impossible task, and she thought perhaps she should refuse to take it on. What if she failed?

She got up and went to the room that had been prepared for her. It was as sumptuous as the other rooms in the prioress's residence – windows of colored glass, tapestries on the walls, a chair with elaborate carvings on its arms, and a large wooden desk with a polished surface that reflected the light from a tall candle in a silver candlestick. She sat on the bed. It was soft, not hard like those on which the sisters sleep.

A noise startled her. Someone was in the prioress's study. She got up, went to the door, and peered out.

The afternoon had worn on, and the study, lit only by a few flames in the fireplace, was in near darkness, but there was enough light to see a nun bending over the prioress's desk. When the woman turned her head to the side, her pale face stood out against the shadows. It was not the prioress.

Christine drew back. The nun was looking through the priory accounts Sister Richarde had left. After a while, she removed a document and tucked it into the sleeve of her habit. She arranged the other papers neatly and left.

Christine sat on her bed and wondered about what she'd seen. She tried to convince herself that she hadn't really observed one of the sisters taking something that didn't belong to her. *There has to be a reasonable explanation*, she said to herself. But she couldn't help thinking that the incident might have something to do with the murder she was supposed to be investigating.

She sat for a while, hesitant to go out because she didn't know her way around the priory. But when the prioress didn't return, she went into the courtyard. She hadn't noticed earlier that there were henhouses there, and she was amused to find herself surrounded by chickens. She walked on, came to the cemetery, and stood looking at the apse of the church. *It's as impressive as the cathedral in Paris*, she thought, and she reminded herself that this should not be surprising. This was a royal priory, richly financed by the king, a home for noble ladies and, once in a while, a commoner like her daughter.

She made the circuit around the apse, came to the public entrance to the church, and stepped in. It was too early for vespers, and the space was silent. She stood for a while in the increasing darkness, wishing she could hear singing, then left and went to look for Thomas and Henri at the priory entrance. She found them there, talking to the *portier* and his grandson.

Thomas ran to her. 'I was worried about you.'

'What could happen to me in a priory?' Christine asked, thinking that a lot could happen in a priory where one of the sisters had been murdered. Henri looked at her slyly. *He knows why I've been asked here*, she thought.

'How did you find the prioress?' Henri asked. 'Is she running this place well?'

Better than you would, Christine thought.

'Look!' Thomas said, pointing to the prioress, who stood at the entrance, holding a loaf of bread out to a man with a disfigured face and sores on his arms.

'So, she talks to lepers,' Henri said. 'Most unusual.'

Christine was amazed. The woman who'd seemed so formidable a while ago gazed on the leper with compassion, her face soft and kind. *Surely I've misjudged her*, she thought. An hour ago she'd considered making some excuse to leave. Now she abandoned the idea. She couldn't refuse to help the noble woman who stood there talking with a leper.

Thomas touched her arm. 'Isn't it dangerous to stand near a leper? Won't she get sick?'

'I don't believe she will,' Christine said.

Henri was impatient. 'We're staying at the inn across the road. Are you coming with us? You can sleep there.'

'I'll be staying with the prioress.'

'Why?' Thomas asked.

'I can't tell you right now. But I will, soon. Meet me here tomorrow.' She turned to go, realizing that she could hardly wait to go back into the church and hear the singing.

The prioress gave the leper some coins and came to Christine's side. She looked formidable again, and Thomas drew back. Henri, on the other hand, stood with his arms folded over his chest.

'There is no need to look so smug, Henri Le Picart,' Mother Marie said. 'It's possible to have compassion as well as a head for business. Does this priory look as though it is going to ruin because we spend too much time caring for the poor?'

'How would I know whether it's going to ruin or not?' Henri asked. 'I'm not allowed inside to look around.'

Mother Marie laughed. 'Well said, Henri. You can ask Brother Michel about what goes on with us, since he is privileged to stay with the friars.'

'I assure you, I will,' Henri said.

Christine blanched. *How dare the man address the prioress like that?* she asked herself. But the prioress was unfazed. She looked Henri in the eye and said, 'You are welcome to come into the church and hear the sisters chant vespers.'

'But not see them,' Henri said. 'So conveniently hidden behind the iron grille. No, thank you.'

'As you wish,' the prioress said. She took Christine's arm and led her through the courtyard and into the church. 'Stay here for a while and listen,' she said. 'Soon I will send someone to bring you to my quarters where you will have supper.'

EIGHT

Let the Abbess's table always be with the guests and the pilgrims. But when there are no guests, let it be in her power to invite whom she will of the sisters.

From a rhymed version of the *Rule of Saint Benedict*, written for English nuns, 1400–1425

The sisters were chanting the liturgy for vespers, and an unceasing flow of song filled the church. When a nun glided to her side and motioned for her to come with her, Christine was reluctant to leave. But the sister beckoned insistently, and she followed, treading quietly so she could hear the music for as long as possible.

They went into the arcaded walkway of a large cloister. It was nearly dark now, but she could see a lawn and, in the center, a huge pine tree, its thick branches, which were laden with water from the recent rain, sweeping the ground. 'That tree is magnificent!' she exclaimed.

The nun smiled. 'I don't think there is another like it anywhere in the world.' Then she moved on, past a large building that Christine knew was a dormitory, and into the prioress's quarters.

The prioress was waiting for her in her parlor, which was lit by a great many candles in sconces on the wall. She was accompanied by four other nuns. 'I thought you would enjoy meeting some of the sisters who care for our community,' Mother Marie said. 'Sister Richarde, our treasuress, you have already met.' Sister Richarde nodded slightly, squinting and unsmiling.

Another nun stepped forward. 'This is Sister Louise, our cellarer. She makes sure we always have enough to eat.' *Sister Louise certainly doesn't go hungry*, Christine thought as she looked at the short, very fat sister with round, red cheeks.

'And this is Sister Claude, our chantress.' The prioress was smiling at a tiny woman with an expressionless face. 'You have heard the results of her labors in the choir.' *How is this unremarkable-looking woman able to inspire such glorious music?* Christine asked herself.

The prioress took the hand of a tall nun with a face so pale it nearly matched the white of her habit. 'This is Sister Thomasine, our subprioress. She makes sure our rules are observed correctly, especially those having to do with the hours of the divine office.' Sister Thomasine appeared to be young, but as Christine looked at her closely, she realized she was older than she'd at first thought. She also realized that this was the nun she'd seen taking a document from the desk in the prioress's study.

All four sisters had puzzled looks on their faces.

'This is Christine, daughter of *Maître* Thomas de Pizan, the renowned astrologer and physician to the late king, and widow of *Maître* Étienne de Castel, who served as secretary to our present king,' the prioress said. 'She is an accomplished scribe, and I have asked her here to make a duplicate of a valuable manuscript. She will stay with me, but she is free to go anywhere she likes.'

Everyone looked uncomfortable. Christine was sure it was unusual to have a stranger living with the prioress and wandering around the priory. She wondered whether the prioress suspected any of these sisters of having something to do with Sister Thérèse's death.

Sister Richarde seemed to be looking down her long, hooked nose at her. *She's thinking that the priory already has excellent scribes and wondering why they need another*, Christine said to herself. She was surprised when Sister Richarde laughed and said, 'I could use a good scribe to decipher the unreadable receipts the bailiff gives me.'

Sister Louise, who looked as though she'd helped herself to a good share of the priory's provisions, guffawed, as did Sister Thomasine, whose pale face transformed itself into a grimace when she smiled. Sister Claude, however, didn't laugh. 'I can give you piles of music manuscripts to copy,' she said. 'There never seem to be enough.' She looked like a timid little bird.

'I'm afraid I am not proficient with music manuscripts,' Christine said.

'Then I'll teach you,' Sister Claude sniffed.

The prioress led her guests into a dining room where a table covered with a snow-white cloth was set with silver salt cellars, silver goblets, and candles in silver candleholders. *The sisters all come from noble families*, Christine mused. *They may have dedicated themselves to lives of prayer, but they still expect to enjoy the luxuries they've been accustomed to.* Nevertheless, she was sure the sisters in the refectory were eating off less costly dishes.

A lay sister served a simple but elegant supper from the prioress's kitchen – a soup of mixed greens and herbs, a soft, creamy cheese from Normandy that Christine recognized because it was one of Francesca's favorites, and excellent bread. Sister Louise insisted on describing how the cheese, called *angelot*, was made, her fat jowls quivering with delight. She was ecstatic when Christine told her how much her mother loved this cheese and how Francesca always searched for it at the market.

The prioress engaged Sister Richarde in a conversation about the priory accounts, talked to Sister Thomasine about one of the novices who seemed not to understand the rules, questioned Sister Louise about the state of some grain that had been delivered, hoping it hadn't been left out in the rain, and congratulated Sister Claude on having acquired a new processional for the choir. Christine noticed that she studied each nun intently as she spoke with her. They all returned her gaze unflinchingly.

As soon as there was a lull in the conversation, Christine seized the opportunity to ask Sister Claude about the music. 'What makes it so different from other chant I've heard?' she asked.

Sister Claude looked surprised. 'Few people would notice. There's a pause in the middle of each verse. Some choirs let this go on too long. We keep it short. That keeps people awake.'

Sister Louise heard this and laughed. 'The important thing is to keep your *singers* awake.'

Sister Richarde complained about the bailiff. 'Can you believe it?' she asked. 'He keeps saying we should start cutting trees in the forest of Saint-Germain-en-Laye. How many times do I have to tell him we are not allowed to cut there? That is stated very clearly in our charter.'

'I don't think the woodsmen would go into the forest, anyway,' Sister Louise said. 'There may be a sorcerer there.'

'Nonsense,' the prioress said.

'I don't believe it's nonsense,' Sister Louise said. 'The sorcerer who was burned in Paris last year had an assistant who ran away.

People are saying the assistant came to the forest here. We shouldn't take that lightly. We may be in danger.'

'Utter nonsense,' the prioress repeated. 'If there is someone in the forest who thinks he's a sorcerer, he will be caught and executed.'

'But Louise is right,' Sister Thomasine said. 'We should be prepared here at the priory in case he tries to work his spells on us.'

Sister Louise picked up her wine goblet and set it down again before she could take a drink. Her pudgy hands were shaking. Sister Claude clutched the arms of her chair. Even Sister Richarde looked frightened.

'Enough of this conversation!' the prioress said, her voice as cold as ice. 'It is sinful to speak of such things. Especially in front of the child.' She pointed to the door, where a little girl stood listening. The prioress motioned for her to come in, and she ran to her and climbed on to her lap. The other sisters curtsied, and Christine realized that this was the king's daughter.

'I want to know about sorcerers,' the princess said.

'There is nothing to know,' the prioress said. 'There are no sorcerers here.' She frowned at Sister Thomasine.

'Yes, there are,' the princess said. She jumped off the prioress's lap and ran around the room, tugging on the sisters' white robes, pretending to look underneath them for a sorcerer. Another sister ran in and scurried around after her, admonishing her to stop.

'That's Sister Denise,' Sister Thomasine whispered to Christine. 'Reverend Mother chose her to look after the princess for a few days while Sister Catherine, her regular guardian, is away. As you can see, it was not a wise choice.'

Sister Denise, a timid-looking woman with a flat face and bulging eyes, did look defeated. It was clear that she was embarrassed at having the prioress see that she couldn't control the child.

Sister Claude caught the little girl in her arms and sang softly to her. The princess became calm and looked around the room, studying each of the nuns and finally fixing her eyes on Christine. Then she began to sing along with Sister Claude, softly at first, and then in a loud, shrill voice.

'You will make a fine addition to the choir when you are older,' Sister Claude said.

'I don't want to sing in the choir,' the princess exclaimed.

All the sisters smiled, as if to say, *This is the king's daughter, and she can do and say whatever she likes*. The prioress was the only one who looked displeased. 'You may be a princess, but that does not give you the right to be insolent,' she said, and she lifted the child off her feet and pretended to spank her.

The princess started to cry, whereupon the prioress took her on to her lap again and whispered a prayer. The child listened quietly and seemed about to fall asleep. She nodded when Sister Denise told her it was time to go to bed. She climbed down from the prioress's lap and followed her to the door.

Perhaps she's not as ill-mannered as she seems, Christine thought.

The princess turned and stuck out her tongue at her.

NINE

The church is divided into two parts by a continuous screen so no man can come into contact with the women. No man may go behind this screen, even accidentally. Those who say the mass and read the gospels are outside with the people of the town, and the pure women are in the nave, singing in high, strong voices.

Christine de Pizan, *Le Livre du Dit de Poissy*, 1400

Christine stood in the dark transept of the church with people from the town, listening to the choir chant compline. Because she couldn't see the nuns, it was easy to imagine that the magnificent sounds flowing around her were produced by one of the heavenly choirs that preachers talked so much about. In the dark transept, she lost her sense of direction and could no longer tell where to find the entrance, but that didn't trouble her; she felt she would be happy to stay there after the sisters had gone to bed and wait for them to come back in the middle of the night for matins.

Her reverie was broken by the voice of the prioress, who said, 'I rarely hear the chanting on this side of the grille.'

'Are you usually with them?'

'Most of the time, unless I have pressing business to take care of. I would rather be in there than anywhere else in the world.'

'I would like to be able to go in there, to understand a little of what it must be like to be part of such a glorious sound.'

'I will take you sometime.'

Christine followed the prioress out into the cloister. The rain had begun again. Water dripped from the branches of the huge pine tree, and the scent of pine needles filled the air. A strong wind came up and pushed at their backs as they hurried through the covered arcade and along a corridor to the prioress's quarters. Christine was suddenly overwhelmed with tiredness. She said goodnight to the prioress and went to her room, where she blew out the candle in the silver candlestick, fell into bed, and knew nothing until the next morning when she opened her eyes to see her daughter sitting in a chair beside her.

'Don't look so surprised, Mama. Reverend Mother said I might come to see you after prime,' Marie said.

'I'm not used to seeing you in your habit.'

Christine got out of bed and went to look out the window. No rays of morning sun lit the colored glass, and rain beat on the panes with an incessant patter. She turned back to Marie and was astonished to see another nun standing beside her. The room was so dark she hadn't noticed her standing in the shadows.

'This is Sister Juliana, Mama,' Marie said. 'She has something to tell you about Sister Thérèse.'

Sister Juliana was of medium height and slim, with a freckled face. She looked very young. 'I don't believe her heart gave out,' she blurted out.

'Why don't you believe it?'

'Because of the way she acted when she came back after her sister's funeral. Before she went home, she was her usual self. She met me in the cloister. We hid under the branches of the big pine. Have you seen the pine?'

'I have. It's extraordinary,' Christine said.

'Well, no one disturbed us there, and Thérèse babbled on and on about her family. We aren't supposed to talk, but she couldn't help it. But when she came back from the funeral, I met her outside the dormitory, and she turned away from me without saying a word. Reverend Mother came and took her off to bed, and that was the last time I saw her. I heard her say to Reverend

Mother that she wanted to tell her something. I think something must have happened at home – something terrible – to make her act like that. Something that caused her to die. Do you know what it was?'

Christine was taken aback. But she couldn't tell the girl that she did indeed know what had caused Thérèse's death. Instead, she asked, 'Did Thérèse like dogs?'

'That's a funny question. But yes, she did.' She smiled, and dimples appeared in her cheeks. 'She told me her brother had a small dog that she liked very much. We aren't allowed to have dogs here, of course. Why do you ask?'

'I was just wondering, trying to understand more about her,' Christine said.

Marie said, 'I had permission to be with you for a while, Mama. Now I must go back.'

'Do you have permission, too, Juliana?' Christine asked.

'No. I'll do severe penance, but I don't care.'

'Are you sure?' Marie asked.

'Your mother is the only person I can talk to.'

'Then tell her everything.' Marie kissed her mother and left.

Juliana stood shifting her feet.

Christine asked, 'What more do you have to tell me about Thérèse?'

'It's really not about Thérèse. I've told you everything I know about what happened to her. It's something else.' She sat down on the bed and started to cry.

Christine sat beside her and put her arms around her. 'Please tell me what's wrong!'

Juliana wiped her eyes and said, 'I just have to talk to someone. Marie said you would understand. She's told me all about you. She says you help people who are in trouble. She says people are always telling you that women shouldn't get involved in such things, but you do it anyway. I don't think it's right for women to be told what they can or cannot do. Women should be allowed to do whatever they want.' Her words came tumbling out so fast that Christine had a hard time following them.

'How old are you, Juliana?' she asked.

'Eighteen. Just like Marie.'

'Have you not been allowed to do what you want?'

The girl stamped her foot. 'Of course I haven't. Here in the priory, we can't do *anything* we want. We have to obey all the rules, and we can't have minds of our own.'

'Does my daughter feel that way?'

'No. She came here because she wanted to. I did not. I don't want to be a nun. Someone told me my family put me here because they're poor and they can't marry me off because they don't have any money for a dowry.'

'You could leave, you know.'

'Where could I go?'

Where could a young girl who had no money go? Christine had to ask herself.

Juliana started to cry again. 'I want to be strong, like you,' she said. 'I'm sure you never let your family make you do anything you don't want to do.'

'That's different. I have to be independent. My husband died when my children were very young. I work as a scribe to support my family.'

Juliana was sobbing now. 'I could be a scribe. I'd do anything to get away from here. Please help me.'

Christine rocked her in her arms. 'Let me think about it. Go back to the choir now. It must be nearly time for terce. I'll tell the prioress I detained you, so you won't be punished.'

'I'm sorry. I'm sure you never cry when things go wrong.'

Christine smiled, remembering all the times she'd wept for her husband, feeling sorry for herself and crying out in the dark that she didn't deserve all her misfortunes. 'Don't be so sure of that,' she said.

Juliana stood up and dried her eyes with the sleeve of her habit. 'Just talking to you has helped.'

'Can't you talk to anyone else?'

'I can talk to Marie. She understands.'

'What about the other sisters?'

'I'm sure you think they are so nice, praying and singing all the time. Don't be fooled. They all look alike, gliding around in their white habits, but they aren't alike at all. And some of them aren't nice.'

Juliana's face was red, and she was shaking. Christine took her arm, led her to the door, and said gently, 'I think you'd better go back to the choir now.'

'I'm sorry. I couldn't help it. I'm so unhappy here.' The girl turned and left.

Christine got dressed and went out to hear the choir chant terce, on the way passing through the cloister, where rain pounded down on the lawn and the huge pine tree swayed in a howling wind. She hurried into the church and was stunned for a moment by the silence. Then she heard rustling sounds behind the grille and knew the nuns were filing in. The rustling stopped, and out of nowhere the chant came. It swirled around her, rising and falling, now soft, now loud, unending. She stood transfixed until she felt a hand on her arm and looked to find Thomas beside her.

'We came to find you, Mama. Henri has something to tell you.'

She looked around and saw Henri Le Picart scowling. 'Don't you enjoy the chant, Henri?' she asked.

'They're singing it too fast.'

'That's the way it's supposed to be,' Christine said. 'The Dominicans sing it differently from other orders. They don't sing it so slowly and drawn out that it lulls you to sleep. Listen for the pause in the middle of each verse and notice how they keep it short so your attention doesn't wander.'

Henri stared at her. 'So now you're an authority on the chant, Christine.'

'I'm learning. Soon I'll know as much as you, Henri.'

Henri laughed. 'You probably will. But tear your attention away from your new-found interest and come outside. As you can see, your son is bouncing up and down with excitement at what we have to tell you.'

Thomas grabbed his mother's hand and pulled her out the door of the church and through the courtyard to the entrance to the priory, where the *portier*, accompanied by his grandson Jacques, let them out. The rain came down heavily, and Henri hustled them across the street to the inn where he and Thomas were staying.

The inn was dark, and it smelled of spilled wine and burnt bread, but at least there was a blazing fire in a large fireplace. 'We might as well have something to eat,' Henri said. They sat at a table, the top of which was covered with crude words customers had carved into it. Several waiters bustled around. One, a skinny man wearing a green tunic, bright pink tights, and a hat with a large peacock feather, seemed to know Henri, and he winked at him. 'Just bring us some bread and soup. Wine, too,' Henri said as he waved him away. The waiter made a mock bow, tipped his hat so the peacock feather nearly brushed Henri's nose, and hurried off.

Henri turned to Christine and said, 'I don't suppose you get much to eat at the priory.'

Christine remembered she hadn't had anything to eat that morning, but she also remembered the elegant supper she'd had the night before.

'You don't think much of nuns, do you, Henri?'

'I wouldn't trust them to serve a good meal.'

'There you're mistaken. Perhaps someday you will learn the truth. But now tell me what's so important.'

'Let me tell her!' Thomas cried.

'Calm down, Thomas,' Christine said.

Thomas leaned toward her and said in a loud voice, 'There really is a sorcerer living in the forest of Saint-Germain-en-Laye.'

TEN

No woman is as naturally sensible as a man. Therefore, women need sensible men to judiciously conduct their affairs.

Humbert of Romans (c. 1200–1277), *Opera de vita regulari*

Suddenly, Michel appeared. 'I heard what you said, Thomas. I'm sure it's not true.'

'But it is!' Thomas cried. 'Isn't it, Henri?'

Henri laughed. 'Why not? There are all kinds of sorcerers at the court claiming they can cure the king. Why not here?'

'All charlatans,' Michel said.

'Do you mention sorcerers in your chronicle, Michel?' Christine asked, referring to the account of the reign of Charles the Sixth the monk was writing.

'As little as possible,' Michel said. He took off his wet cloak and shook it. The skinny waiter appeared with the bread, soup, and wine Henri had ordered and bent over the table as he set everything out. 'Bring more. We have another guest,' Henri said, turning his head to avoid the peacock feather. The waiter started to go away, then stopped behind Henri's chair and made a face.

Michel sat down. 'Sorcerers!' he snorted. 'It's unfortunate that so many people feel free to call in those scoundrels to practice their false remedies on the king.'

'Like the two monks who were decapitated last year,' Thomas said.

'Yes, like those two.'

'I hope you'll write everything about how they were punished,' Thomas said. 'I hope you'll write about how they were led through the streets with paper crowns on their heads and pieces of parchment on their shoulders with all their crimes listed.'

Henri laughed. 'It sounds as though you followed the procession, Thomas.'

'I did. I watched them get beheaded, and I saw their heads stuck on to lances and held up for everyone to see.'

'What did your mother say about that?' Henri asked, looking at Christine.

'I told him not to go, but he insisted. He even wanted to take his little cousin, who is much too young to witness such things,' Christine said.

'Lisabetta cried because you made her stay home,' Thomas said. He looked at Michel. 'If you write about it in your chronicle, then she can at least read about it someday.'

'I write about what happens to sorcerers so people will know not to believe their poisonous lies, not because I enjoy the gruesome details,' Michel said.

'So you won't write about Jean of Bar, the king's doctor who was burned at the stake for practicing sorcery in the woods in Brie?' Thomas asked.

'The two apostate monks are enough.'

'But Jean of Bar is important,' Thomas said. 'Or at least his assistant is.'

'What are you talking about?'

'Jean of Bar had an assistant, and he's right here, in the forest of Saint-Germain-en-Laye.'

'How do you know?'

'The *portier*'s grandson told me.'

The skinny waiter brought the bread, soup, and wine, sneered, and left. Michel asked Henri, 'Do you believe what the boy says?'

'It is true that Jean of Bar had an assistant who ran away and was never caught. Why couldn't that assistant be here? The *portier*'s grandson wouldn't know anything about Jean of Bar, but he would probably recognize a sorcerer if he saw one.'

'I'm going to the woods to find out!' Thomas cried.

Christine gasped. 'That's too dangerous, Thomas!'

'Dangerous in what way?' Henri asked. 'If there really is a sorcerer there, he wouldn't hurt Thomas. He'd just try to get him to help him work his spells. I'm sure Thomas is too intelligent to let himself be persuaded to do that.'

'So I am,' Thomas said proudly.

'This is ridiculous,' Christine said. 'I forbid you to go, Thomas.'

'You can't tell me what to do. I'm too old now.'

'Perhaps I'll go with him,' Henri said. 'It would be amusing.'

'It has nothing to do with what we're here for,' Christine said.

'It might,' Henri said.

Just as I thought, Christine said to herself. *He's only been pretending not to know what's going on at the priory. He knows very well.*

Michel said, 'Enough about sorcerers. We have to talk about the prioress's suspicions that Sister Thérèse did not die because of a bad heart.'

Michel knows, too! She turned to him angrily. 'Why didn't you tell me you knew why the prioress invited me here?'

'We were waiting until you'd talked to her yourself,' Michel said.

Thomas's ears perked up. He tugged on Christine's sleeve. 'You promised to tell *me* why you're here.'

'Everyone else seems to know. You might as well know, too.'

'Does it have to do with sorcerers?'

'No. It has to do with murder. One of the nuns at the priory was stabbed. The prioress has asked me to find out who did it.'

'You can do that! I know you can!'

'I'm not so sure, Thomas.'

'I'll help you if you'll just let me know what's going on. I'm old enough now that you don't have to keep secrets from me.'

Christine looked at her son and it seemed he had suddenly become a young man. 'I promise I'll tell you whatever I can.' She turned to Michel. 'Did the prioress tell you about the dog collar she found in the cloister?'

'She did. And she asked me to try to find out from the friars who live at the priory whether they'd seen a dog on the grounds.'

'A dog?' Thomas cried. 'What are you talking about?'

'The prioress found a dog collar in the cloister next to Sister Thérèse's body,' Christine said.

'The *portier*'s grandson Jacques will know if there was a dog at the priory. He knows everything that goes on there.'

'I'm sure he does,' Henri said. 'Does *he* have a dog?'

'He does,' Thomas said.

'It might have been that dog.'

'I'll ask him,' Thomas said. He ran out of the inn before anyone could stop him.

The waiter came back and looked at their untouched food. 'Is something wrong?' he asked, shaking his head so the peacock feather came dangerously close to Henri's cheek.

'Not at all,' Christine said. 'We've been talking.' She dipped her spoon into her soup. The others started to eat, too, and by the time they'd finished, Thomas was back, bringing with him the *portier*'s grandson, who tugged at the collar of a large brown dog that shook himself vigorously and splattered everyone with muddy water.

'This is Jacques,' Thomas said. 'And Humbert.'

Henri started to laugh. 'Humbert? What kind of a name is that for a dog?'

Michel was holding his hand over his mouth. 'Don't you know?' he asked, suppressing a giggle. 'Humbert of Romans was the fifth master general of the Dominican order.'

'How would Jacques know about him?' Christine asked.

'Jacques is always with his grandfather at the entrance to the priory,' Thomas said. 'He hears everything the prioress says when she comes there, as she often does. Isn't that right, Jacques?'

Jacques threw out his chest. 'I don't miss a thing.'

'Why would she have said anything about Humbert?' Christine asked.

Michel suppressed a smile. 'Humbert died more than a hundred years ago, but he left many writings on how the Dominicans should conduct themselves. He wrote in one of his treatises that nuns are not capable of managing their communities on their own. Mother Marie is incensed about this. She'll tell anyone who will listen that women are just as capable of managing their affairs as men.'

Good for her, Christine thought. *I would have told Humbert that, too, if I'd known him.* But at that moment she was more interested in what Humbert the dog wore around his neck – a wide brown collar, perfectly intact. The collar the prioress had found in the cloister was small and narrow and broken – certainly not something that would have ever been around the neck of this huge animal. 'This isn't the right dog,' she said.

Henri tousled Jacques's hair. 'Take Humbert and go back to your grandfather now.'

Jacques grabbed the dog's collar and dragged him back across the street to the priory entrance. Henri turned to Christine and asked, 'Have you been able to find any suspects at the priory?'

'I've been there for less than a day.'

'I'm surprised at you. I would have thought you'd have the murderer by now. And you haven't even come up with a suspect.'

Christine bristled. 'Have *you* come up with a suspect?'

'Not yet. That's why I think someone should go and find Jacques's sorcerer.'

ELEVEN

The song of rejoicing softens hard hearts.

Hildegard of Bingen (1098–1179), *Scivias*

C hristine stood up. 'How dare you encourage Thomas to go into the forest and look for a sorcerer who isn't even there?' She slammed her hand down on the table, making the soup bowls and wine cups rattle. She marched out of the inn, hoping the others wouldn't follow her. But they did, and they made a bedraggled little procession as they dashed through raindrops into the priory courtyard – Christine holding her hands over her starched linen headdress, Michel wincing as his feet turned wet and cold in his waterlogged sandals, Henri jumping over puddles in a vain attempt to keep his elegant poulaines dry, and Thomas marching along, calling out, 'I'm not afraid of a little rain. And I'm not afraid of sorcerers.'

When they reached the church, Thomas decided to go back to the priory entrance so he could ask Jacques more about the sorcerer, and Michel hurried off to the friars' quarters to put on dry sandals.

Henri trailed after Christine into the church. She couldn't tell him to leave without disturbing the people who were listening to the sisters chant the noon office, so she just tried to concentrate on the music.

Henri stood with his hands on his hips, shaking his head. 'Don't they ever stop?' he whispered.

'Of course not,' she hissed. 'It's their calling. That's why this priory was founded, so the sisters would offer endless prayers for the royal family and all of France. But you wouldn't understand that.'

'It's boring,' Henri whispered.

'It's not boring! Don't you know how complex the sung liturgy is? Just be quiet and listen,' Christine said, her voice rising. Several people turned around to look at her, and she moved as far away from him as she could. The music surged around them. Henri was so quiet that she wondered whether he'd left. She turned and saw that he'd done what she'd suggested. He stood motionless and, for once, didn't say a word. The chanting had captivated him, too.

All of a sudden, everything stopped. The break in the music was so startling that Christine felt as though she'd been slapped. They could hear crying and the nuns moving around behind the grille. She and Henri stared at each other.

Then the chanting began again, louder and more insistent than before. Henri started to laugh.

'What are your pious sisters doing back there?'

'I'm sure it's not a common occurrence. Mother Marie would never allow it.'

They stood for a while, listening. Then the office was over. Henri followed her out into the courtyard, and before she could tell him to go away and stop bothering her, the prioress came toward them. 'Were you listening?' she asked.

'Yes. What happened?'

Mother Marie shook her head. 'You've probably heard there's a tomb with an effigy of our founder, King Philippe le Bel, in the choir. The king's body is not in the tomb; it's buried at the Abbey of Saint-Denis. But his heart is here, buried in a vault below the tomb. Sister Adelie says she can hear the heart beating. Today she says the beating became so loud she couldn't concentrate on the music. She had a fit and fell to the floor, crying and holding her ears. We had to take her to the infirmary.'

'Women get like that,' Henri said under his breath.

The prioress shook her finger at him. 'We get tired of hearing men say such things, Henri. Sister Adelie is not well. Have a little compassion.'

'I've had enough of women's problems for one day,' Henri said. He turned on his heel and left.

'How do you know him?' Christine asked the prioress.

'I've known him for many years. I used to see him at the palace when my sister was alive. I saw you at the palace, too. You were just a young girl at the time. He wanted to marry you, you know.'

Christine felt herself blushing. She'd suspected that about Henri, but she'd tucked the thought far away in the back of her mind. She was embarrassed as well as amazed that this man who always seemed to be insinuating himself into her life and insulting her, a man whom she disliked and distrusted, had ever had anything other than disparaging thoughts about her.

'He respects you,' the prioress said.

'You'd never know it from the way he talks to me.'

'He talks to all women that way.'

'I'm astounded that he dares speak to *you* that way.'

'He doesn't know how to express anything other than disdain when he talks to women. We try to keep him out of our affairs here. I am not pleased that he was privy to what happened during the office today.'

'Tell me about Sister Adelie,' Christine said.

'Sister Adelie is a burden. She has fits, and she has visions. She says King Philip leaves his body in Saint-Denis and comes here, looking for his heart. She goes into trances and claims she's talking to him.'

'Do any of the other sisters have visions?'

'No. Although I've begun to wonder whether Sister Thérèse might not have experienced something like that when she got up in the middle of the night and went into the cloister.'

The rain began to come down heavily, and Christine and the prioress hurried into the prioress's quarters. There they found a very agitated sister waiting for them.

'This is Sister Geneviève,' the prioress said to Christine. 'Our infirmaress.'

Sister Geneviève barely nodded to Christine before she launched into a diatribe against Sister Adelie. 'This can't go on!' she cried, her small, squat body shaking with rage. 'First she interrupts sext, and now she's upsetting all the other patients in the infirmary. You have to do something, Reverend Mother!'

The prioress sighed and sat down at her desk. 'Tell me calmly what you want me to do, Geneviève.'

Sister Geneviève stood in front of the desk, placed her hands flat on it, and leaned over so her face was close to that of the prioress. 'You tell *me*, Mother.'

'Adelie is from one of our noblest families,' the prioress said. 'When she came here, her family gave us a large sum of money and a priceless gold chalice. Even now, they contribute large sums of money yearly.'

'I am well aware of that,' the infirmaress said. 'But if this goes on much longer, the priory will be so unsettled we will not be able to continue our mission.' She stamped her foot. 'What if the king finds out? We'll lose our support. What will you do then?'

Perhaps the king already knows, Christine thought. *Perhaps that's why he was so insistent that I come here. There may be more to this than the death of a nun.* 'I would like to speak to Sister Adelie,' she said to the infirmaress.

'You? Who are you to ask such a thing? This is priory business.' The infirmaress shook with rage.

Mother Marie stood up and said to her, 'Let me introduce you to Christine. She is the daughter of *Maître* Thomas de Pizan, who was, as I'm sure you remember, the renowned physician and astrologer who served the late king. I have asked her here to help us find out who murdered Thérèse.'

The infirmaress looked from the prioress to Christine. 'I thought we weren't going to tell anyone how Thérèse died.'

'That is true, Geneviève. We agreed to keep what we know about Thérèse's death to ourselves. But Christine can help us. She is the widow of *Maître* Étienne de Castel, who served as secretary to our present king, and she is herself an excellent scribe. I have told the others she has come to copy a manuscript for me. That gives her an excuse to be here. I'm hoping she will be able to uncover the truth.'

Sister Geneviève started to remonstrate, but the prioress interrupted. 'Do you recall, a number of years ago, when one of the king's knights died and his wife was wrongly accused of poisoning him?'

'Of course. Everyone talked about it.'

'I was in Paris to visit my nephew, the king, at the time, and I was privy to what happened. The wife was condemned to die at the stake, but at the last minute she was saved.'

'Yes, I remember,' Sister Geneviève said. 'The woman's name was Alix de Clairy. I was so happy when I learned she had not died.'

'She didn't die because the woman standing before you discovered she was not guilty. Christine went to the king and tried to convince him of this, but poor Charles, who'd gone mad the summer before, wouldn't listen. Then, at great risk to her own life, Christine went after the real murderess. When the truth finally came out, because of what Christine had done, the murderess was burned at the stake, and Alix de Clairy is alive today because of Christine's bravery.'

The infirmaress stood staring at Christine with her mouth open. 'Was it really you?'

'I had a lot of help,' Christine said.

The prioress smiled. 'Brother Michel told me how he arranged your disastrous audience with the king, and how you refused to give up, even though everyone tried to discourage you.'

'Michel did more than that,' Christine said. 'He convinced me to go on even after it seemed there was no longer any hope of saving Alix.'

'Are you talking about Brother Michel from the Abbey of Saint-Denis, the one who is writing the chronicle of the reign of King Charles?' Sister Geneviève asked the prioress.

'The very one,' the prioress said. 'Actually, he's here at the priory now. He's staying with the friars.'

The infirmaress stepped closer to Christine. 'Is he here to help you discover what happened to poor Thérèse?'

'Yes,' Christine said. 'But he won't be allowed into the cloistered area where you sisters live. So I'll need all the help I can get from you. That is why I would like to talk to Sister Adelie.'

'All right. But I have to warn you: Adelie is a strange one. Are you prepared for that?'

'I am,' Christine said, wondering whether that was true. She'd imagined the priory would be a place of peace and quiet. Her illusion had been shattered, and she wasn't sure she was ready for any more shocks.

TWELVE

To kepynge of the seke in the fermery, schal be depute suche a suster by the abbes that dredethe God, hauyng a diligence about hem to . . . ofte change ther beddes and clothes, geue them medycynes, ley to ther plastres, and mynyster to them mete and drynke, fyre and water . . . wasche them, and wype them, or auoyde them, not angry nor hasty, or unpacient thof one haue the vomet, another the fluxe, another the frenzy, whiche nowe syngeth, nowe cryethe, nowe lawghethe, now wepethe, now chydethe, nowe fryghththe, now is wrothe . . .

Rule of Syon Abbey, fifteenth century

The three women left the prioress's apartments and walked through passages and courtyards to the infirmary, which was next to a small cloister with a garden of medicinal herbs. The garden was a muddy mess, nearly washed out by the rain, and Sister Geneviève walked quickly past it.

In a large, open room under a high vaulted ceiling, the infirmary nuns hurried about, caring for women who lay in narrow beds, some very ill or asleep, others sitting up, waiting for nurses to bring them bowls of soup or medicines. Whenever one of the nurses passed carrying a tray, Sister Geneviève examined what was on the tray and rearranged it.

In a far corner, a tiny nun sat on the edge of her bed, waving her arms about and talking to herself. She had an untidy bandage on her right hand. 'That is Sister Adelie,' the infirmaress said.

'What happened to her hand? Did she hurt it when she fell in the church today?' Christine asked.

'No. She says she slipped on the wet tiles of the cloister walkway. I don't think she hurt herself badly. She won't let me look at the hand, and I don't want to force her; it would upset her too much. I wish she would at least let me attend to the makeshift bandage she's wrapped around it. It's getting dirty and frayed.'

Christine stared at the little nun. She had such a wrinkled face that she thought at first she was very old, but when she looked more closely, she could see that she was about the same age as her daughter.

'Let me approach her first,' the infirmaress said.

Christine was only too happy to allow her to do so, for Sister Adelie looked completely deranged. She'd pulled her habit up above her knees, and she kept pulling her veil down over her face as though she wanted to hide behind it. The infirmaress approached her slowly, talking softly, as though to a frightened animal.

'Adelie has visions,' Mother Marie said. 'And she thinks she hears things no one else can hear.'

'Like the king's heart?'

'Exactly. We've tried to explain that it is impossible for the heart to beat, that it has no life. After she'd had a number of attacks, we kept her out of the choir for a while. She seemed better, so we let her join the sisters today for sext. You heard what happened.'

'What about her visions?'

'She thinks she sees King Philip. She says he's short and stooped, and he has a hole in his chest where his heart should be.'

'King Philip is reputed to have been tall and handsome. That's why he's called "Philip the Fair."'

'I know.'

Sister Geneviève motioned for Christine and the prioress to approach the flailing nun. Mother Marie took the bandaged hand in hers. 'Why don't you let me look at it, Adelie?' she asked.

Adelie drew her hand away. She looked at Christine and covered her face with her other hand.

'You don't need to be afraid,' Christine said. 'I just want to talk to you about what you heard in the choir.'

'It was the king's heart,' Adelie moaned. She uncovered her face and stared at Christine with unblinking grey eyes. 'It's under his tomb. It wants to go back into his body.' Beads of sweat appeared on her forehead.

The prioress said, 'I've told you many times, Adelie, King Philip's body isn't in that tomb. It's in a tomb at the Abbey of Saint-Denis.'

'But his heart is here. It wants to go back into his body.'

'What's underneath the tomb?' Christine asked the prioress.

'There's an underground chapel. We never go there. It's cold and damp because we are so close to the river. The king's heart is supposed to be down there somewhere, in a small vault. No one has ever been able to find it.'

'The heart *is* there,' Adelie moaned.

Sister Geneviève stood nearby, holding a damp towel she'd folded into a neat square. The prioress took it and gently pressed it against Adelie's forehead. 'We'll go and look, Adelie. Will that reassure you?'

Adelie grabbed the towel and threw it on to the floor. Then she buried her face in a pillow.

'You see? Nothing helps,' Sister Geneviève said as she picked up the towel, shook it out, and folded it into a tight little square again.

'Come with me,' the prioress said to Christine as she turned and walked to the door. On the way out, she stopped at each of the beds and spoke to the occupant. One of the sick nuns seemed particularly distressed about Sister Adelie. 'I don't like having her here,' she said. 'She's frightening me.'

'She is not well,' Mother Marie said. 'You must have compassion for her. As we all must.' She took Christine's arm and led her through a series of passageways to a kitchen where cooks were preparing the evening meal. The afternoon was getting on, and it was growing dark. 'We'll need some light,' she said as she took a candle from a sconce. They went through a large dormitory and back to the church, entering by way of a door that led into the public space. She stopped to show Christine six sculpted figures against the wall at one end of the transept.

'Those are some of Saint Louis's children,' she said. She held the candle high above one of them. 'This is Isabelle, who died after losing her father and her husband, one right after the other. I love her because she has such a pretty face, and she looks so young and so sad. Also, because she hides something for me.' She reached into a deep fold at the bottom of the figure's gown and took out a large key. Then she went to a heavy wooden door in the wall at the entrance to the nuns' choir and unlocked it. A steep flight of stairs led down to the underground chapel. Mold, dust, and cold, damp air rose to greet them.

They descended cautiously, their way lit by the light of the candle, into a small room with nothing but thick columns supporting a vaulted ceiling and an altar with a statue of the Virgin Mary holding the Christ Child. On one side of the empty space, a series of arched openings covered with grilles opened to the outside. The prioress looked closely at the openings and frowned. 'When the water in the river gets high, it seeps through those grilles. I'm afraid that's happening now.'

Christine shivered. The place was dank and musty, and she couldn't imagine that anyone ever came here to worship. 'You have no idea where the king's heart is buried?' she asked.

'It might be under the altar. It's said to be in a pewter urn enveloped in a cloth with golden fleurs-de-lis on a red background. That sounds lovely, but none of us will ever see it. Of course, Adelie thinks she can *hear* it, but that's another matter.'

Christine looked around. Besides the altar and the statue, the chapel was empty. There was no place where a person could hide.

'Who knows where you keep the key?'

'Not many other people. I really don't want anyone else to come down here. I don't want anyone to get sick; we have enough problems with damp air, being so close to the river.'

They stood quietly for a moment, as though by an unspoken agreement they'd decided to listen, to make absolutely certain there were no heartbeats except their own. Then the prioress turned and started up the stairs. Christine took one last look around, saw nothing but a bare, forlorn space, and followed her.

THIRTEEN

Listen to the little nun who just wants to have some fun.

Eustache Deschamps (c. 1340–1404), *Virelai* 752

It was dark when Christine and Mother Marie returned to the prioress's quarters. There they found Sister Juliana, sitting at the prioress's desk with her head in her hands.

'Ah, Juliana. I forgot you asked to see me,' the prioress said as she stirred the fire with a poker. 'Why are you not in the refectory at supper with the others?'

Juliana started to say something, but before she could get the words out, she burst into tears and ran from the room. Christine grabbed a candle from a sconce on the wall and ran after her – down the stairs, through a narrow passageway, and into the empty dormitory, where the girl had flung herself on to her bed and lay weeping bitterly. Christine let her cry for a while and then sat down beside her.

'Why did you run away from Mother Marie? She's a kind woman.'

'I know she's kind. But she doesn't want to hear what I have to say.'

'You can tell me.'

'I already told you. I don't want to be here.'

'Where else would you rather be?'

'Anywhere.'

'What would you do?'

'I could learn to be a scribe, like you.'

'It's not an easy life.'

'I could be a minstrel: I could play the harp, and I could sing. I'd rather sing love songs than chant in the choir all day. I'd sing love songs for noble ladies, even for the queen. Will you introduce me to the queen?'

'What makes you think I know the queen?'

'You wouldn't be here if you didn't. The king and queen and their children come here, as well as other nobles. They have their own quarters. But you're not nobility. So you must have come because the queen asked you to.'

'That's an interesting deduction, Juliana. But I don't believe you figured it out all by yourself.'

'All right, I didn't. But don't think I eavesdrop; I just overheard some of the sisters talking about you.'

Christine laughed. 'No one ever admits to eavesdropping.' *Except Alips*, she thought. She missed the dwarf, who had ways of gathering information. She missed Marion, too, and longed for her help.

Juliana was watching her. 'What are you thinking?' she asked.

'Do you want to do something for the queen?'

'You mean play the harp for her?'

'No, not that. But you're right. I'm here because the queen asked me to come. And I think you know why.'

'It has something to do with Thérèse, doesn't it?'

'Yes. Mother Marie wrote to the queen and asked her to send me here because she knows Thérèse didn't die of a weak heart.'

Juliana's eyes sparkled.

'This is serious, Juliana. You must never repeat what I'm going to tell you. If I find out you've told someone else, I'll make sure you are severely punished. On the other hand, if you keep the secret and help me, I'll see what I can do to help you leave the priory.'

Juliana jumped up from the bed, lifted the skirt of her habit above her ankles, and did a little dance. 'That's all I want,' she cried. 'To get away from here!'

She certainly isn't cut out to be a nun, Christine mused. She felt her heart lift as she watched the girl whirl around the room.

Juliana wheeled to a stop in front of her. 'Tell me what to do!'

'First of all, calm down.'

Juliana sat on the bed. She winced. 'I hate this mattress. I'll never have to sleep on it again.'

'I said I'd *try* to help you, Juliana.'

Juliana folded her hands in her lap and looked at Christine expectantly. 'So tell me.'

'Thérèse's heart didn't give out. She was murdered.'

Juliana gasped.

Perhaps I've made a mistake, Christine said to herself. *Perhaps she's too young for this.*

But Juliana caught her breath and said, 'Now I *really* want you to let me help you. Did someone here at the priory kill her? Was it one of the sisters?'

'That's what we have to find out. That's how you can help me. You know all the sisters, so you can tell me about them.'

'Where do you want me to start?'

'Let's start with Adelie.'

'She thinks she hears things. Like King Philip's heart beating under the nuns' choir. That's impossible. If she heard a heart beating today, it was mine.'

'Why do you say that?'

'I was scared. I'd done something stupid, and I was terrified I'd get caught.'

'What did you do?'

'There's a tomb in the nuns' choir. Have you seen it?'

'Ordinary people aren't allowed into the nuns' choir. We listen to the music on the other side of the grille.'

'I don't see the sense of that. For women, at least.' She tried to bounce on the hard bed and made a face. 'Anyway, the tomb is for a king who lived a long time ago. He isn't even in it, but there's a statue of him on top. He's wearing coronation robes and holding two scepters. There's an ivory hand of God making a blessing at the top of one of the scepters.' She giggled. 'I did something terrible to that hand.' She looked at Christine slyly. 'You won't tell anyone, will you?'

'It depends on what it is. I'm not your confessor.'

'I'll tell you anyway. We do embroidery in our free time. We're supposed to leave everything when we're done, but I like to keep my thimble.' She giggled again. 'I had it today when we filed into the choir for sext. I leaned over and put it on God's thumb.'

Christine tried to keep a straight face. 'Did anyone see it?'

'Before anyone could discover it, Adelie went into her fit, and while they were all trying to calm her down, I snatched the thimble away.'

'That *was* a terrible thing to do, Juliana. You're right. You're not suited to convent life.'

'I'm glad you think so.'

'You were going to tell me about Adelie's fits.'

'She claims she hears things. Sometimes she has visions and she goes into trances. It's all an act. She wants people to think she's special. Perhaps she thinks she'll be made a saint someday.'

'How do you know she's pretending?'

'When she thinks no one is watching, she stops, just like that. No one who's really in a trance or having a vision would be able to return to normal as fast as that.'

'Have you told Mother Marie about this?'

'She knows. She just doesn't want to do anything about it yet. I think she's waiting to see if Adelie will change.'

'Do *you* think she'll change?'

'I don't know.'

'Does anyone else have visions or trances?'

'Are you thinking of Thérèse? You're wondering what made her get up in the middle of the night and go into the cloister. Perhaps she did see something. If she did, you can be sure she didn't make it up. She would never have done anything like that.'

'You knew Thérèse well. Tell me about her family.'

'They come from a town not far from here. Her father was wealthy at one time. Then one of his sons went off on the crusade to Nicopolis and was captured. His father paid a tremendous amount of money in ransom, but it wasn't enough. The son is still a captive, and the father doesn't have any more money.'

'I thought the Duke of Burgundy had paid the ransom money for all those captured at Nicopolis.'

'Evidently not. Thérèse told me that the duke won't help her father. She didn't know why.'

'Tell me again what happened when Thérèse came back from her sister's funeral.'

'She was different. She wouldn't talk to me. She wanted to tell Mother Marie something, but she died before she could do it.'

'We have to find out what she wanted to tell her,' Christine said.

'How are we going to do that?'

'I don't know. I hope you'll be able to help me figure it out.'

FOURTEEN

Nuns pretend that their fathers, sisters, brothers, cousins, and relatives are ill and failing so they can go outside the cloister.

Lamentations of Matheolus, late thirteenth century

The next day, Christine decided to visit the infirmary again and talk with Sister Geneviève. As she walked through a drizzly rain from the prioress's apartments to a complex of buildings reserved for lay sisters and all the people who served the needs of the nuns, she thought about the size of the priory, and what a responsibility it was for the prioress. She mentally shook her fist at Humbert of Romans, who'd written that women were incapable of handling their own affairs. *He would not say that if he could see how Mother Marie presides over this vast enterprise*, she said to herself.

In the infirmary, Sister Geneviève was attending to Sister Adelie, who seemed to be in a stupor. 'I gave her a special mixture of herbs,' she said. 'I hope I didn't give her too much.' Just then, Adelie moaned and tried to sit up, and the infirmaress breathed a sigh of relief.

'Can you leave her for a while? I would like to speak with you.'

Sister Geneviève nodded and led Christine to a room lined with shelves on which were handsome ceramic bottles arranged with the precision Christine had come to associate with this tidy little nun. When Geneviève saw her visitor looking at the label on one of the bottles, she took it down and caressed it lovingly. 'This contains the potion I gave Adelie. It's an old remedy one of my teachers told me about.'

'What's in it?'

'Valerian, hellebore, mint, poppy juice, and sleeping nightshade. It's very strong. That's why I was afraid I might have given her too much.'

'Can it be used for headaches? My mother suffers from them.'

'Heavens, no. It's much too potent for that.' She picked up another bottle. 'This contains an infusion of roses, lavender, sage, and hay. That's what I give the sisters for their headaches.' She set the bottles back on the shelf and turned them round so their labels lined up perfectly. 'Now, what did you want to speak about?'

'Sister Thérèse,' Christine said. 'Mother Marie has told me you and she are the only ones who know she didn't die because her heart was weak.'

Sister Geneviève went to the one window in the room and peered out. She sighed and turned to her visitor. 'She was stabbed. We were able to conceal that fact from the others because the doctor who came was not our regular doctor. He was just a substitute, young and timid. I told him Thérèse had always been frail and that her weak heart had finally given out. He didn't dare contradict me. He accepted that as the cause of her death without examining her body.'

'Is he still here?'

'He's been dismissed; I made sure of that.'

I'm sure you did, Christine said to herself.

'Do you have any idea who could have stabbed her? There are so many people here I don't know where to begin.'

Sister Geneviève gave a little mirthless laugh. 'I'm sure there were many people here who would have liked to be rid of Thérèse. She had haughty ways, and she was disrespectful to the lay sisters and the other people who serve us. Just recently, I heard her berate the poor laundress because she'd been unable to remove a spot from her habit. I happen to know the habit was soiled because Thérèse had been walking in the orchard; we've had so much rain, and everything is so muddy, only a fool would go for a walk in the orchard.'

'Was it her custom to walk on the grounds?'

'Yes. The other sisters do go into the orchard and the gardens, but only when the weather is good. Thérèse just couldn't resist the temptation to go wandering around. She thought she didn't have to act like everyone else.'

'Do you think one of the sisters killed her?'

'I just don't know. I don't want to believe it.'

'There are many other people working here. Do you suspect any of them?'

The rain had begun to come down harder than before, and it drummed against the window. Sister Geneviève traced a haphazard design in the moisture that coated the glass. 'I'm going to tell you something even Mother Marie doesn't know. This information could be very damaging to her and to the priory. I'm trusting you with it in case it's something that will help you solve the problem of Thérèse's murder.'

'You can trust me not to tell anyone else about it unless it's absolutely necessary.'

'There is no reason for anyone else to know.' She stepped close to Christine and said in a low voice, 'Thérèse was pregnant.'

Christine gasped. 'Are you sure?'

'Do you doubt me? I'm a nurse. I know about such things.'

'Why haven't you told the prioress?'

'Don't you realize what a terrible position that would put her in? It's her duty to ensure that all our rules are followed and that all the sisters are pure and innocent. Surely you know that many people believe nuns are corrupted. At a priory like this, which receives so much money from the king, we have to be especially careful not to commit *any* indiscretion. We have to be perfect, and it's Mother Marie's responsibility to see that we are. If anyone found out that one of us had sinned, she would be blamed.'

Christine thought of the prioress's humility. Perhaps that was a weakness. Perhaps in her desire to minister to the poor, she was lax in her other duties. But she just couldn't believe it.

As if reading her thoughts, the infirmaress said, 'Prioresses are elected by the other sisters. Of course, our mission is to offer prayers and chant for the royal family and for all of France. But the prioress also has to be an astute businesswoman.'

'Isn't Mother Marie exactly that?'

'Of course she is. But she is also the king's aunt. She became prioress the year Charles became king. Some of the sisters wonder about it. There is someone among us who would like to take over her position. If it were known that one of the sisters had committed a terrible sin, there would be calls for Mother Marie to be replaced.'

Christine couldn't imagine that happening, but she appreciated the nun's concern.

'It is very important that you discover who murdered Thérèse,' Sister Geneviève said. 'Mother Marie is a superb prioress and an admirable person. Her reputation must be protected at all costs.'

'Do you think it's possible Thérèse had relations with any of the friars here?'

'Of course not! I know all the friars, and there is absolutely no way any of them would have stooped to such a thing!'

'I had to ask.'

Sister Geneviève went to one of the shelves and started rearranging bottles that were already lined up like soldiers. She said, 'It would make a good story, though, wouldn't it? People are always looking for ways to prove that monks and nuns are debauched.' She moved a few bottles, put them back where they'd been, and turned to face Christine.

'There's a more likely possibility. Thérèse often went to visit her family. Her relatives always seemed to be sick or dying.'

'Mother Marie told me she'd just returned from her sister's funeral.'

'For once, the illness was real. Thérèse had visited her sister several times during the past few months. It must have been on one of those visits that she got pregnant. She must have had a lover – someone her parents wouldn't let her marry.'

'Do you know her family?'

'I only know they live in Archères, not far from here. She had two sisters and two brothers. One of the brothers went on the crusade to Nicopolis and didn't come back. I've heard he's being held hostage there.'

'Someone should visit the family and talk to them,' Christine said.

'Henri Le Picart can do it,' Sister Geneviève said.

'You know Henri?'

'Doesn't everyone know Henri?'

'Even at the priory?'

'Of course. Don't you know that Henri has a daughter here?'

Christine had to brace herself against the wall. 'Did I hear you correctly?'

'I thought you knew, since Mother Marie seems to have told you everything.'

'She didn't tell me that. I didn't even know Henri was married.'

'As far as I know, he isn't and never has been.'

'You mean, Henri Le Picart has an illegitimate daughter?'

'That's exactly right.'

'Who is she?'

'Sister Juliana.'

Christine nearly slumped to the floor. 'How long has she been here?'

'Since she was a small child. She doesn't know anything about Henri. I'm sure she's never even seen him. She only knows she was put here when she was very young.'

'Who brought her here if it wasn't her father?'

'A nursemaid.'

'Who is her mother?'

'No one knows. You look as though you are about to faint. Shall I get you some water?'

'No, no. I'm just so surprised. I've known Henri for a long time, and I would never have suspected this. Does he come here often?'

'He comes, but he doesn't see Juliana. He always makes a large donation to the priory when he leaves.'

'But this is a place for women from noble families. Henri is not a nobleman. And I wouldn't have thought an illegitimate girl would be admitted.'

'You aren't nobility, either. Your daughter is here.'

'She had special permission from the king. My father was a royal astrologer, and I have worked as a scribe for the queen for many years.'

'Well, Henri has connections at the court, too. The king is fond of him. So is the king's brother, Louis.'

Louis likes him because he lends him money, Christine thought.

'Juliana has no idea who her father is?'

'None at all.'

'Juliana tells me she hates it here and wants to leave. She thinks she would like it better out in the real world. I wonder how she knows there's a world out there that she would prefer, since she's been cloistered for most of her life.'

'What makes you think this is not a real world?'

Christine felt herself blushing. 'I didn't mean it that way.'

'Many of the sisters were formerly in that other world. We're supposed to follow the rule of silence, but it's a hard rule to keep, and we talk about what we remember. And then there was Thérèse. She and Juliana were friends, and I'm sure Juliana learned a lot from her.' She sniffed. 'A lot she shouldn't know.'

'Do you think Juliana should stay here if she doesn't want to?'

'That's not a question for me. Ask the Reverend Mother.' She laughed. 'Remember, Henri gives a lot of money to the priory. What do you think he'd do if his daughter left?'

Who knows what would Henri do about anything? Christine asked herself.

FIFTEEN

There were beautiful orchards with more than seventy pairs of trees from which came much good fruit. There were gardens, a pleasant paradise where they had everything they needed. In this beautiful refuge, closed all around by handsome walls, there were loudly singing birds, lively fallow deer, goats running wild, many hares and rabbits, and two ponds well stocked with fish.

Christine de Pizan, *Le Livre du Dit de Poissy*, 1400

Christine left the infirmary in need of fresh air and a quiet place to think. The rain had stopped, and although the grass was wet and water dripped from the trees, she sought out the orchard. There, next to the high wall that encircled the priory, she sat on a bench – not minding that the seat was damp – put her head in her hands, and tried to make sense of what she'd just learned.

First, she thought about the murdered nun. Someone would have to talk to the family. The infirmaress had suggested Henri. Henri, who had an illegitimate daughter at the priory! She couldn't fathom it. She watched a gardener and his assistant prune an apple tree. The rasp of a saw against wood set her nerves on edge. A small bird hopped around in the branches over her head, making soft chirping sounds and pecking at the bark. *I should be a farmer's wife*, she thought. *Then I might have peace.*

She leaned against the wall, ignoring the cold seeping through the stones, and closed her eyes. She had a vision of a young Henri Le Picart frolicking with a pretty girl. He'd thrown off his black cape with the ermine collar, and he pranced around in a red jacket and tight silver hose. A very young Henri. She started to laugh. 'I can't wait to tell Marion,' she said out loud.

'Tell Marion what?' The voice seemed to come out of nowhere, and she nearly fell off the bench. 'I didn't mean to frighten you,' Brother Michel said. He was standing beside her, his round eyes blinking furiously. 'This is no place to sleep.'

'I wasn't sleeping. I was trying to make sense of things. I've had a shock, Michel.'

'Tell me about it.'

'Henri has a daughter. She's a nun here.'

'I know.'

Christine jumped up from the bench. 'You know, and you've never told me?'

'Why would I tell you? You dislike Henri so much; why would you want to know anything about him?'

'I don't want to know anything about him. I wish I'd never met him.'

'So, then, what does it matter whether he has a daughter or not?'

'It matters to somebody. Think of the poor girl, shut up here where she doesn't want to be. And there's Henri, going around like a nobleman, making money by unknown means, sticking his nose into everyone's business, especially mine.'

'He's not that bad, Christine.'

'Bad enough. Why won't he acknowledge his daughter?'

'Perhaps he thinks she's better off here than out in the world where she would be shunned because of the stigma of illegitimacy.'

'Shouldn't that be for her to decide? I've talked to this girl, Michel. She's very unhappy. I'm going to tell her what I know.' She started to walk away.

Michel grabbed her arm and pulled her back. 'You can't do that, Christine. This is not your business.'

'It *is* my business. Anything that has to do with the way women are treated is my business. I'm not going to let a woman be treated as a chattel.'

'You don't know what you're saying, Christine.'

'I do know. You have your chronicle, where you can say what you like. I can say what I like, too.'

'I don't make judgments in my chronicle. I just write what I observe.'

'I happen to know that's not entirely true, Michel. You've told me that in your chronicle you condemn the sorcerers who say they can cure the king. That's a judgment. You've told me you write that you believe the Duchess of Orléans was falsely accused of being a sorceress. That's a judgment.'

'Those are only small parts of the chronicle.'

'What about our friend Eustache Deschamps who lives at the court and makes judgments in his poetry about everything he sees? What about all the men who judge women and condemn them as descendants of Eve, who made so much trouble for them by eating an apple?'

'All that may be true, Christine, but you will make yourself ill if you carry on so about it.'

'I thought you were my friend, Michel.'

'I am. I'm trying to help you. And now I think the best thing you can do for yourself and others is to solve the mystery of this murdered nun.'

Christine leaned back against the wall and closed her eyes again. 'Do you have any information that will help me do that, Michel?'

'Unfortunately, no.'

'Then go away. I have to think.'

She didn't open her eyes, but she knew the monk had left when she heard the tree pruners greet him as he passed by them on the way out. Then she sat for a long time, getting colder and colder, yet unwilling to get up and go back inside. Finally, she fell asleep and dreamed she was sinking under the ice in a large fishpond next to the orchard. A sound woke her, and she opened her eyes to see Jacques, the *portier*'s grandson, standing in front of her.

'Ha! I caught you. You were sleeping,' the boy said. 'Don't you know it's raining?'

It was indeed raining. Her clothes were soaked.

'You're not very smart,' Jacques said.

'If you tell me that's just like a woman, I'll spank you,' she said.

'I don't know what you're talking about. I don't know anything about women.'

'You ought to, since you live here at the priory.'

'I'm not allowed to come in here.'

'That doesn't make any sense. If you aren't in here, where are you?' Her teeth were chattering, and she realized she wasn't making any sense, either.

'Well, I'm not supposed to be.' He clapped his hand over his mouth when he realized what he'd said. 'I mean, I'm not allowed to go into the part where the sisters are enclosed.'

'Have you been in there? Tell me the truth.'

The boy's face got red. 'Well, hardly ever. No one has ever seen me.'

'Your grandfather doesn't know?'

'You won't tell him, will you?'

'We'll see.'

Jacques fingered the buttons on his yellow tunic.

'If you really don't want your grandfather to know, then you have to help me.'

The boy twisted a button so hard it came off in his hand. 'What do you want me to do?'

'Tell me if you've ever seen anyone come in here who isn't supposed to.'

'Well, I have seen someone. I think it's the sorcerer who lives in the forest.'

'Is that so?' Christine sighed. She needed help, but she wasn't going to get it from this imaginative little boy. She missed her friends in Paris who always helped her when she had a mystery to solve.

'You can go now,' she said. Jacques stood shuffling his feet. 'Don't worry. I won't tell your grandfather.' He raced away.

She sat and thought about Alips, the queen's dwarf, and Marion, the prostitute who said she'd changed her ways. *What are they doing now?* she wondered.

SIXTEEN

Do not stir fire with a sword.

Old proverb

In Paris, everyone was on edge. The king claimed he felt swords
pricking him, a sign his madness was catching up with him
again, and he was terrified.

Alips the dwarf was frightened, too – for Christine as well as for
the king. Early in the morning the day after Christine left for Poissy,
she wandered around the palace, wondering why the king had sent
her friend to the priory. *There's trouble here at the court, and there
must be trouble at the priory, too*, she thought. *Is all this somehow
connected?*

Alips wasn't the only one who was agitated at the Hôtel Saint-Pol
that morning. The king had flown into a paroxysm of despair, and
when the queen had tried to comfort him, he'd pushed her away
and turned on his courtiers. 'Someone among you has put a spell
on me!' he shouted, tears running down his cheeks. 'Whoever it is,
I beg you to stop.' The courtiers just looked at each other, shaking
their heads.

Isabeau fled to her rooms. Her ladies-in-waiting tried to calm her
with comforting words and offerings of her favorite sweets, but she
brushed them away. When her minstrel played a soothing melody
on her lute, she grabbed the instrument and threatened to break it.
Her fool thought she'd be amused if he did an absurd little dance
with her monkey, and that was the last straw.

'Enough!' Isabeau shouted as she strode to the fool, put her hands
on his shoulders, and pushed him to the floor. He sat up, put his
head in his hands, and pretended to cry.

She became even more agitated when she noticed that one of her
ladies was missing.

'Where is Symonne du Mesnil?' she demanded to know.

The ladies shifted their feet and looked at the floor.

'Tell me!'

Little Catherine de Villiers, her voice quivering, spoke up. 'The Duke and Duchess of Burgundy sent her away.'

The queen was speechless for a moment. Then she became very red in the face and stamped her feet. 'Order the Duchess of Burgundy to come to me immediately!' she hissed at one of her maids.

The maid hurried from the room. 'You leave, too!' Isabeau barked at everyone else. They all crept out of the room. Alips, however, hidden behind a big pillow on a window seat, stayed where she was.

The queen flung herself down on her bed and wept. Alips knew from the way she shielded her eyes with her hand that she had one of her painful headaches. Her greyhound tried to jump on the bed with her, but she pushed him away, and he lay on the floor, whimpering.

The room, which had grown very dark, was illuminated by a sudden streak of lightning. A storm was approaching, and when the Duchess of Burgundy strode in, she was accompanied by a loud clap of thunder.

'What is the meaning of this?' the duchess raged. 'Instead of calling for me and taking up my valuable time, you should be caring for the king.' She quivered with anger, and her gold chains and necklaces jangled.

'Where is Symonne du Mesnil?' the queen shouted. 'You had no right to send any of my ladies-in-waiting away!'

The duchess stamped her foot. The gold chains and necklaces rattled and clanked. 'I will do whatever I like!'

'You will not!' Isabeau screamed. She jumped up from the bed. Her long black hair swirled around her face.

The duchess sneered. 'You can't help the king, and you can't even manage your ladies.'

'My ladies are devoted to me. None of them would dream of leaving me, except for Symonne. She is really *your* lady, not mine. You brought her here, never asking me whether I wanted her or not. And now you send her away. How dare you?' Her black eyes flashed.

The duchess thrust out her arm as though she would hit the queen, then realized what she was doing and let the arm fall. The sudden motion frightened the greyhound, who rose to his feet and lunged at her. The queen caught his collar and pulled him back. The duchess usually hurried from the room when the greyhound threatened her, but this time she stood her ground.

'I'll dare anything I want. You have no sway here.' The duchess nearly spat in the queen's face.

'You are making a great mistake,' the queen said, her voice suddenly icy cold. She dragged the greyhound close to the duchess. 'Get out, before I let him go!'

The duchess shook her fist at the queen, picked up the skirt of her black gown, and strode from the room, shouting, 'You will pay for this, you foolish woman!'

Isabeau sank on to her bed and buried her face in her hands.

For once, Alips didn't have the courage to go to her. She crept out of the room.

The duchess was charging down the hallway, and Alips followed her as she clumped down a staircase and stormed through passageways and galleries until she came to an empty room and went in. Alips waited a moment, then peered around the open door. The duchess stood before a cold fireplace, hammering the ashes with a poker and mumbling angrily to herself. A door on the other side of the room opened, and the Duke of Burgundy entered.

'Where have you been?' the duchess raged at her husband.

Alips moved a little closer.

The duchess seized her husband's arm. He was a large, corpulent man, but he was nearly bowled over by her attack. She clung to his arm and shook it.

'What is troubling you, my dear?'

'The queen is upset because Symonne has gone away. I didn't think she'd notice. Now she's making a fuss about it. You have to do something!'

The duke brushed his wife's hand away. 'You are as foolish as the queen. This never would have happened if you'd listened to me. There was no need to make Symonne one of the queen's ladies.'

The duchess sat down heavily on an elaborately carved chair. 'I did what I thought was right. I thought I was helping you.'

'You didn't take the time to think that the queen might not like it.'

'The queen is stupid.'

'You think all women except you are stupid. I agree. Most of them are. But not Isabeau.'

'You're right. The queen isn't stupid. That's why I became worried when I found out she'd sent that meddlesome Pizan woman to Poissy.'

The duke snorted. 'Do you really think Christine is smart enough to find out anything?'

Alips could see just far enough into the room to know that the duchess was sitting with her head in her hands, and her husband was standing over her.

'She's a clever one,' the duchess said.

'You can stop worrying. I sent Symonne du Mesnil to Poissy to find out what she's doing and stop her if she starts to make trouble for us.'

'The queen is so angry. She may be the one to make trouble.'

'Forget about the queen. She has no power.' The duke helped the duchess up, and they stood before the cold fireplace, lost in their thoughts.

Alips crept away, her head spinning. She had no idea what it was they didn't want Christine to find out, but she was sure of one thing: her friend was in danger. She walked slowly through the great gallery to the door of the palace, passed the *portier* without greeting him, and stepped out into the street.

'You'll get into trouble out there,' the *portier*, who'd never seen the dwarf leave the palace before, called after her. She was so preoccupied that she didn't hear him. She bumped into a woman carrying a large satchel.

'You dwarfs have to watch where you are going,' the woman said as she reached down to keep her from falling.

'I didn't see you, Marion,' Alips said, not at all offended that Marion thought dwarfs had to pay more attention than other people to where they were going. She liked Marion, Christine's friend who had been a prostitute but was now a respectable embroiderer who sold her wares to the queen and her ladies.

'Why are you out here, Alips?' Marion asked.

'I don't know. Where are *you* going?'

'To see the queen. I'm delivering new purses.'

'I don't think the queen will want to see you today. She's upset. The king thinks he's about to have another of his attacks.'

'You're upset, too. I can see that. What happened?'

'Do you know that Christine went to Poissy yesterday? The prioress at the priory asked for her to come and copy a manuscript. The king said she had to go.'

'I didn't know.'

'I heard the Duke and Duchess of Burgundy discussing it just now. It seems that when they learned Christine had gone to Poissy, they sent one of the queen's ladies-in-waiting to find out what she's doing there.'

'Which lady-in-waiting? I know them all.'

'Symonne du Mesnil.'

'That one! She's strange.'

'I know. I've learned a lot about all the others, but I've never been able to find out anything about Symonne.'

Marion smiled. She was well aware that Alips knew everything about everyone at the palace. She'd often wondered what it must be like to be so small that you could be in a room and no one would know you were there.

'The queen and the duchess had a terrible argument about Symonne,' Alips said. 'The queen was very angry that the duchess sent her away. I longed to tell her not to show her anger to the duchess; things only get worse when you irritate an angry person. But I didn't want them to know I was in the room. The duchess left in a huff, and there's no telling what the horrible woman will do next.'

It started to rain. 'We have to get inside,' Marion said. She took the dwarf's hand and pulled her across the street to the palace stables. The stable master called out, 'Hello, Marion. Who's your friend?'

'Someone who needs to be around the horses instead of the nobility for a while,' Marion called back.

The stable master burst out laughing.

'This is a good place to be,' Marion said to Alips. 'The horses and the people who work here are much nicer than the people at the palace.'

The stable master came over to them. 'Do you have any news of Colin?' he asked Marion.

'Of course not, Yves. None of those who were lost in the battle at Nicopolis will ever be heard from again.'

'I feel so guilty. He wasn't the worst stable boy I've had. I shouldn't have dismissed him. If I'd been kinder, perhaps he wouldn't have decided to go off on the crusade.'

Marion put her hand on the stable master's arm. 'It's not your fault, Yves. Here, meet my friend, Alips. She's the queen's dwarf.'

'Welcome to the stables, *Madame*,' Yves said, bowing to Alips. 'Do you like horses?'

'I've ridden in carriages, but I've never met any of the horses that draw them.'

'I'll introduce you to some.'

'Not today,' Marion said. 'We came in here so we could talk without getting soaked. It's pouring out there.' She gestured toward the open door through which they could see the rain coming down heavily.

'Then I'll leave you to it.'

'He's gruff, but he's really very kind,' Marion said as they watched the stable master walk away.

'So I see,' Alips said. 'As I remember, Colin was the brother of Christine's hired girl, Georgette. What happened to him?'

'He never came back from the crusade against the infidels.'

'Are they sure he's dead, and not just a captive? The Duke of Burgundy pays ransom for the men who were captured alive at Nicopolis, you know.'

'No one's said anything about ransom for Colin. That means he's dead.' Marion shifted her satchel from one hand to the other. She was wearing a crimson cape, but she'd left the colorful beads she usually wore in her red hair at home. She was admitted to the palace because she made beautiful embroidered belts and purses for the queen and her ladies, but she'd been a prostitute, and she didn't want anyone to be reminded of that. 'Tell me more about Christine going to Poissy and this business with Symonne du Mesnil,' she said. 'If Christine went to the priory to copy a manuscript, why would she be in danger?'

'It's the way the duke and duchess were talking. There's obviously more to this than a manuscript. The prioress must have lots of scribes. Why would she need Christine? And I forgot to tell you: the king sent Brother Michel and Henri Le Picart with her.'

'Henri?' Marion handed Alips her satchel. 'Here. You deliver these purses to the queen for me. Tell her I'm sick or something.'

'Where are you going?'

'To help Christine.'

Alips staggered under the weight of the satchel. 'How can you help her?

'I'm going to Poissy.'

SEVENTEEN

With my becke bent, my lyttyl wanton eye, my fedders freshe as is the emrawde grene, about my neck a cyrculet lyke the ryche rubye . . .

John Skelton (c. 1460–1529), *Speke Parott*

Marion was sure the Duke and Duchess of Burgundy were up to no good. The duke was out to gain power at any cost, and his wife was a cruel, heartless woman who did nothing that was not in her own interests. When she heard they'd sent Symonne du Mesnil to Poissy, she knew she had to help Christine, because she wasn't sure that Henri Le Picart, a man she thoroughly disliked, would protect her.

Henri owned a lot of houses and rented out rooms in some of them. Marion lived in one of those rooms, on the rue Saint-Honoré. She was not pleased to have Henri as her landlord, but the room was cheap, and now that she was supporting herself with her embroidery, it was all she could afford. It was too late to start out for Poissy that day, so she got up at the crack of dawn the next morning and dressed for the ride. Babil, her green parrot, cocked his head and made anxious clucking sounds as he climbed up and down the bars of his cage, watching her with his red-rimmed eyes as she put on a brown smock with long sleeves, a short-sleeved kirtle with a plain brown belt to which she attached one of her embroidered purses, and sturdy boots.

'Don't worry, Babil, I've got the perfect place for you to stay while I'm gone, and I haven't forgotten you'll need something to eat while you're there.' She put on her crimson cloak, grabbed a sack, picked up the cage, and went out and around the corner to the house of a man who rented out horses.

'What is it this time, Marion?' the man called out as he saw her coming down the street. 'I've got a new stallion. He needs breaking in.'

'No, thanks. I'd rather come home in one piece.'

The man called to his stable boy, 'Bring the little white palfrey. The lady's not the best rider.'

'I ride well enough.'

'Are you bringing that thing in the cage with you?'

Babil let out a loud squawk. 'Here, you hold him,' Marion said as she thrust the cage into his hand. Then, with the help of the stable boy, she got up on to the palfrey, leaned down, retrieved Babil, and rode away.

The sight of Marion in her crimson cloak riding a white palfrey and holding a cage with a green parrot turned heads in the streets of Paris. Marion paid no attention. She rode up the rue Saint-Honoré to the rue des Bourdonnais, tied the palfrey to a post, and walked down a cul-de-sac, carrying the cage. When she came to a small door, she opened it and called out, 'Hello, Mahaut!'

'I've been expecting you,' a ghostly figure said.

Marion stepped into a windowless room lit by dozens of candles, set the cage on the floor, and gave the apparition a hug. She'd first met Mahaut three years earlier when she'd been helping Christine discover who had left a disfigured baby in the palace gardens. At first, she'd not trusted the woman, who was referred to by street people as the 'white woman' because of her deathly white skin and her nearly white hair. But Mahaut, who sold all manner of curious items to people who practiced magic and sorcery, had intrigued her. Among the woman's many wares were herbs and seeds – some poisonous, others just right for a hungry parrot. Marion had begun to buy food for Babil from Mahaut as an excuse to get to know her.

'So, I see you've brought the bird with you this time,' Mahaut said. She limped over to Babil's cage, stared in through the bars, and made clucking noises. Babil responded with excited squawks. 'I'll bet you get tired of seeds,' she said. She rummaged around on a shelf and found a box with small holes in it. She brought it close to the cage and opened it. 'Maybe you'd like some of these,' she said as she tipped it up so Babil could see. He cocked his head, opened and closed his bright red beak, and made gurgling sounds.

'He doesn't eat meat!' Marion cried when she saw what was in the box – dozens of live worms.

Mahaut laughed. Her pale blue eyes sparkled. 'I've got grasshoppers and spiders, too,' she teased.

'Just give me some chickweed and hemp seed.'

Mahaut closed the box and put it back on the shelf. 'Are you going somewhere, Marion? Taking the bird with you?'

'I'm going to Poissy. I'm leaving Babil with a friend.'

'Poissy, you say? I have a sister there. Perhaps you'll see her.'

'Does she live in the town?'

'She's a nun at the priory.'

'I don't mean to call you a liar, Mahaut, but I happen to know those nuns come from noble families.'

'Why do you assume I don't come from a noble family?'

'Do you?'

Mahaut laughed. 'Do you know how the nobility get rid of daughters they don't want?'

'I've heard they put them in convents.'

'That's right. I wasn't having any of that. I ran away.'

'To this dark room? To sell things like this? What kind of a life is that if you come from a wealthy family?'

'The first thing I did after I ran away was become a prostitute, like you. But I gave it up after I was beaten by one of my customers. That's where I got this limp. But now I've done all right for myself. It's better than being a very unhappy nun.'

'I'd like to hear all about it,' Marion said. 'But not today. I have to be on my way while it's still early.'

'And I'd like to tell you all about it,' Mahaut said. 'It's always good to talk to someone who understands.' She measured out the hemp seed and pulled a stalk of dried chickweed down from a collection of herbs hanging from the ceiling. 'Be sure to soak all this in water before you give it to him,' she said as she put everything into a bag.

'I always do,' Marion said as she paid Mahaut and stuffed the box into the sack she'd brought.

Mahaut had a sly smile on her face. 'If you see my sister in Poissy, give her my greetings.'

'How will I know which sister she is? They all look alike.'

'You'll know her.'

Marion picked up the cage and went out the door with a puzzled look on her face.

'You forgot to tell me why you're going there!' Mahaut called after her. But Marion was already out in the street, and she didn't hear her.

* * *

When she arrived at Christine's house, Marion called for Thomas to come and help her down from the palfrey. But instead of Thomas, Georgette appeared, looking very awkward and uncomfortable.

Marion, who hadn't seen the girl for a while, started to laugh. 'I heard you got married. It didn't take long for your belly to swell.'

Georgette waddled over to her. 'You're just jealous.'

'You misunderstand me, Georgette. I have nothing but admiration for you. You know I'll never find a husband.'

Georgette's face turned bright red. She's heard Christine tell Francesca many times that Marion had become a prostitute because she'd been raped as a child, and that no man would marry her because of that.

Marion laughed. 'It's all right, Georgette. I don't want a husband. Here, hold Babil.'

Georgette reached up and took the cage.

'Where's Thomas?' Marion asked as she clambered down from the palfrey.

'The king and queen sent Christine to Poissy, to copy a manuscript for the prioress.'

'I know.'

'Well, Thomas decided to go with her. It was Henri Le Picart's idea.'

'I'm sure Christine wasn't happy about that.'

'She wasn't. But Thomas went anyway. He's old enough to do what he wants.' She set the cage on the ground so she could pull up her apron, which kept slipping down over her big stomach. 'Why are you here?'

'I'm going to Poissy, too.'

'Were you invited?'

'Of course not. But I've learned something that makes me worried about Christine.'

'Don't tell Francesca. She'd be even more upset than she already is.'

'It can't be helped. I need someone to look after my parrot.'

Just then Francesca appeared at the door. When she saw Marion, she frowned. 'What are you doing here?'

'I need you to take care of Babil for a while. I'm going to Poissy.'

Francesca crossed herself. 'That is where *Cristina* has gone! Has something happened?'

'I'm not sure. I think she might need help.'

Francesca crossed herself again. 'I knew she was putting herself in danger!' She started to weep. Babil made squeaking noises as he climbed up and down the inside of his cage. 'You be quiet!' she shrieked at him.

'He'll be good company for you while I'm gone,' Marion said. She picked up the cage and thrust it into Francesca's arms. 'Here's his food.' She handed Georgette the sack with the chickweed and hemp, and climbed back up on to the palfrey.

'You have not even told me what is happening!' Francesca cried.

Marion hesitated. She couldn't think of anything to say that wouldn't alarm Francesca further. She dug her heels into the palfrey's sides and rode off down the street.

EIGHTEEN

One friend watches over and cares for another.

Old proverb

It was a misty day, but the rain held off until Marion reached the forest of Saint-Germain-en Laye. Then she drew her cloak over her head and spurred the palfrey on, trying not to look at the huge trees that lined the path, their newly leafed branches swaying menacingly in the wind. When a limb touched her cheek, she buried her face in the little horse's neck and told herself not to be afraid; but dusk was falling, and she couldn't help thinking that a sorcerer named Jean of Bar had been arrested in a forest, and musing that forests would be good hiding places for all manner of miscreants. Then, before she could let herself become thoroughly frightened, the palfrey started to trot across an open field. They'd come out of the woods, and the rooftops and church spires of Poissy were visible in the distance. She let out a cry of relief and urged the palfrey into a gallop.

But once they'd passed through an open city gate, she drew the horse to a halt. She had no idea what to do next. She supposed Christine was staying with the prioress, but she didn't know whether she should knock at the door of the priory. She knew the nuns were strictly cloistered, and men were not allowed to visit them. As for women, she had no idea.

The palfrey picked his way through crowds of people and animals. 'I'm sure you're hungry,' she whispered to the little horse, and he neighed softly as though he understood. When they came near the walls of the priory, she heard someone shout her name, and Thomas came running to her side. 'What are you doing here, Marion?'

'I'm not sure. I just felt I had to come.'

'That doesn't make sense.'

'I know.' The rain came down heavily now. 'Can we go somewhere dry?'

'We can go into the inn,' Thomas said as he took hold of the palfrey's bridle and led him across the street. 'Henri Le Picart and I are staying there. Maybe Henri will be able to get you a room, too.'

Marion climbed down from palfrey. When her feet touched the ground, her legs gave out, and she nearly fell. 'I don't often go for long rides,' she said.

'Weren't you afraid – a woman all alone? Especially going through the forest?'

'I must admit, I was a little fearful when all those big trees started threatening me.'

'The trees aren't dangerous, Marion. But something else could be. There's a sorcerer there.'

'Do you really think so?'

'I know so. I'm going to find him.' He threw the reins of the palfrey's bridle over a post and led Marion into the inn. Heads turned when men sitting at tables with cups of wine saw the tall, red-headed woman wearing a crimson cloak. Thomas blushed.

'Don't worry, Thomas,' Marion said. 'This isn't Paris, where everyone knows me.'

Thomas stood tall, and Marion smiled. *He's old enough to think it might be a fine thing to be seen with a prostitute*, she thought. They sat at a table next to a window. The thin waiter wearing a green tunic, pink tights, and a hat with a large peacock feather came over and leered at Marion. Thomas snapped his fingers. 'We want some wine!' The waiter bowed deeply, and the peacock feather brushed Marion's face. He snickered and hurried off, flapping his arms like a bird.

'Now, tell me why you're here. Has something happened in Paris?' Thomas asked.

'I'm not sure. I only know what Alips, the queen's dwarf, told me. When the Duke and Duchess of Burgundy learned that your mother had been sent here, they decided that one of the queen's ladies-in-waiting ought to be here, too. They're afraid your mother is going to find out something they don't want anyone to know. Do you have any idea what it could be?'

'All I know is the prioress asked my mother to come because one of her nuns was murdered. It has something to do with a dog.'

'A dog? What does a dog have to do with it?'

'I have no idea.'

'What do Henri Le Picart and Brother Michel have to say about it?'

'Not much.'

'I'm not surprised.'

'Henri does have one suggestion. He thinks we ought to find the sorcerer who's hiding in the forest.'

'Are you sure there's a sorcerer?'

'The grandson of the old man who lets people in and out of the priory says so.'

'That's all the proof you have? The word of a child?'

'Henri believes him.'

The waiter returned. He bowed to Marion again, making sure the peacock feather brushed against her face, and plunked down a jug and some cups. Some wine spilled on to the table. He laughed.

Marion stood up and shook her fist at him. '*Crétin!* What kind of inn is this?' She poked the tabletop with her finger. 'Have you seen what's carved into this? Disgraceful.' She pointed to the floor. 'Those rushes haven't been changed since the Flood.' She reached up to the window, collected some dust, and blew it in his direction. He put his hand to his face and sneezed.

'And your pink tights are torn.'

He looked down at his legs. 'In the back, *imbécil*.' He stalked away. Thomas was doubled over with laughter.

Marion sat down. 'Did you notice the gold ring with the big ruby he's wearing?' she asked as she poured wine into the cups.

'I did,' Thomas said. 'I wonder where he got it.'

'Not around here, I'm sure. Now, let's decide what we're going to do.'

'Who's the lady-in-waiting the duke sent here?'

'Her name's Symonne du Mesnil. Your mother will know who she is. Alips told me she's never been able to learn anything about her past. That seems strange. Alips has always been able to ferret out information about everyone else at the court.'

'You were right to come here, Marion.'

'I think so, too. I've been around the court long enough to know that the Duke and Duchess of Burgundy are treacherous. The duke is power-hungry, and his wife is even worse. She succeeded in getting the wife of the king's brother driven out of Paris, and I think she would do the same to the queen if she could. That's why I'm here. I'm very fond of your mother. She's in danger, and I don't want anything to happen to her.'

NINETEEN

Music comforts those who despair and brings joy to those who are downhearted and troubled. It calms angry hearts and diabolical rages.

Christine de Pizan, *La Mutation de Fortune,* 1403

C hristine was listening to the nuns chanting nones, letting the sound of the tightly woven voices engulf her and wash away her anger and confusion. When she felt a touch on her shoulder, she ignored it. But then someone squeezed her arm, and she came out of her trance. Marion was standing beside her. She gazed at her, open-mouthed.

'At least you could say "hello," and thank me for coming,' Marion said. 'I don't often go into a church.'

'Has something happened at home?'

'Not at your house, unless Babil has bitten your mother.'

'Babil? My mother? I don't understand.'

'I couldn't leave him alone. I think he and your mother will become friends.'

'Babil is at my house?'

'God's teeth. Weren't you listening? That's what I said.'

Christine grabbed Marion's arm and dragged her out of the church. 'You can't talk like that in there, Marion.'

'I was just beginning to enjoy the music.'

'You can go back later. How did you get in here, anyway?'

'Thomas told the *portier* to let me in. Thomas seems to know everybody. You'd better be prepared, Christine: Thomas is growing up to be a fine-looking young man.'

'You don't have to tell me. I worry about him. I wish he wouldn't spend so much time with Henri Le Picart.'

'I can understand that.'

'You'll understand even more when I tell you what I've just learned about Henri. But first I want to know how you got here.'

'I rode, of course. Just like you.'

'But why did you come?'

'Alips overheard the Duke and Duchess of Burgundy talking, and I became concerned. The prioress didn't summon you just to copy a manuscript, did she?'

'No, she didn't. One of the nuns died. She was stabbed. The prioress wants me to find out who did it.'

'God's beard! Nuns murdering each other. What's the world coming to?'

'I'm not sure it was one of the sisters. But so far I have no idea who it could have been.'

'Maybe what Alips overheard those two old connivers talking about has something to do with it. They're not happy that you're in Poissy. They've sent Symonne du Mesnil to find out what you're doing.'

'The lady-in-waiting no one knows anything about?'

'The very one. She's mixed up in whatever is going on, I'm sure.'

Christine tried to picture Symonne. She'd seen her often over the years: a slender woman who was younger than the queen's other ladies-in-waiting and who always wore plain gowns and simple starched white headdresses. She giggled sometimes, a trait Alips said was the result of drinking too much wine at dinner, but other than that she'd always been a shadowy presence.

'Do you know Symonne?' Christine asked.

'When I bring my embroidery to the queen, her ladies are usually around the queen. Symonne always stays in the background, as though she wants to make herself invisible.'

'Alips told me the Duchess of Burgundy brought her to Isabeau. No one seems to know who she is or where she came from.'

'The duke and duchess must be using her for something. We have to find out what it is before you get hurt. Tell me what's going on.'

'As I said, one of the nuns was murdered. She got up in the middle of the night and went into the cloister. Someone stabbed her. The prioress found a broken dog collar near the spot where she died. She had no idea why a dog would have been there.'

'Who else knows she was murdered?'

'Only the infirmaress. She and the prioress are letting the other nuns think her heart gave out. They don't want to frighten them.'

'What's an infirmaress?'

'She takes care of the sick nuns. She told me something she hasn't told the prioress: the murdered nun was pregnant.'

'God's balls! So it's right, what they say about nuns.'

'Don't say that, Marion. People, especially men, love to slander nuns.'

'Does the infirmaress know who the father was?'

'No. But she's sure it wasn't anyone at the priory.'

'That should be easy to figure out since there aren't any men there.'

'But there are. There are friars who say mass and hear the nuns' confessions. And there are doctors and workmen – all kinds of people. The infirmaress is certain it wasn't any of them. But she says the murdered nun often got permission to go home and visit supposedly sick family members. She thinks she must have had a sweetheart on the outside.'

'I suppose that makes sense. Where does her family live?'

'In Archères, not far from here. The infirmaress thinks Henri should go and talk to them.'

'How does she know Henri?'

Christine started to laugh. 'Brace yourself, Marion. You won't believe this. The infirmaress told me that Henri has an illegitimate daughter who's one of the sisters here.'

Marion grabbed Christine's arm to steady herself. 'Henri? I don't believe it!'

'She didn't make it up. Michel knows about it, too.'

'He never told you?'

'He knows how much I dislike Henri. I dislike him even more

now that I know about his daughter. Henri had her brought to the priory when she was just a little girl. She has no idea who her father is. He comes, gives money, and leaves. He never sees her at all.'

'Just like Henri. No consideration for anyone else.'

'That's true. I've met this girl. She hates it here.'

'Why doesn't she leave?'

'Where would she go – a young girl with no money and no family? No family she knows about, anyway.'

The prioress came toward them, her arms full of loaves of bread to give to a group of lepers who'd congregated at the priory entrance. When she saw Christine and Marion, she stopped and looked at them questioningly.

Christine wished Marion hadn't worn her ostentatious crimson cloak. At least she didn't have beads in her red hair. 'This is my friend Marion, Reverend Mother. She just arrived from Paris.'

Marion did a little curtsy.

'Welcome,' the prioress said. 'Did you come by yourself?'

'Yes. I rented a nice little palfrey.'

'It's a long ride, and it's late. Where are you going to stay tonight?'

Marion looked at Christine. 'Thomas said Henri may be able to find me a place at the inn where they're staying.'

'That's fine,' the prioress said. She smiled at Marion.

Does she know she's talking to a prostitute? Christine wondered.

One of the loaves started to fall and Marion caught it. 'Here, let me help you. I suppose you're taking the bread to those poor souls outside.'

'I am,' the prioress said. 'Would you like to accompany me?' Marion took a few more loaves the prioress was about to drop, and the two of them went off toward the entrance. Christine followed, her eyes wide with amazement.

The *portier* looked worried. 'It's dangerous, the prioress standing so close to the lepers,' he said to Christine.

'She's a brave woman,' Christine said as she watched Mother Marie place a loaf of bread in a leper's outstretched hands. Marion was doing the same thing. She'd taken off her crimson cloak and slung it over her arm, and Christine was pleased to see that underneath it she'd worn practical clothes, suitable for a long ride. She also noticed one of her elegant embroidered purses hanging from her plain brown belt.

The prioress dispensed the last of the bread and turned to go back into the priory. Then she noticed the purse.

'That is beautiful,' she said.

Marion untied the purse from her belt and handed it to her. The prioress examined it closely. Then she held it up for Christine to see. It was decorated with delicate flowers and Marion's favorite subject, her green parrot, Babil. Christine had a purse just like it, as did Francesca.

'The sisters would like to see this,' the prioress said. 'It would inspire them to work harder on their own embroidery.'

Marion looked surprised. 'You mean the sisters do embroidery? I thought they only prayed.'

The prioress laughed. 'They have some spare time. Embroidery gives them something useful to do.'

'Women aren't useful for anything else,' said Henri Le Picart, who'd come through the priory gate when they weren't looking and had been standing behind them, listening.

'Son of a—' Marion clapped her hand over her mouth. She glanced at the prioress, but the prioress turned her face away; Christine could see that she was trying to suppress a smile.

'Not pleased to see me, Marion?' Henri asked.

'Not many people are,' Marion said.

'Embroidery is an art, Henri,' the prioress said. 'You might try it yourself. It teaches patience.'

'Actually, I know a lot about it,' Henri said.

Naturally, Christine said to herself.

'It's the colors.' Henri took the purse from the prioress's hand. 'Do you see the parrot's red beak? The red ring around his throat? His red eye? Marion has captured that red perfectly.' He made a small bow in Marion's direction. 'I've made it my business to learn about red dyes.' He winked at the prioress. 'I could teach your sisters all about it if you'd like.'

'Very clever, Henri,' the prioress said. 'But you will not be invited in.'

'I'm heartbroken.' He handed the purse to Marion. 'Come with me, Marion. I've reserved a room for you in the inn across the street.'

Marion looked at Christine. Christine shook her head.

'*Merde*,' Marion said under her breath as she stomped off after Henri.

'I know she'd rather stay here,' the prioress said. 'I'd like to have her here, too. But she'll just have to put up with Henri. I'm sure that if anyone can take it, she can.'

TWENTY

A solitary captive maid, in the flower of youth my summers fade.

A Nun's Lament, early sixteenth-century Spain

Thehe next morning, Christine went to the church to hear the nuns chant terce. It was early, so she wandered to the far end of the transept and looked at the six statues the prioress had shown her.

'Those are Saint Louis's children,' said Juliana, who suddenly appeared at her side.

'Are you supposed to be here?' Christine asked. 'This is the public space.'

'And I might meet a man, God forbid,' Juliana said. 'But you're the only one here now, so I'm safe.'

'You didn't answer my question. And besides, shouldn't you be with the others for terce?'

Juliana pointed to the statues. 'Do you know who these people are?'

'No. Do you?'

Juliana put her hand on a foot of the first of the figures. 'This is Louis, named after his father, the saint this priory is dedicated to. The poor boy was supposed to become king after his father, and they made him spend his whole childhood learning what kings are supposed to do, and then when he was only fifteen, he died. His father must have been very upset.'

'I'm sure he was.'

Juliana went to stand in front of the next statue. 'This is Philip the Bold. They called him "bold," but he really wasn't. He was great at riding horses, but he lost all the battles he fought in.' She moved on to the next. 'This is John Tristan. He was called "Tristan" because he was born in Egypt while his mother and father were on a crusade, and two days after he was born, his father was captured, and everyone was very sad.'

'How do you know all this, Juliana?'

'The novice mistress makes us learn about these people. Actually, it's kind of interesting. The next one, for example, is Isabelle. She went on a crusade with her father, and he died. Then her husband died, and she was so downhearted that she died two months later.' Christine wondered whether Juliana knew about the key the prioress kept hidden in the folds of Isabelle's gown.

Juliana moved on. 'Here's Pierre d'Alençon. He died on one of his father's crusades, too.'

Then she came to the last of the statues, a man in a cap holding a staff and a pair of very large gloves. She stroked the man's foot. 'This is Robert of Clermont. He's the saddest of all, because he got hit on the head in a tournament and lost his wits. I think those are the gloves he wore in the tournament.'

Robert had a silly smile that belied the suffering he must have felt. Christine couldn't help thinking of poor mad King Charles.

'Look there,' Juliana said, pointing to the transept crossing where two statues stood in front of the choir screen. 'Those are the parents, Saint Louis and his wife. The whole family is here.'

'Not quite all,' Christine said. 'Saint Louis had eleven children. I wonder why some of them were left out.'

'Maybe there wasn't room for them. Sometimes parents leave out the children they don't want. After poor Robert went mad, they probably didn't want him anymore, either.'

Christine had to smile at the girl's ingenious concept of history.

'Doesn't Robert's story make you think of our king?' Juliana asked. 'He's lost his wits, too. But in his case, it's because he's been bewitched.'

'He hasn't been bewitched. The people who say that don't know what they're talking about.'

'But there really are sorcerers, you know. They put spells on people. They say there's a sorcerer living in the forest close to the priory.'

'I'm sure you find that idea intriguing, Juliana. But I doubt it's true.'

'People say they've seen him.'

'Who?'

'Thérèse for one.'

'Who else?'

'There's a strange man who comes here. He has a little black beard, and he wears a black cloak with a long hood and an ermine collar. Thérèse said he looked like a sorcerer, and I agreed.'

Christine had a hard time not registering shock. *So she has seen her father, and she doesn't even know it.* 'Where did you see this man?'

'He was walking in the orchard with Mother Marie. She can go there whenever she wants, but the rest of us have to have permission.'

'Which you didn't have, I'm sure.'

'Of course I didn't. Thérèse was with me, and she didn't, either. So we saw this man, and I'm sure he's a sorcerer. I had a dream about him afterward. He was doing all kinds of amazing things, like conjuring up evil spirits and imprisoning them in crystal balls.'

'Do you think that's what sorcerers do?'

'Thérèse told me. She heard about it from her brother.'

'You know, Juliana, people who say they are sorcerers claim they can do all kinds of mysterious and evil things. But none of it is true. Do you know a man was burned at the stake in Paris last year for making such claims?'

'I didn't know anything about it. We never find out what's going on out there in the world.'

'Don't you think you're happier not knowing about all the terrible things happening beyond the walls of the priory?'

'Not at all. Please, I do so much want to get away from here! You promised to help me.'

'Did I?'

'Well, sort of. Have you thought about how you are going to do it?' Juliana looked so unhappy that Christine felt tears come to her eyes. The girl said, 'I can tell you understand. You wouldn't want to be locked up here, either. I just know it.'

'I would enjoy it. I would love the peace and quiet. I could get on with my writing.'

'You mean the writing you do for the queen?'

'No. My own writing. Just poems so far. But I have other ideas.' She didn't want to tell Juliana what those ideas were because they were too close to what Juliana was complaining about – ideas about how men kept women from being educated and forced them to fulfill roles they thought proper for them, such as housekeeping and

childbearing and making them become nuns when they couldn't
think of anything else to do with them. She said quietly to the girl,
'Perhaps I can help you.'

Juliana threw her arms up in the air and twirled around.

'But first *you* have to help *me*. You have to help me find out who
killed Sister Thérèse.'

TWENTY-ONE

The fifth virtue a nun must have is Solicitude or Diligence . . .
With diligence you can master all your senses, including bodily
sleep, for even nature can be mastered and tamed by this virtue.
Which is to say that through the use of great will power, the
spirit can be made to control the body, which is a very neces-
sary thing for a good nun.

Christine de Pizan, *Le Livre des Trois Vertus*, 1405

They could hear someone moving around on the other side
of the grille. 'Sister Claude goes in there to make sure the
music manuscripts are in order,' Juliana said. 'She's very
protective of her precious manuscripts.'

'As well she should be,' Christine said. 'I'm sure they're beautiful
– and costly.'

'You wouldn't think they were so wonderful if you had to sing
from them all day long.'

'But the chant is lovely.'

'For you, standing on this side of the grille. Imagine what it's
like for us. Seven times a day we file in like sheep, with the prioress
and the chantress right behind us like shepherds, and we find our
places in those manuscripts and we chant, on and on and on. I'm
always losing my place, and Sister Claude hits me.'

'Surely not!'

'She does. She hits us when she wakes us in the middle of the
night for matins and lauds, too, if we don't jump right out of bed.
She was especially hard on Thérèse.'

'But isn't that an essential part of your life, getting up to chant the divine office?'

'Of course it is. But knowing that doesn't make it any easier. We have to sleep with our clothes on, you know, so we can get to the church faster. You've been in the dormitory. You've seen how hard our mattresses are. I never get enough sleep.' She opened her eyes wide and stared at Christine. 'Do you see the bags under my eyes?'

'Your eyes look fine to me.'

'I'm exhausted.'

'You know, Juliana, you can train yourself to stay awake. That's what nuns are expected to do.'

'I can't. I have to get away from here. You *have* to help me.'

'I told you, you have to help me first.'

They could hear the sisters filing in on the other side of the grille. 'We can talk later. You have to go in now,' Christine said.

Juliana hung her head. 'I don't want to.'

'But you must. You'll be punished!'

'I don't care. I know where we can go and talk. Come!'

Juliana ran out of the church through a small door at the side of the transept. Baffled, Christine followed her. The rain had started again, and she slipped and nearly fell as they dashed through the cloister and out into a large walled courtyard. In one corner of the wall, there was a building. 'Over there!' Juliana cried as she ran across the muddy courtyard and opened a small door. 'There are laundry rooms on the other side of this, but the laundresses never come in here.'

They hurried into a room filled with clothes that were certainly not laundry – embroidered houppelandes, gold-trimmed kirtles, velvet mantles, silk chemises. 'Whose are these?' Christine asked.

'Sometimes when a woman comes here to become a nun, the chambress puts the clothes she wore in the outside world in here. Later, she gives them away to the poor, but before she does that, I come here and try them on.'

Juliana rummaged through the discarded garments and held up an emerald-green houppelande with a wide lace collar, long sleeves trimmed with pure white miniver, and big purple flowers embroidered down the front. Before Christine could stop her, she cast off her habit and veil, and slipped the elegant houppelande over her head. Then she dove into the pile of garments again and came up with a ruffled veil. 'So much prettier than the plain old things we have to wear,' she murmured as she put it on. She pranced up to Christine.

'How do I look?'

Christine was scandalized, but she couldn't lie. 'Like a princess. Now take it off before someone comes in here and sees you. Otherwise, I'll report you to the prioress.'

Instead of doing what she was told, Juliana picked up a gold belt and fastened it around her waist. Christine stamped her foot. 'I told you—'

'I heard you.' Reluctantly, Juliana lifted the dress over her head and put on her habit. 'Do you know how scratchy this is?' she asked. 'Here, feel it. Our habits can't be made of anything other than wool. Undyed wool, of course. It feels even worse now because it got all wet in the rain.'

'Do you know what happened to the clothes you had on when you were brought here?'

'Of course not. That was a long time ago, when I was just a child. I don't expect they were very fine. I don't think my parents had any money. Otherwise, they would have kept me.'

Henri Le Picart was never poor, Christine thought. *Why did he have to give his daughter away? How cruel. Here is this unhappy girl, trying to imagine parents who were too poor to take care of her, and all the while her real father is someone who just can't be bothered.*

Juliana was adjusting her veil. 'Are you satisfied? Now I look like all the others.'

'You don't like the other sisters, do you?' Christine asked.

'Most of them are all right. But some are as mean as can be. They are all well educated, of course. Anyone who enters here has to be able to read and write. And sing.'

'Did Sister Thérèse sing well?'

'Not that well. She had trouble reading the music, and Sister Claude used to get very angry when she made mistakes. Sister Thomasine helps lead the singing, and she'd get angry, too. They made Thérèse cry. Then Thomasine would stomp off, muttering to herself that she'd like to be rid of the girl. I think she was going to talk to the prioress about expelling Thérèse: no one is supposed to be admitted here if she can't sing.'

Christine thought of her daughter. She'd never really heard Marie sing, but she supposed she must have some talent for it; otherwise, she wouldn't be allowed to stay. 'What about my daughter?' she asked Juliana.

'Don't you know? She has a lovely voice. I admire her. She likes singing. It makes her happy here. She doesn't seem to mind all the rules. Was she like that as a child?'

Christine smiled, remembering that Marie had always been the one to reprimand the others when they'd done something wrong. Especially Thomas, who was *always* doing something wrong. 'Marie was a steadying spirit in our family,' she said.

'Then this is a good place for her.'

'But not for you and Thérèse?'

'Definitely not.'

'Tell me everything you know about Thérèse.'

'I only know that her family lives in Archères and she often went home to see them, because they always seemed to be sick.'

'Doesn't that sound a bit suspicious to you? Doesn't it suggest that she'd thought of a good excuse to get away from the priory for a while?'

'It does. I wish I had a family that was always sick.'

Christine thought of Henri, and she disliked him more than ever. Why wouldn't he want to have the companionship of this lively girl? *Would it bother Henri to know that his daughter is so unhappy?* she asked herself. *Probably not.*

'But Thérèse's sister really did die, didn't she?'

'Oh, yes. Thérèse had a real reason to go home the last time.'

'How did the others feel about her? Did they resent her for being able to go home so often?'

'The other novices liked her. She could make a jest of anything. She even memorized the lives of the saints and retold them in amusing ways. Especially Saint Dominic, the founder of our order. The novice mistress, Sister Petra, heard her one day, and she got very angry and accused Thérèse of making fun of the lessons. I wasn't there, but I heard she made Thérèse lie face down on the floor and repeat some silly prayer a hundred times. When Thérèse got up, Petra slapped her and shoved her out of the room. I was told that Petra and Thérèse looked as though they could kill each other.'

'Who else didn't like her?'

'Sister Richarde didn't. She was very angry when she caught Thérèse imitating the way she has of squinting and looking down her long nose at the papers she's always carrying around. Richarde reported her to the prioress.'

'It sounds as though Thérèse was always getting into trouble.'

'It's true. Even Sister Louise, who's so good-natured, used to get mad at her. Thérèse would go into the hen yard next to Mother Marie's residence and run around scaring the hens. Louise claimed that every time Thérèse did that, the hens stopped laying.'

Juliana was searching through the collection of discarded clothes again. She pulled a yellow cotte, examined it, and thrust it aside. 'I don't like yellow.' A purple velvet houppelande and a green wool cloak with beaver lining got the same treatment. Christine watched her for a while, wishing she could assure the girl that she would find a way to take her out of the priory. But that was not what she was here for. She took an embroidered red houppelande out of her hands. 'We have to talk, Juliana.'

Juliana sat down on the pile of clothes. 'This sounds serious.'

'It is. I've told you that Thérèse was murdered. But I haven't said how. I'm going to tell you now, but this is something you must not repeat. I'm only telling you because I think you can help me. She was stabbed.'

'How terrible!'

'It is. Could any of the sisters have acquired a knife around here somewhere?'

'Of course. The kitchens are full of them.'

'Do the sisters go into the kitchens?'

'We're not supposed to. The cooks and the lay sisters do all the cooking. Of course, the prioress and her henchmen go there all the time.'

'Like Sister Claude and Sister Petra?'

'Exactly. Are you thinking it could be either of them?'

'I'm not thinking anything. I'm just asking questions.'

They could hear someone moving around outside. 'I know who it is,' Juliana said. She opened the door and drew in a little nun who was so short she barely came up to her shoulders. It was Sister Adelie. Her hair was wet, her white habit was covered with mud, and she looked even more deranged than when Christine had seen her in the infirmary.

'How did you get out?' Juliana wanted to know.

'It was easy. I just walked out when Sister Geneviève wasn't looking.'

'This is Adelie,' Juliana said to Christine. 'She's the only one who knows I come in here.'

Adelie looked at Christine. 'I remember. I met her in the infirmary.'

'She's come because Thérèse died.'

'It was her heart,' Adelie said.

'You see – that's what they want us to believe,' Juliana whispered to Christine.

'It wasn't strong like the king's heart,' Adelie said.

'She means the heart that's buried under the choir,' Juliana said. 'Not King Charles's heart.'

Adelie nodded. 'King Charles has a good heart.'

Christine wondered what she meant. Most people thought of Charles as a madman, not a person with a good heart.

'King Charles wouldn't hurt anyone,' Adelie said. 'Not like Sister Petra.'

'Does Sister Petra hurt you?' Christine asked.

'She hits me. She says I'm too ugly and stupid to be here.'

'She hit Thérèse, too, didn't she?' Juliana asked.

'She said Thérèse was too poor to be here. She said her father had wasted all his money. One time I saw her strike Thérèse with a switch. She had other things to hurt people with, too.'

Adelie reached into the sleeve of her habit and drew out a knife. 'Like this. I found it under her pillow.'

TWENTY-TWO

These are they who wickedly corrupt the holy psalms: the dangler, the gasper, the leaper, the galloper, the dragger, the mumbler, the foreskipper, the forerunner, and the over leaper.

John Bromyard (d. c. 1352), *Summa Praedicantium*

Christine took the knife from Adelie. It was a kitchen knife, the kind her mother used.

'This is exciting,' Juliana said. 'We're going to catch the killer!'

'It's not exciting. It's dangerous, and neither of you must say anything about it. Can you both promise that?'

Juliana nodded. She put her arm around Adelie. 'You'll be good, won't you, Adelie? You won't tell anyone else about the knife.'

Adelie nodded.

'Won't you get into trouble if you're not back for sext?' Christine asked.

'We're going to be in trouble no matter what we do,' Juliana said.

Christine handed Juliana the knife. 'Can you hide this in the pile of clothes for a while?'

Juliana lifted the discarded garments and put the knife under them. 'You'll have to come for it before the chambress takes these things away.'

'I'll try. If I can find my way back here.'

'Don't worry. I'll be around to show you.'

I'm sure you will, Christine thought. *You're just like Thomas – you don't want to miss anything.*

Juliana opened the door and peered out. 'It's stopped raining. Hurry. Before the laundresses come out.'

In the courtyard, Christine looked around and saw that there was a small door in the wall, a door that led out into the open space around the church. *That could be useful*, she said to herself as they went back to the cloistered area of the priory. Along the way, they passed a large kitchen where the cooks were preparing the nuns' evening meal.

'I don't know why they look so busy. It'll be just bread and watered wine,' Juliana said. She took Adelie's arm. 'Come on. We'll go to sext. If you hear the king's heart beating, keep it to yourself, or they'll put you in the infirmary again.'

Christine went into the public space of the church and let the beautiful sound of the nuns' chanting float around her. Her trance was interrupted when she sensed someone beside her.

'Where have you been?' Marion asked. 'I've been looking every-where for you.'

'I'm glad you're here. I need your help. Let's go out.'

Some townspeople were entering the church to hear the nuns chant the noon office. Christine pulled Marion to one side.

'I need you to get into the priory.'

'I'm in here now.'

'I mean into the part where the people who work for the nuns go, the part where you aren't supposed to be. Let me show you how you can do it.' She led Marion along the outside of the church until they came to the back of the building that housed the laundry room. 'Do you see the door in the wall? Go through it, and you'll be in a courtyard behind the nuns' choir. That's how the friars and the people who come to work here get in.'

'What do you want me to do?'

Christine mentally pictured where Juliana had taken her. 'Go to the middle of the courtyard and turn right; there's an opening there that will take you out into a long passageway. Follow that until you come to another wide passageway to the left. Go down that, and you'll come to a kitchen.' Christine knew there were several kitchens at the priory. She could only hope this was the right one.

'I want you to find out whether the cooks are missing a knife – a knife like the one my mother uses to cut up chickens. If they are, see if you can find out who took it.'

'Won't they know I don't belong there?'

'If you can get past the *portier* at the front entrance, you'll be able to think of something.'

'I've made friends with the *portier*. He saw me helping the prioress hand out bread to the lepers, and he thinks I'm a friend of hers.'

'If you take off your cloak, you'll look like the women from town who come here to work for the nuns. Go first thing in the morning.'

Marion went back to the inn, and Christine went to the prioress's quarters for the noon meal – civet of hare, fine cheese, fruit, and pastries: nothing like the bread and water Juliana said she anticipated. *Do all the sisters eat like this?* she wondered. *They probably do. Juliana likes to exaggerate.*

The prioress had invited Sister Claude, Sister Thomasine, and Sister Petra, the novice mistress. After hearing Juliana's description of Sister Petra, Christine was eager to talk to the woman, but Sister Claude dominated the conversation with complaints about the sisters in the choir. 'They're impossible!' she said. 'They yawn and go to sleep, and when I tap them on the shoulder to wake them up, they gasp and go too fast and skip ahead, or go too slow and repeat where there is no repeat. Today was especially bad.'

'I was listening,' Christine said. 'They sounded wonderful to me.'

'They lose their place. And they don't open their mouths wide; they just mumble.'

Christine couldn't make Sister Claude's description of the choir nuns fit with the ethereal sounds she'd heard coming from behind the grille. But it wasn't easy to associate tiny Sister Claude, with her bland, expressionless face, with those sounds either.

'You have to understand that we have a mission, given to us in our foundation charter. We sisters are obligated to chant the divine office throughout the day, offering endless prayers. How can those prayers reach God when they're sung carelessly?'

The prioress put her hand on Sister Claude's arm. 'You are exaggerating, as usual, my dear Claude. Christine is right: the singing is lovely. Don't be so hard on your choristers.'

Christine turned to Sister Petra. She was the thinnest woman she'd ever seen, and everything about her seemed forbidding, from her threadlike eyebrows to her pinched lips. *No wonder Juliana resents her*, she thought.

'I understand you train the novices. It must be difficult to keep all those young women focused on their studies.'

'It's not so difficult,' Sister Petra said. 'They think I have a stout switch. I really don't, but it scares them.'

Christine glanced at the prioress and saw her blanch.

'Some of them are insolent,' Sister Petra continued. 'Like the one who died. She always argued with me.'

'Thérèse had her good qualities,' the prioress said. 'I was particularly impressed with her devotion to the founder of our order.'

'She just liked the stories of his life,' Sister Thomasine said. She was standing by a window, and the rays of the sun, which had suddenly come out, cast soft colors on to the smooth white skin of her face.

Sister Petra said, 'She had a vivid imagination. Unfortunately, she didn't bother to learn all the things a novice is supposed to learn, especially our rules. Not that she would have followed them.'

'We need to be stricter here,' Sister Thomasine said, glaring at the prioress.

The prioress looked away. Christine wondered whether she was bothered by the criticism. But before she had time to think about it, the little princess bounded in. The sisters all curtsied. Sister

Denise hurried in and apologized to the prioress. 'She won't take her nap,' she said. She tried to catch the princess in her arms, but the child ran to the prioress and ducked behind her chair. Sister Denise pulled the little girl out and held her tight.

'Disgraceful,' Sister Thomasine said.

The princess pointed her finger at Christine. 'Why is she here? She's not one of the sisters.'

'She's here because I invited her,' the prioress said. 'She is the widow of *Maître* Étienne de Castel, who served as your father's secretary. She has made some beautiful copies of your mother's manuscripts.'

'You have lots of beautiful manuscripts, too. I see one over there.' The little girl ran to the desk and picked up the *Life of Saint Dominic*. It was heavy, and the prioress lifted it from her hands before she could drop it.

'Here, we'll look at it together,' she said as she laid the manuscript on the desk and opened it.

Christine and the other nuns gathered around. 'Saint Dominic was the founder of our order,' the prioress explained to the child. 'See, here are pictures of all the major events of his life, from his birth to his death.'

The princess yawned. 'I'm sleepy.'

'Then you should have your nap. Wasn't that what Sister Denise was trying to get you to do?'

'Sister Denise can't make me do anything I don't want to do.'

'You are an insolent little girl,' the prioress said, pretending to spank her.

'You see,' Sister Thomasine whispered to Christine. 'Things are too lax here.'

Sister Denise picked the child up and carried her away for her nap.

Christine stood looking at the first picture in the manuscript. She'd seen it before. Now there was something about it that troubled her, but she couldn't think what it was. Sister Claude brought her out of her reverie. 'I hope you will come to hear nones. My singers aren't nearly as bad as I make them out to be,' she said.

TWENTY-THREE

Be glad in your heart if ye suffer insolence from Slurry, the cook's boy, who washeth dishes in the kitchen.

The *Ancrene Riwle* or *Guide for Anchoresses*,
thirteenth century

Marion lay awake on an uncomfortable bed in the inn across the street from the priory and worried that she wouldn't be able to find the kitchen and do what Christine had asked. Besides being disagreeable because of the lumpy bed, her room was on the street, right where she could hear all the arguments and fights that went on during the night. After listening for a while to a dispute over a loaf of bread, she got up, put on her cloak, and went out. She found two young women fitted out with fake deformities – a bloody bandage around the head of one and a crooked patch over one eye of the other – just like some of her reprobate friends in Paris.

'*Hé*, mopsies!' she cried. '*Tais-toi!* You're keeping me awake!'

A third woman, who wore a tattered brown mantle with a big hood, approached and pointed to Marion's crimson cloak. 'Who are you to tell us what to do? You're not from around here with a cloak like that.'

Marion was about to tell them that where she came from was none of their business when she had an idea. 'What's your name?' she asked the woman.

'Luce.'

'Do you like this cloak, Luce?'

The woman nodded.

'Then I'll let you wear it for a while if you'll lend me your mantle.'

Luce's eyes sparkled. She took off the mantle and held it out to Marion. Marion took off the crimson cloak. 'Remember, I'm only lending it to you. Be here tomorrow so you can give it back. And don't think you can run away with it. If you do, I'll tell the authorities and have you arrested. Do you understand?'

The woman nodded.

Marion went back to her room and slept soundly through the rest of the night, for now she knew how she was going to do what Christine had asked.

The next morning she went to the priory, carrying Luce's ragged mantle under her arm.

'Where's your pretty crimson cloak?' the *portier* asked as he let her in.

'I lent it to a friend.' She waited until his back was turned, and then crept around the side of the church until she came to the little door. She went in, put on Luce's mantle, stuffed her red hair under the hood, and walked through the courtyard and along the passageways Christine had told her about until she came to a large kitchen.

The door was open because it wasn't raining and it was a warm day. She peered in. She'd expected to see nuns in white habits and black veils preparing bread and water, so she was surprised to see what looked like any normal kitchen scene. A stout woman in a blue cotte and a big white apron – obviously, the head cook – stood on a platform giving orders to her helpers, some of them lay sisters, others lay people from the town. A small boy stoked the fire in a large fireplace, and an even smaller boy stood on a box washing dishes. The boy on the box glanced around and saw her. He winked and flicked soapy water in her direction.

The meal being prepared looked delicious: huge kettles of soup – for which a woman in a bright green kirtle and a yellow apron was cutting up vegetables – and omelets of eggs, cheese, and herbs that several lay sisters cooked in big pans over the fire. Marion smelled the cheese and herbs, and her stomach started to rumble. When a boy who was sweeping the floor came near her, she leaned in and asked, 'Can you spare a bit of bread?'

'Cook doesn't like beggars,' the boy said. He looked her up and down and went on with his sweeping.

One of the cooks, a fat woman in a flour-dusted cotte, who was making crust for apple tarts at a table near the door, begin to swear and shout at the boy.

'I told you to find that knife. It's been several weeks since it disappeared. What's the matter with you, dolt?'

'I've looked everywhere for it,' the boy wailed. 'I hope you don't think I stole it.'

'No, I don't think you stole it. You're too stupid to know what to do with it.'

Another boy heard the argument and said, 'I don't know where the knife is, but I know who took it.'

The head cook heard, and she shouted, 'Why didn't you say something?'

'Why should I? You cooks are always yelling at us.'

The other cook grabbed his arm and shook him. 'You'd better tell us. Right now.'

'One of the sisters took it.'

'Which sister?'

'How should I know? They all look alike.'

The boy on the box jumped down and ran over to Marion. 'Actually, they don't all look alike,' he whispered.

'Do *you* know who it was?' Marion asked.

'No. But she was shorter than some of the others. At least the ones I've seen. Most of them never come here.'

'But lots of other people come into this part of the priory, don't they?'

'Sure. Even beggars like you.' The boy laughed and ran back to his box.

Marion went into the courtyard in front of the entrance to the church, hoping to see Christine. But Christine was not there, so she went across the street to get her cloak back. She found Luce prancing around, showing it off as though she owned it. She was about to tell her to give it up when she had another idea. She'd come to Poissy to find out what Symonne du Mesnil was up to, and she figured it would be easier to ask questions if she wasn't conspicuous in her crimson cloak. She went up Luce and grabbed her arm.

'Don't forget who that cloak belongs to,' she said.

'Do you want it back so soon?'

'You can borrow it a little longer. I'm going to walk around the market. You can return it when I come back.'

Luce let out a little whoop of joy and skipped back to her companions.

Marion stood for a while, unsure what to do next. In Paris, it was her reprobate friends to whom she often turned for information, so she looked to see if there were any beggars in the crowds of people who'd come to town for the cattle market. She found some standing by the door of the inn. Their costumes were no more original than those of her Paris friends: bandages stained with fake blood, sham tumors, ragged eye patches, makeshift crutches, wooden legs. There was even a man who rolled himself along on a little cart, pretending he had no legs. She studied them all, trying to decide which one to approach. Then she noticed a woman wearing a green kirtle with a wide embroidered belt. She moved closer and looked at the belt. She was sure it was one of hers. She pulled the hood of Luce's mantle down over her face, crept behind a large cart parked in the middle of the street, and watched. When the woman turned, she saw that it was Symonne du Mesnil.

TWENTY-FOUR

To presume can be deceptive; much harm can come from trusting too much.

Christine de Pizan, *Proverbes Moraux*, 1400

Marion ducked farther back into the shadow of the cart and watched as Symonne threw a coin into a beggar's tin cup and walked away. She waited a moment, then stepped cautiously into the street and followed. She was sure the woman hadn't seen her.

It was a market day, and as Symonne wound her way through the throngs of people, she had to stop to let a herd of cattle go by. Marion stopped, too. The sound of terrified animals filled the air, and the smell of blood and excrement reminded her of the slaughterhouses and butchers' shops around the Châtelet in Paris. *It would be easier to follow her there, because I know all the streets and places to hide*, she thought. *But I trust my instincts. She'll never know I'm behind her.*

Symonne moved on, and Marion crept after her. They came to the banks of the Seine, where cattle drivers herded their charges down to the river to drink, bracing themselves on the slippery grass to keep from falling into the high water. Close by was a bridge with many arches, and men, sheep, and cattle on their way into town trudged over it, jostling a band of traveling musicians heading in the same direction. The cacophony of bleating sheep and lowing cattle mingled with the shrill sounds of bagpipes and shawms.

As soon as the band of musicians stepped off the bridge, Symonne walked into their midst and disappeared. Marion tried to go after her, but a juggler blocked her way, tossing balls at her and laughing. She stepped around him and collided with a man strutting about with a bear on a chain. The bear held out a cup; she threw a coin into it and hurried on.

Venders of meat pies and onion tarts hawked their wares, some of them sheltering under tents to keep off the rain that had started to fall, and peddlers strolled through the crowds, getting in everyone's way. She slipped on the wet street as a man leading a huge bull pushed her aside. Then a flock of bleating sheep ran by, followed by a dog that nipped at their feet and a small boy who cried desperately that they were supposed to wait for him.

She came upon a group of traveling players who'd set up a stage and were about to put on a show that needed participants from the audience. The hood of Luce's ragged mantle fell back, revealing her red hair, and the players noticed her.

'You're just who we need,' one of them shouted, and they all gathered around, beckoning to her.

'Not in the rain,' she said, and she walked away, struggling to get through the crowds and bumping into people at every turn. An old woman holding a puppy she wanted to sell held the poor animal out to her. She looked so desperate, and the puppy had such pleading eyes, that she was tempted. She mentally slapped herself and brushed past the woman without acknowledging her.

By this time, Marion was sure she'd lost Symonne. Then she spotted her ahead. She hurried forward, but her way was blocked by a herd of cows that had stopped in the middle of the street and refused to move, even when their handler lashed out at them with a whip. She tried to step around them and found herself in a very narrow and dark blind alleyway. In her haste to get out, she brushed against a wall, bruising her hand and tearing Luce's mantle. By the time she'd regained the street, she'd lost all sense of direction. She looked around frantically for Symonne, but she was gone. *At least she didn't see me*, she thought. *I'm sure of that.*

Marion looked down at the tear in Luce's mantle and decided it didn't matter – the mantle was so full of holes to begin with. She went back to the beggars in front of the inn. Luce was still there, showing off the crimson cloak. 'It's time to give it back,' Marion told her.

Reluctantly, Luce took off the cloak. Marion put it on, gave Luce the ragged mantle, and went toward the door of the inn, intending to get out of the rain. A group of horses stood tied to a post, and as she passed them, Symonne du Mesnil stepped out from their midst and said, 'You thought I didn't see you. You're too trusting. Be more careful next time.' She slipped around the corner of the inn and was gone.

TWENTY-FIVE

There is a Latin proverb that men use to defame women. It says, 'God created women to weep, speak, and spin.'

Christine de Pizan, *Le Livre de la Cité des Dames*, 1404–1405

Early the next morning, Christine found the prioress in her study with a letter in her hand.

'I want to speak with you about this,' Mother Marie said. 'Sit over there by the fire. It's still cold in here.'

Christine sat on a bench in front of a newly laid fire, picked up a poker, and stirred the logs. Flames leaped up and sent points of light sparkling on the silver platters and crystal goblets on the shelves.

The prioress put the letter on her desk, rubbed her hands together to warm them, and said, 'When Thérèse came here, her father, Tassin of Archères, gave us a silver chalice. Now he's written asking me to return it. I will certainly do so. The chalice is of little worth, but perhaps he can sell it. I know he needs the money.'

'That is kind of you,' Christine said.

'There is a reason why I am telling you this. I would like you to deliver the chalice. If you meet Thérèse's family, you may learn something that will help solve the mystery of her death.'

'Gladly.'

'I thought I might ask Henri Le Picart to accompany you.'

Christine sighed. She tried to cover her mouth with her hand so the prioress wouldn't notice. But of course she did. She had a sly smile on her face.

There was a knock at the door, and before the prioress could answer it, Sister Richarde charged in.

'That man Picart again! He has no business telling the bailiff we should have a steward to oversee our finances!' she fumed.

'You don't have to worry,' the prioress said. 'You've read our foundation charter. You know it says we don't have to account to anyone for how we conduct our business.'

'I know. But every time that man comes here, he goes around saying that we must be mismanaging our affairs.'

How like Henri, Christine thought. She was so angry that she dropped the poker. The noise startled Sister Richarde, who hadn't noticed her sitting by the fire.

'We shouldn't be talking about this in front of your guest,' the treasuress said.

The prioress smiled and said to Christine, 'You are welcome to join our conversation. I know that anything having to do with Henri Le Picart interests you.'

Christine rose from the bench. 'It's unfair of him to assume that women are incapable of managing their own affairs.'

'The worst of it is, all men seem to feel that way,' Sister Richarde said.

'Not all. My father didn't,' Christine said. 'He taught me to read and write. Because of that, I am able to support my family, not sit in a corner crying about my misfortunes.'

'*Brava!*' Sister Richarde cried. 'Then you understand why Henri Le Picart upsets me so much.'

'I understand very well,' Christine said. 'I have known Henri for years. He doesn't think women have minds.'

The prioress smiled. 'We have to make allowances for Henri. I believe he is a good person at heart.'

Christine wondered how she could say that when Henri had forced his daughter Juliana into the priory. She said, 'Henri's attitude toward women is certainly not to my liking. He acts as though we are inferior beings who must defer to men in everything, even when they are wrong.'

'And they are often wrong,' Sister Richarde said. 'I'll give you an example. The bailiff bought some sheep last week, and this morning he told me he was going to pasture them in the forest of Saint-Germain-en-Laye. I told him he couldn't do that, and he started arguing with me, as though I didn't know what I was talking about. I had to point out to him that our foundation charter states that we have the right of pasturage in the king's forests with the *exception* of the forests of Laye and Coucy. I don't think he believes me. I'll have to bring him here so you can show him the charter, Reverend Mother.'

The prioress started to laugh. 'Just tell the shepherds about the sorcerer who's supposed to be hiding in the forest. They won't go anywhere near it.'

'Do you think there really might be a sorcerer there?' Sister Richarde asked.

'Of course not.'

'The sorcerer who was put to death in Paris last year had an assistant who ran away. Perhaps he came here.'

'My dear Richarde, you know better than to keep repeating that foolish notion!'

'I've heard that Jean of Bar made an image for the Duke of Burgundy. The duke was going to use it to cure the king. The image wasn't found with Jean's other paraphernalia, and no one knows where it is. Perhaps it really does have magical powers, and the assistant is hiding it in the forest.'

The prioress stamped her foot. 'Enough! I'm sorry I mentioned this non-existent sorcerer. You know very well that the Church denounces magic and superstition. That is why Jean of Bar was executed.'

Christine listened to all this without saying a word. She didn't believe in the sorcerer, but she had other thoughts about the Duke of Burgundy. If the duke had an image made, he might have intended to use it to harm, not help, the king.

Sister Richarde picked up the documents on the prioress's desk and looked through them, squinting as she did so. Christine remembered Juliana saying that Thérèse had angered her by imitating that look.

'Have you removed any of the receipts for last week's timber sales?' Sister Richarde asked the prioress.

'Certainly not.'

'One of them is not here. I can't imagine what could have happened to it. But I'll look for it later. Right now, I have to go and talk to the bailiff again.'

'If you have a problem, send him to me,' the prioress said.

'I'll send Henri Le Picart, too. He's the one who's causing all the trouble. You have to enlighten him about women, Reverend Mother.'

Good luck with that, Christine said to herself.

After Sister Richarde had left, the prioress said to Christine, 'Have you learned anything that can help us determine who killed Thérèse?'

Christine wasn't ready to tell the prioress about her visit with Juliana and Adelie. Instead, she said, 'Thérèse was killed with a knife. Would any of the sisters have a knife?'

'There would be no need. But there are many knives in the kitchens. Do you want me to ask the cooks if any of them are missing?'

'It would be better if you didn't get involved. I have other ways of finding out.'

The prioress smiled. 'I'm sure you do. I have to tell you, you are a perfect foil for Henri Le Picart. I hope he realizes that.'

The little princess appeared at the door. She ran in and climbed on to the prioress's lap. 'I heard you talking about knives,' she said.

'It's nothing you need to know about,' Mother Marie said.

'But I know who has a knife,' the princess said.

TWENTY-SIX

Lies can be used not for falsehood but to protect something.

Christine de Pizan,
Le Livre de la Prod'hommie de l'Homme, 1402

Christine and the prioress stared at the princess.

'Who has a knife?' the prioress asked.

The princess started to speak but stopped when Sister Denise came into the room. 'I've been looking for her everywhere,' she said.

The princess buried her face in the prioress's chest.

'Tell us about the knife,' the prioress said.

'I forgot,' the child said in a small voice.

'How could you forget? If you saw someone with a knife, you must tell us who it was.'

The princess bit her lip. 'The cooks have knives.'

'Who else?'

'I told you. I forgot.'

'Are you afraid someone will get into trouble if you tell us?'

The child looked away.

'Why does she look so distressed?' Sister Denise asked.

'She'll be all right,' the prioress said. She shook the little girl gently. 'You told us you know who has a knife, and now you tell us you've forgotten who it is. That is a lie. You know it is wrong to tell a lie.'

The little girl started to cry.

'All right,' the prioress said. 'We'll leave it for now.'

There was a knock on the door and Sister Claude came in, bringing with her Sister Louise and a very tall nun who limped to the prioress, shook her fist at her, and cried, 'It's an outrage.'

'Calm yourself,' the prioress said. 'What has happened?'

'You must come to the refectory and see for yourself.'

'This is Sister Dorian, our fratress,' the prioress said to Christine. She handed the princess to Sister Denise. 'Please take her to her quarters. We'll talk to her later.'

Sister Dorian was looking at Christine doubtfully. 'It's all right,' the prioress said. 'This is Christine, widow of the king's secretary, Étienne de Castel. She will come with us. Please lead the way.'

The refectory, which was next to the church and could be entered directly from the prioress's residence, was a huge space with a floor made of tiny colored stones and two rows of pillars supporting high pointed vaults. Against the walls, under high windows, were dozens of long tables and narrow benches. Christine pictured one hundred twenty nuns sitting on the benches, resting their backs against the stone walls until the fratress saw them and poked them to make them sit up straight.

At one end of the vast space was a raised platform on which stood a lectern with a book, ready for the nun who would read while the others ate in silence. Christine glanced at the book and saw that it contained the story of Saint Dominic's life. *How many lives of this saint do they need?* she asked herself. But she didn't have long to ponder this because Sister Dorian herded them forward.

'When I came in here a little while ago, I discovered *this*,' she said, pointing to something that had been carved into the top of one of the tables. It was the crude figure of a bird.

'Do you know who did this?' the prioress asked.

'No,' the fratress said. 'It was done while we were all at prime.'

'Do any of you know what this figure means?' the prioress asked.

Sister Dorian shook her head.

'Claude?'

Sister Claude was silent.

Sister Louise said, 'It's evil.' She began to cry. 'The sorcerer who lives in the forest must have done it.'

'That is utter nonsense, Louise,' the prioress said.

'It is not! There is a sorcerer, and he is coming out of the forest to harm us.'

She sounds just like my mother, Christine thought.

'Perhaps one of the novices did it,' Sister Dorian said.

Sister Claude, looking very small next to the tall fratress, said, 'I know you don't like the novices, Dorian, and I complain about them a lot, too, but I just can't believe any of them capable of such mischief.'

Sister Dorian turned to the prioress. 'What do you think, Mother?'

'I think this must be taken to the carpenters' shop. They will be able to scrape this revolting figure away.'

'But you can't erase the fact that it was done!'

'I know. Nevertheless, it is best if the others know nothing about it. You must all keep this to yourselves.'

'But we must warn the others!' Sister Louise exclaimed.

'And upset everyone?' the prioress asked. 'Let's suppose for a moment that there *is* a sorcerer, Louise. Do you think he did this just to frighten *you*?'

'Not just me. He knew that everyone in the priory would see it,' Louise said, her fat cheeks quivering. 'He wants to frighten us all.'

'So, if you tell the others, the whole community will be terrorized and you will have helped him accomplish his goal. Do you want that?'

'You're right. It would be a sin to assist a sorcerer,' Sister Louise muttered.

'I'm glad you understand, Louise. Let me repeat what I said before: you must *all* keep this to yourselves.'

'Does that order include your guest?' Sister Dorian asked, shaking with rage.

'I would not have asked her here if I did not have complete confidence in her discretion,' the prioress said calmly. She ran her hand over the figure of the bird and shook her head sadly. 'Dorian, please have the carpenters remove this as soon as possible.'

Sister Dorian glared at her for a moment, then limped out the door. Sister Claude and Sister Louise stood looking after her with tears in their eyes. 'How could this be happening here?' Sister Claude asked. 'We have always been so peaceful and secure.'

The prioress put her arms around her. 'We will be so again, Claude. Please believe me.' She motioned to Christine to follow her, and they returned to her quarters. It was mid-morning, but it was raining, and her study was nearly as dark as it had been at dawn. None of the crystal goblets on the shelves glittered, and the noble ladies in the tapestries on the wall faded into their flowered backgrounds. The prioress sat on a seat in front of the window and leaned her forehead against the moist glass. 'I've heard something about a bird like that,' she mused. 'I don't remember what it was. But there is someone who would know.'

She went to her desk and picked up the letter from Tassin of Archères. 'As I said earlier, Christine, I was considering having Henri Le Picart accompany you to Archères. I think it's a good idea. Don't you agree?'

Christine didn't agree. But what could she do? She nodded.

TWENTY-SEVEN

Note that the hoopoe is possessed of great virtue for necromancers and invokers of demons.

From a fifteenth-century manual of demonic magic,
Bayerische Staatsbibliothek, Munich, Clm 849, fol. 17v

'Come with me,' the prioress said, and she led Christine out of the cloistered area to the priory entrance. There they found Henri.

'Do you need my help after all?' he asked.

'I do,' Mother Marie said. 'But first I want to show you something.'

They went back to the priory and through many courtyards and passageways until they came to a shop where carpenters were at work repairing broken benches. The defaced refectory table had been brought there, and one of the men was examining the figure that had been carved into it.

'Come and look at this, Henri,' the prioress said. 'It should interest you.'

Henri stepped up to the table and bent over the figure of the bird. He looked puzzled for a moment and then he began to laugh.

'You must recognize this, Christine,' he said.

'I do not.'

'Sorcerers love this bird,' Henri said. 'It's not very well done, but it's recognizable because of the big crown of feathers on its head. It's called a hoopoe.'

'Why would anyone carve the figure of this bird into one of our refectory tables?' the prioress asked.

'Isn't Christine here to solve problems like this?'

'Perhaps you can help, too, Henri.'

'Christine should at least know about the superstitions surrounding the hoopoe. Didn't your mother ever tell you that sorcerers sacrifice hoopoes when they summon demons?'

'My mother doesn't practice sorcery.'

'Oh, well. The hoopoe is not always a symbol of evil. Some parts of the bird can be useful. Especially the eyes, if you carry them around in a little bag. Did your mother ever tell you that?'

She fought back the urge to lash out at him.

'Perhaps the sorcerer could carry the eyes in one of Marion's embroidered purses,' Henri added.

Christine turned and was about to leave, but a look from the prioress held her there.

'Tell us, Henri, how do the eyes help?' Mother Marie asked politely.

'They ward off evil spirits.'

'What about the other parts of the bird?'

'Put the powdered head of a hoopoe under your pillow, and you'll dream of hidden treasure. If you have a hoopoe's heart under there, too, you'll see where to look for the treasure.'

'Do you believe those things?'

'I don't. But most women do. Some women put hoopoe feathers on their heads to cure their headaches. I've even heard of a woman who thought she could make herself invisible if she mixed the blood of a hoopoe with—'

'All right, Henri,' the prioress said. 'I'm sure you have a lot more of this nonsense to share with us, but that's enough. That is not why I invited you here.'

'Why did you invite me here?'

'I wanted someone to identify this bird. Now that you've done that, I need to find out who carved it into the table.'

'You know, Reverend Mother, your priory is not as cloistered as you think. Oh, yes, the nuns' choir, the cloister, the chapter house, the nuns' dormitory, and the refectory are off-limits to strangers, especially men. But there is so much more to the priory – the places where the friars, lay sisters, and all the people who care for you live and work. This carpentry shop, for example. Do you really think you and your nuns are completely cut off from the world? Do you really think no one could breach the walls of your enclosure?'

'Of course, I know all that,' the prioress said. 'Why do you think it is necessary to tell me?'

'Because I don't think you realize the danger you are in,' Henri said.

The prioress's eyes flashed. *She certainly does know*, Christine thought. *But she's shrewd. She needs his help, and she knows it won't do to antagonize him, as much as she might wish to. But what does she think he knows that she doesn't?*

The prioress said calmly, 'Your lecture on the hoopoe was interesting, Henri. There were one or two things about the bird I'd not heard before.'

Henri made a mock bow. 'Thank you, Reverend Mother.'

The prioress looked at the carpenter, who was waiting to resume work on the table. 'Do you think you can get rid of the figure of the bird without damaging the surface?'

'With a little labor, Reverend Mother, this table will look as good as new,' the man said.

'Then we'll step outside and let you get on with it.'

They went out into a courtyard and stood near the great bell that was rung to summon the sisters to office. The prioress said, 'I asked you here, Henri, because I do need your help. I think the hoopoe scratched into the table may have something to do with Sister Thérèse's death.'

'Why do you think that?'

'It's just an idea. We have to look into anything unusual that happens here if we're going to find out who killed her.'

'There is reason in that,' Henri conceded.

The prioress said, 'I have received a letter from Tassin of Archères, Thérèse's father. He asks that I return a chalice he gave the priory. I need someone to deliver it. Christine has agreed to do it because it will give her a chance to observe Thérèse's family. She needs an escort. Will you go with her?'

Henri looked at Christine. 'I don't think she would like that.'

'You're right,' Christine said. 'I wouldn't.'

'Do you really expect me to agree to accompany her when my company is so distasteful?' Henri asked the prioress.

Mother Marie held up her hand. 'Enough of this squabbling. You must both accede to my wishes, regardless of your personal feelings.'

TWENTY-EIGHT

The baroness should have knowledge of everything, for as the philosopher says, no one is wise who does not know something about everything. Furthermore, she should have the courage of a man.

Christine de Pizan, *Le Livre des Trois Vertus*, 1405

The next morning, the prioress handed Christine a blue velvet sack. 'The chalice is in here. When you hand it to Tassin of Archères, tell him I return it to him gladly.'

Christine went to the entrance to the priory and found Henri talking to the *portier* while Jacques held the bridles of her palfrey and Henri's big destrier. 'Take me with you,' the boy cried.

Henri smiled and tousled his hair. 'Not today,' he said.

Christine handed the velvet sack to Henri. 'You'd better carry this.'

'Ah, yes, the priceless chalice.' Henri slung the sack over his shoulder. Christine shuddered. He climbed into the saddle and started off without waiting for her.

Jacques helped Christine up on to the palfrey and walked sadly back to his grandfather's side.

The sun appeared, and the day promised to be pleasant. The village of Archères was less than a league up the river from Poissy, and Christine looked forward to a pleasant journey on a road flanked on one side by the Seine and on the other by the forest of Saint-Germain-en-Laye. Finches and jays chirped and screeched from the branches of the great oak and chestnut trees, a magpie chattered, and crows flew overhead, drowning out the other birds with their harsh cries. On the river, which had risen alarmingly high, a group of ducks bobbed up and down, their emerald-green heads as bright as the blue of the water.

Henri, whose mood seemed worse than usual, wasn't enjoying any of this. 'You aren't happy to be going to Archères?' Christine asked.

'Certainly not. Tassin of Archères owes me a lot of money. I sold him some land a few years ago and he's never paid me.'

'Tell me about him.'

'He's only a baron, but he fancies himself a great lord. He'll never be that, now that he's lost all his money trying to ransom a son who got himself captured at Nicopolis.'

'Why won't the Duke of Burgundy pay the ransom? Does he have some grudge against Tassin of Archères?'

'Tassin is certainly a man who provokes people to hold grudges. You may like his wife, though. She's your type of woman.'

'What do you mean by that?'

'You'll see.'

They rode slowly along the riverbank. A few barges circumvented islands in the river, setting waves lapping against the shore and making tall grasses bend and sway. Everything was calm and pleasant, except Henri. Christine decided to ignore him and enjoy the outing. Soon they approached a walled village with an ancient church. Just outside the village was a hill, and on top of the hill stood a large manor house and a few dilapidated barns and outbuildings. A wall surrounded the demesne, but many of its stones had fallen, and what had once been a means of fortification was rapidly becoming a pile of rocks. As they rode across planks that bridged a half-hearted attempt at a moat, Christine looked down and saw nothing but a ditch filled with litter.

They came to the heavy wooden door of the manor house. Henri banged on it until a man in a tunic too large for his small frame opened it and demanded to know who they were and what they wanted.

'To see your master, of course,' Henri said. 'We have something for him.' He looked back at Christine, saw that she was still sitting on the palfrey, but didn't offer to help her dismount. The man came out and offered her his hand. As she dismounted, she noticed that his tunic was threadbare, his shoes were shabby, and there were holes in his hose.

A tall woman in a blue houppelande came to the door. 'Good morning, Madame Marguerite,' Henri said, suddenly polite. 'I've come to see your husband and I've brought with me Christine, widow of the king's secretary, Étienne de Castel.'

Madame Marguerite looked behind her and beckoned to a small, weasel-like man who started to turn away when he saw Henri.

'I'm not here to ask for my money, Tassin,' Henri snorted. 'I've brought you something from the prioress at Poissy. God knows, you don't deserve it.'

Tassin of Archères grabbed the sack from Henri's hands and was about to flee, but his wife stopped him.

'That is no way to treat our guests, Tassin.' She turned to Christine. 'Welcome. Please come in and have some refreshment.'

'You are most kind,' Christine said as she followed the baroness into the great hall of the manor house. The floor of the large, almost empty space was covered with greasy rushes, the walls were bare, and the oiled cloth covering the windows was torn. Even on a warm spring day, the space was cold, and no one had lit a fire in a large fireplace built into one of the walls.

At one end of the hall stood a large table and a few benches. The baroness clapped her hands to call a pretty maid in a dingy white apron who carried in a tray on which were mismatched pewter cups and plates of tarts. 'Please be seated,' Madame Marguerite said to Christine and Henri. 'We have little to offer, but you are welcome to it.' While her husband cowered in the corner, giving Henri dirty looks and surreptitiously peering into the blue velvet sack to make sure his chalice was there, the baroness poured wine into the cups and served the tarts. Christine bit into a tart and found it delicious.

Two children came running in. One, a pretty girl who looked to be about twelve, ran to her mother and hugged her. The other, a large, surly-looking boy in his late teens with a black patch over one eye, stood glaring at his mother and her guests. Christine was dismayed to see that both children's clothes were as threadbare as those of the man who'd opened the door for them. Even the rope collar of a mangy little dog that slouched in after them was frayed.

The baroness, seeming not to notice the alarming condition of her children's clothes, graciously introduced them. The girl, Suzanne, curtsied politely. The boy, Guy, nodded and slouched off to the corner to join his father, followed by his dog.

Where is the rest of the household? Christine wondered. There was no steward, and no butlers, chamberlains, or any other staff necessary for the upkeep of such a large manor house. *The baroness must be doing all the work herself,* she thought. She watched the woman, who sat holding her daughter, and felt immense pity as well as admiration.

'I was so sorry to hear about your daughter Thérèse's death,' Christine said. 'I have three children of my own. I cannot imagine how it would feel to lose one of them.'

'It is very hard,' Madame Marguerite said. 'To make it worse, Thérèse was the second child I lost. The last time I saw her was when she came home to attend my other daughter's funeral. I'd made myself so ill with grieving for Martine I was not able to make the journey to the priory for Thérèse's funeral.' She put her hand over her eyes to hide her tears.

Christine couldn't think of a way to ask any of the questions she had on her mind. Obviously, no one in the family knew Thérèse had been murdered. *Does her mother know she was pregnant?* she wondered.

'Was Thérèse happy at the priory?'

'The last time she was here, she was so eager to get back she left without waiting for Guy to accompany her.'

'I'm sure the sisters were good to her.'

'She didn't like some of them. She felt they were overly strict. But they must have been good teachers. She told us about the things she learned, especially about the Dominican order and its founder.' She smiled. 'Thérèse was always regaling us with stories about Saint Dominic.'

'Did anything happen to upset her when she was here the last time?'

The expression on Lady Marguerite's face was guarded. 'Naturally, she was upset about her sister's death.' She glanced over at her husband, who was glowering in the corner.

Christine waited, hoping the baroness would say more, but Madame Marguerite looked at the empty plate of tarts and clapped her hands for the maid.

'I can understand her love for the priory,' Christine said. 'It is a beautiful, peaceful place.'

'You have seen it?'

'Yes. I am staying there. It gives me a chance to see my daughter, who is one of the novices.'

The baroness looked puzzled.

'I work as a copyist. After my husband died, I took up that work to support my family. The prioress has asked me to copy a manuscript for her.'

The baroness still looked puzzled.

'I'm sure you are wondering how it is that my daughter, who is not from a noble family, was accepted at the royal priory.'

The baroness held up her hand. 'Please accept my apologies. I did not mean to imply that your daughter was not worthy.'

'I can understand your confusion. There is nothing to apologize for. My daughter was accepted because my family has many ties to the court. My father was physician and astrologer to the king, and before that, his father.'

Lady Marguerite's eyes widened. 'Was your father Thomas of Pizan?'

'He was.'

'I know all about him. My father was one of Charles the Fifth's chamberlains, and he told me that Thomas of Pizan was a great man. I am so pleased to meet his daughter.'

Tassin and his son sat in the corner, arguing about something. Guy had his arms around his dog, shielding the mutt from his father, who was shaking his fist. Henri, who had not said a word, got up, went to sit on a bench by the cold fireplace, and watched them.

'I would like to hear about your work as a copyist,' the baroness said.

Christine was about to describe some of the beautiful books she'd copied for the queen when the maid came in with the tarts. From the corner, Guy called out in a mocking, lewd voice, 'Come over here, Berta.' The girl set the tray down and ran from the room. Guy laughed. Christine turned to look at him and was shocked by the leer on his face.

Henri stood up and indicated that it was time to leave.

'I am reluctant to let you go,' the baroness said. 'We have so few visitors here.'

Christine would have liked to stay, too. She felt great sympathy for the woman. She looked over at the father and son again. Guy's little dog was trying to lick Tassin's hand. Tassin kicked him. Guy picked up the dog and slunk out of the room. Tassin made no sign that he was aware the visitors were leaving.

Outside, Henri mounted his destrier, while the man in the threadbare tunic helped Christine on to the palfrey. Tassin stayed in the house, but the baroness came out to wish them a pleasant journey. They rode away, and when they came to the dry moat, Christine looked down and saw Guy throwing stones at a few pigs snuffling around in the litter.

'What a sad family,' she said to Henri. 'What happened to the son's eye?'

'Guy's a big boy, but he's not strong. He's also a bully. He taunted some boys from the town last year, and they gave him a severe beating.'

'I thought perhaps his father might have done it. Tassin of Archères looks like a brute.'

'He is. He treats Guy miserably. He even tried to kill his dog. The older son, Bernart, is his favorite. Tassin has spent all his money on ransom for him. Such foolishness. Bernart is never going to come back.'

'How do you know?'

Henri didn't reply. He looked up and shook his fist at the magpie, which was still chattering from the top of an oak in the forest.

'That bird sounds almost human,' Christine said.

'It's just a lot of noise.'

'Don't you like birds, Henri?'

'Not particularly. I find what people say about them amusing, though.'

'What do you mean?'

'Like the hoopoe. All those myths about it. People pay money to buy the bird's brains and blood because they think they have supernatural powers.'

Christine felt a chill.

'The hoopoe does have some good qualities,' Henri mused. 'There's something I neglected to tell you about that bird, Christine.'

'I think you've told me enough. Poor bird. Hunted down and killed just to satisfy people's need to practice evil.'

Henri laughed. 'I don't know how many hoopoes are actually caught. And anyway, how does anyone know whether the little brain he's bought comes from a hoopoe or a crow? How does he know the vial of blood he's spent all this money on doesn't come from a butchered cow?'

'I thought you were going to tell me something pleasant about the hoopoe.'

'People say that when young hoopoes see their parents getting old, they care for them, preening their feathers and staying close to them to keep them warm. Supposedly, this rejuvenates the old birds.'

'What a lovely idea,' Christine said.

'I thought you would like it. I see how you argue with your mother, Christine. But I also see how well you care for her.'

Christine was so surprised that she nearly fell off her horse.

Henri looked up at the magpie. 'Got to get that damned bird's noise out of my head,' he muttered, and he started to hum.

TWENTY-NINE

The most humble lady [*Marie de Bourbon*] . . . *in whom there is modesty, goodness, sound judgment, and nobility.*

Christine de Pizan, *Le Livre du Dit de Poissy*, 1400

The day had been pleasant when they'd started out, but now clouds thickened and threatened rain. Henri spurred the destrier, and Christine's little palfrey hurried after him as a strong wind came up, causing the river to swell with waves that rocked the barges and drove the ducks up on to the bank to hunker down in the reeds and tall grass. The trees in the forest swayed and bent, and moaning sounds seemed to come from deep within. Henri turned around in his saddle and called back to Christine, 'It's probably the sorcerer.'

'I don't find that amusing,' Christine called back. The palfrey quickened his pace.

The rain started to fall as they approached the walls of the town. By the time they arrived at the entrance to the priory, they were soaked. The prioress was standing with the *portier*, sheltering under her black cloak. As soon as Jacques had helped Christine down from the palfrey, the prioress motioned for her to follow her.

'I have no time for you now, Henri,' Mother Marie said as they hurried away.

Slipping and sliding as they tried to dodge the raindrops, they made their way through the courtyard and into the prioress's parlor. A fire blazed in the fireplace, and the prioress's cook was placing warmed wine and tarts on the table.

'We will have these later,' Mother Marie said. 'Now you must put on dry clothes.'

Christine went into her room and did as she was told, relieved to be out of her wet garments. She took a moment to sit and think about all that had happened that day, putting her thoughts in order so she could present them to the prioress in a clear manner. Then she went into the parlor, where she found Mother Marie sitting at the table, resting her head in her hands.

'Is something wrong?' Christine asked.

The prioress raised her head. Her eyes were red and she looked very tired. 'I will tell you in a moment. But first, have some refreshment and tell me your impressions of Thérèse's family.' She handed Christine a cup of wine and a tart.

'It was a sad day,' Christine began after she had taken a sip of wine and a bite of the tart. 'You were right to return Tassin of Archères's chalice. I am afraid he is very much in need of money.'

'Tassin of Archères was never good at managing his finances. And once he decided to try to ransom his son, he ruined himself. Madame Marguerite would have handled things differently, I am sure.'

'I suspected that, too, from what I saw. But I feel so sorry for the children, especially the girl.'

'You have seen what kind of home Thérèse came from. Did you see anything that would give us a clue as to why she was murdered?'

'The baroness told me that after her sister's funeral Thérèse was so anxious to get back to the priory she left without waiting for her brother to accompany her. I suspect Madame Marguerite may know why, but she changed the subject before I could ask her about it. All I can say is that after having visited her family, I am certain Thérèse was happier here than at home.'

'It was just a wild hope I had, that you would see something that would enable us to find out who stabbed her. We have to solve this mystery before word of a murder here in the priory gets out. Anything that sullies our reputation hurts us, and the king, too. That is something he cannot bear in his present state.'

'I am aware of that.'

'You must know, too, that many people resent us because we are protected by the king. We employ people from the town and the neighborhood, giving them the means to support their families. But there are others who would like to see us fail. People are ready to condemn us at the slightest hint of impropriety or scandal.'

The fire blazed, its light reflected in the silver platters on the table, the crystal goblets on the shelves, and the gold and silver threads in the robes of the ladies in the tapestries on the wall. These priceless objects made a striking contrast to the prioress in her simple white habit and black veil.

'People think we are greedy because we are so richly endowed,' the prioress continued. 'Most of the sisters here come from noble families, as you know. The king makes exceptions for some, like your daughter, but those are few. When they enter the priory, we receive rich gifts. Our treasury is filled with gold and silver chalices, reliquaries, and jeweled crosses. Everyone knows about these precious objects and wonders about them.'

The prioress smiled. 'You may have heard that when Princess Marie entered, there was some controversy. Brother Michel remembers. On the day she was received, she wore a magnificent gold crown set with priceless jewels. I assumed the king was making us a gift of the crown, but, unfortunately, it was only on loan from the Abbey of Saint-Denis. The monks were very upset. They said I was avaricious and not to be trusted, and they made a great deal of noise about it, which was not necessary since once I realized the mistake, I gave the crown back. In return, the king gave us a large sum of money. Brother Michel and I had a good laugh about it, but I fear he is still not entirely convinced we weren't trying to steal the crown.'

'I'm sure Michel doesn't blame you. He's one of the most reason-able people I know.'

The prioress smiled sadly. 'Michel and I will always be good friends, no matter what happens. I wish I could say that for all the sisters here.'

'Surely everyone here respects and honors you!'

'Not everyone. There are sisters here who say I would not have been made prioress if I had not been the king's aunt.'

They are wrong, Christine thought. *No one is better suited to be in charge of a large community of nuns than this extraordinary woman.*

'There is ambition here, just as in the world outside,' the prioress said. 'There are some here who would like to take my place and would do anything to accomplish that end. Something that happened while you were gone makes me more certain of that than ever.'

The prioress rose, went to her desk, picked up a large book, and held it close to her chest. 'As you know, among the many gifts we receive are manuscripts of immense value. This is one of them – an antiphonary we received last year. Gifts like this are given to us with the understanding that we will care for them and preserve them. We are well aware of what a privilege it is to be able to use such precious objects in the choir every day. No one can ever accuse us of handling them carelessly.' She held the manuscript out, but covered it with her hand so that Christine could not see it clearly. 'This manuscript rests on a lectern in the center of the nuns' choir. It is large enough that everyone in a small group of singers can see it, and it is in plain sight at all times. This afternoon, when Sister Claude went into the nuns' choir after nones to prepare for vespers, she found this.'

She held the manuscript up so Christine could get a good look at it. Its leather binding was torn and its spine was broken. She opened it, and Christine gasped. The pages were wrinkled and torn.

'What happened?' she asked, her voice breaking with emotion. The sight of a priceless manuscript in tatters appalled her.

'Someone took it off the lectern, threw it on to the floor, and walked on it,' the prioress said.

THIRTY

Books, clothing, and other things belonging to the monastery
shall be kept carefully.

Constitutions for Dominican Nuns, c. 1300,
Bayerische Staatsbibliothek, Clm 10170, fol. 137v

C hristine stood dumbfounded. After a long while, she asked,
'Was there a time when no one was in the nuns' choir?'
'Between sext and nones all the sisters were in the chapter
house.'

Christine placed her hand gently on one of the pages of the ruined
manuscript. It was crumpled, but the musical notes were still visible,
rising up and down through furrows put there by a cruel foot. A
gilded illumination in one corner had not been damaged. The text
identified it: *Missus est Gabriele.* 'Gabriel was sent,' she murmured.

'The Annunciation,' the prioress said.

The picture showed Mary in a walled garden, seated on the ground
among roses, violets, and snowdrops, looking up in surprise at her
heavenly visitor.

'I love that picture,' the prioress said. 'The Virgin looks so young
and innocent, beautiful yet sad. She reminds me of young girls when
they first come here, unhappy because they're leaving the world,
yet happy because they know they are entering an even lovelier
place.'

The prioress traced with her finger the outline of the figures of
Mary and the angel of the Annunciation.

'Do you have any idea who did this?' Christine asked.

'None at all. Everyone here knows the immense value of this
manuscript. Anyone in our community would quake with fear to
think she had destroyed it and dishonored the spirit of Saint Dominic
and of our past master generals, especially Humbert of Romans.'

'Can you think of anyone here you might have wronged? Anyone
who would want to get revenge?'

'I am absolutely certain that none of the sisters did this,' the prioress said.

Christine wasn't so sure. But she wasn't ready yet to tell the prioress who she thought might be the culprit.

It was not yet time for vespers when Christine left the prioress's quarters. She went to the laundry building, her anger growing with every step, because she couldn't get the image of the destroyed antiphonary out of her mind. When she didn't find the person she wanted to talk to in the room with the discarded clothes, she stormed back to the cloister. But she wasn't there either. *You can't escape me forever, you little devil*, she muttered to herself. She remembered the orchard. The rain had stopped, so that would be a good place to hide. *Not that it matters to her*, she thought. *She'll stay out in the pouring rain if she has to.* She marched to the orchard, and there she found her, talking to one of the gardeners.

'You know you aren't supposed to be talking to a man,' she said as she took Juliana's arm and pulled her away.

'I don't care. Let them put me in prison.' Juliana started to cry.

'You have a lot to answer for, Juliana,' Christine said.

'You're angry with me. You weren't angry with me before.'

Christine practically dragged her out of the orchard, through the muddy courtyard, and into the little room next to the laundry.

'Why shouldn't I be angry with you, Juliana?' she said. 'If you think what you've done is a way to free yourself from a situation you don't like, you're mistaken. I was ready to help you, but now I have to take you to the prioress and tell her what you've done. I don't know what your punishment will be, but it will be harsh, I can assure you.'

'I don't know what you're talking about!'

'That's a lie, and you know it. Look, Juliana, I don't believe you killed Thérèse, but I know about the tricks you've been playing.'

Juliana was weeping. 'If you're thinking of the trick I was going to play with the statue of the king, I told you I removed the thimble before anyone could see it. Isn't that enough?'

'That was nothing compared with what you did today. Don't you have any respect for the things of value the priory has been given?'

Juliana fell to her knees and put her arms around Christine's legs. 'Please, tell me what you're talking about.'

Christine looked down at the girl and felt a pang of guilt. *Could I be wrong?* she asked herself. *Have I let my anger get the better of me?*

'Stop crying and look at me, Juliana. Did you or did you not deface one of the refectory tables? Did you or did you not go into the nuns' choir and throw the antiphonary that was on the lectern on to the floor and walk on it?'

Juliana stared at her open-mouthed. 'What table? What manuscript?'

'Yesterday someone carved something into one of the tables in the refectory. Today that person went into the nuns' choir and threw the antiphonary down and stepped on it. The antiphonary is now unusable.'

'It wasn't me. I swear it wasn't me. I didn't go for a meal in the refectory today, and I didn't go into the nuns' choir, either. I didn't go there! I just couldn't stand it any longer.'

'Where were you?'

'In the orchard, where you found me. I've been there all day.' She tightened her grip on Christine's legs. 'If you turn against me, I'll kill myself.'

'I don't believe you would really do that.'

'I have a knife right here, and I'll use it.' She sprang up, went to the pile of clothes, reached in, and pulled out the knife Adelie had brought. She held the point to her chest. Christine grabbed it from her hand.

'Did you use this knife to deface the refectory table, Juliana?'

'I didn't do anything with the knife. I haven't touched it since we were last here. Give it back to me so I can kill myself.'

'You know you aren't going to do that. But you are in a lot of trouble.'

'It's not fair! You're accusing me of carving something into the table. At least tell me what it was.'

What if she really doesn't know? Christine asked herself.

'It was a hoopoe.'

'What's a hoopoe?'

'A beast with black fur and long horns.'

'Does it live in the forest? Should we be afraid of it?'

Juliana seemed genuinely puzzled. *She really doesn't know what a hoopoe is*, Christine thought. *If she did, she would surely inform me that I have it all wrong.*

Juliana put her hands together in prayer. 'Please believe me. Whatever it is, I didn't do it!'

'I don't believe you did deface the table. But there is still the matter of the antiphonary. Will you swear to me by God and all the angels that you aren't the one who destroyed it?'

Juliana fell to her knees again. 'May God strike me dead if I'm lying. I never did it!' She threw her arms around Christine's legs and wept uncontrollably.

Christine sank down beside her. 'Then I apologize, Juliana, with all my heart.'

Juliana reached out to the pile of clothes, grabbed a velvet houppelande, and wiped her eyes with it.

'Put that houppelande back before you ruin it,' Christine said. 'While you're at it, hide the knife under those clothes again.'

Juliana took the knife and did as she was told. 'At least you didn't accuse me of killing Thérèse,' she said.

'No, I didn't do that.' Christine stood up and pulled the girl to her feet. 'Forgive me, Juliana. The sight of the destroyed manuscript made me so angry, I lost my reason.'

Juliana threw her arms around her. 'I understand. I get angry like that sometimes. Actually, I feel angry like that most of the time.' She stepped back and looked at Christine intently. 'You can make up for falsely accusing me. Help me get away from here.'

'I've been trying to think how I could do it, Juliana. It's not so simple.'

'It *is* simple. You'll find out who killed Thérèse. And who defaced the table and destroyed the manuscript. And then you'll take me away.'

Christine felt utter despair. The girl had too much faith in her abilities.

'One person probably did all those horrible things,' Juliana said.

'I'm sure you're right,' Christine said. 'But I hate to disappoint you. I'm no closer to learning the identity of that person than I was before.'

THIRTY-ONE

Make an image in the form and likeness of the one to whom you wish evil.

Picatrix, ninth-century Arabic book on magic,
translated into Spanish and Latin in 1256

On the day Christine and Henri went to Archères, Marion
went to the priory to tell Christine about her visit to the
priory kitchen and her sighting of Symonne du Mesnil.

'Your friend isn't here,' the *portier* said. 'She's gone off with
that little man with the black beard.'

'Do you know where they went?'

'I heard them talking about Archères.'

Jacques bounced up and down next to his grandfather. 'I got to
hold the horses!'

Marion turned away and found Thomas behind her. 'I don't know
why they didn't take me,' he said. 'They're going to find out things,
and I want to know, too.'

'We'll do some investigating ourselves,' Marion said. 'Have you
seen a woman in a green gown with an embroidered belt like the
ones I gave your mother and grandmother?'

'I have seen a woman like that. I noticed her because of her belt.
It looked expensive. Why do you ask?'

'We're going to follow her and see what she's up to.'

'It shouldn't be hard to find her. There aren't many women around
here with belts like that. Everyone in this town is poor, it seems to
me. Except for the nuns in the priory, of course.'

'That's a pretty astute observation, Thomas. When did you last
see this woman?'

'This morning. She was over by the inn. Who is she, anyway?'

'Symonne du Mesnil, the lady-in-waiting I told you about. The
one the Duke and Duchess of Burgundy sent here.'

'Then we have to find her! Let's go!'

It was not a cattle market day, but everyone was out to see the traveling players, and there were throngs of people in the streets. Jugglers and acrobats wove their way through the crowds, making jokes about the people they encountered. The man who'd seen Marion previously recognized her.

'Such a handsome cloak, *ma biche*. Won't you come up on to our stage and show it off?'

Marion looked at the rickety wheeled platform on which they performed their plays and shook her head. 'Not on that. It doesn't look as if it would hold a couple of fleas, much less a bunch of fat sots like you and your pals.'

The man laughed and signaled to his companions that it was time to start the play.

'I'll bet they aren't as good as the players I've seen in Paris,' Thomas said.

'Don't be so sure. Their stage looks flimsy, but we might be in for a treat.'

The man she'd talked to jumped on to the platform and announced that they were about to see a play they would never forget, a play that would show them the errors of their ways, a play so edifying that they would go away changed forever.

'They're going to do *The Seven Deadly Sins*,' Marion said.

The announcer stepped aside as a man in a floppy beaver hat and a houppelande with ermine-lined sleeves appeared, bringing with him a woman in a low-cut gown covered with beads and flowers. The woman began to arrange her hair under a huge jeweled chaplet while the man held up a mirror so she could admire herself.

Marion laughed. 'That's Pride. The queen's ladies do their hair like that.'

Next came a priest, wheeled in on a bed covered with pillows. He snored loudly and wouldn't get up, even when an acolyte rang a large bell next to his ear. 'I know who that is,' Thomas said. 'It's Sloth.'

Sloth was wheeled out, and Gluttony, a very fat man, came in and sat down at a table where he proceeded to stuff himself with roast pig and cheese tarts. Every now and then, he stopped to take a drink of wine from a huge goblet, drinking so fast that wine dribbled down his chest. His plump wife and tubby children waddled in, grabbed food from the table, and ate until they all fell to the ground in a stupor.

Lust, another woman in a low-cut gown, minced in and nudged

Gluttony and his family with the tip of her dainty shoe, sending them rolling to the side of the stage. Four young men offered her bowls of fruit, jeweled necklaces, and gold coins. She pretended to seduce them, beckoning them with a crooked finger, then pushing them aside. She looked out at the crowd of spectators, noticed Thomas, and winked at him. He blushed and turned away. Marion took him by the chin and turned his head back so he wouldn't miss Sloth being wheeled in again so that Lust could try to entice him to get out of bed.

Greed was a portly man in a red velvet surcoat from which dangled dozens of gold coins. He crept up behind Lust, stole more coins from her purse, and then took even more coins from an open sack that lay beside Sloth's bed. Envy, in a green kirtle, pranced in on bare feet and pulled at the coins on Greed's surcoat, folding her hands in a praying motion, begging him to give her some.

Last of all came Wrath, a large man in a black cape who carried a copper image of a bearded man with staring eyes. He banged on the figure with a large hammer, indulging in such a paroxysm of hate that one of the figure's arms fell off and rattled across the stage.

Throughout it all, devils dressed in red from their horned heads to their long, pointed shoes waited under the stage holding enormous frying pans. At the completion of the tableaus, the players danced about in a frenzy, shaking the stage so much they lost their balance and fell off into the skillets. The audience roared with laughter.

The players crawled out from under the stage and circulated through the crowd, asking for money. Marion threw a coin into the cap of the man who'd tried to get her to participate in the show and began scolding him for making comments about her crimson cloak. Thomas looked away and saw a woman wearing a green kirtle and a wide embroidered belt approach the stage on which lay the players' props – the bed, the coins, the frying pans, the bowls of fruit, the hammer, and the copper figure on which Wrath had vented his anger. He reached back and tugged on Marion's sleeve, trying to get her attention without taking his eyes off the woman. But Marion was so engrossed in her conversation that she didn't notice. He turned around and grabbed her arm. 'I've found her!' he cried. 'Over there!'

Marion turned and looked where he pointed, but the woman was gone. And so was the copper figure with the missing arm.

THIRTY-TWO

*Why is it that so many different men, including learned ones,
say or write in their treatises such wicked and disparaging
things about women?*

Christine de Pizan, *Le Livre de la Cité des Dames*,
1404–1405

T he next day, Christine went to the public entrance of the
church and found Marion.

'I've been looking for you!' Marion cried.

'We can't talk here,' Christine said. 'Let's go to the inn.'

They sat at a table, and Marion studied the words that had been
carved into the wood. She laughed. 'Look here. It says—'

'I don't want to know,' Christine said. 'Where's the skinny
waiter?'

'Over there.' Marion pointed to the other side of the room, where
the tip of a peacock feather could be seen sticking up from behind
a wine cask. She got up, walked over, and stood with her hands on
her hips. 'Afraid of me, *grosse tête*?'

The waiter jumped up. 'What's to be afraid of? You're just a
harpy in a crimson cloak.'

Marion laughed. 'That's an accurate description. Bring us two
cups of wine.'

He looked her up and down. 'I like the cloak, but not what's
in it.'

'Get lost!' Marion said. He snickered and strode away.

Marion sat down and said to Christine, 'Thomas and I have seen
Symonne du Mesnil. She's wearing one of my belts.'

'Where was she?'

'The first time I saw her, she was with a group of beggars. When
she walked away, I followed her for a while, and then I lost her. I
didn't think she'd seen me. But she had. She hid behind some horses
and jumped out at me. She told me I should be more careful. Then,

yesterday, Thomas saw her with a group of players. She was there, and then, all of a sudden, she wasn't. She'd snuck away, and she took something with her.'

'What do you mean?'

'The players were performing *The Seven Deadly Sins*, and one of them depicted Wrath by hammering on a copper image of a man. He hammered so hard that one of the figure's arms fell off. When the play was over and the players were circulating in the crowd and no one was looking, the figure disappeared.'

'And you think Symonne took it?'

'She was standing right by the table where the players put their props. Thomas looked away for a moment, and when he looked back, Symonne and the figure were gone. Why would Symonne du Mesnil want the copper figure of a man with a missing arm?'

'I can't imagine.'

'I have to tell you what I found out about the stolen knife, too. I went around to the kitchen, just as you told me to. One of the boys who works there said he saw a nun take it.'

'Did he know which nun it was?'

'No. He said she was shorter than the others he's seen, but that doesn't mean much. He sees only the ones that go into the kitchen, and he admitted that most of them never go there.'

The waiter reappeared and set two cups of wine on the table with a bang. 'No need to be so surly,' Marion said. The waiter gave a mock bow and pranced away.

'I've got some news for you, too, Marion,' Christine said. 'Yesterday the prioress sent me to Archères to talk to the family of the murdered nun.'

'I know. The *portier* told me. He said you went with the "little man with the black beard." Was Henri of any help?'

'All he did was taunt me.'

'So what did you find out?'

'Not much. Thérèse's family was once wealthy, and now they're poor. The mother is a noble, gracious lady. The father and his son are brutes. The last time Thérèse was home, she was so anxious to get away, she left without waiting for her brother to go with her. But that's all I know. I still don't have any idea why she was murdered.'

'So that's that, I guess.'

'But I have more to tell you. Someone carved a figure of a hoopoe into the top of one of the tables in the refectory.'

Marion choked on her wine. 'Slow down. What's a refectory? What's a hoopoe?'

'The refectory is the room where the nuns eat. A hoopoe is a bird. Some people believe it has magical powers. Henri knows a lot about hoopoes. He couldn't wait to tell me.'

'Why would anyone carve such a thing into a table?'

'That's what I'd like to know. And there's something else. When I got back from Archères, the prioress was very upset. Someone had gone into the nuns' choir, taken a valuable antiphonary off a lectern, thrown it on to the floor, and stepped on it.'

'What's an antiphonary?'

'A book of chants for the divine office. The manuscript is damaged beyond repair.'

'God's holy little fingers! Do you think one of the nuns did it?'

'At first, I was sure it was Juliana, Henri's daughter. She hates being a nun, and it seemed to me she might have decided to vent her anger by destroying things that belong to the priory. But she swore up and down she didn't do it, and I believe her.'

'So where does that leave us? Are we any closer to discovering who killed the nun?'

'No. And to make things worse, Henri mocks me because I haven't solved the problem yet. He thinks women don't have minds. He even taunts the prioress and the nun who handles the priory business. He thinks only men can deal with such complicated matters.'

Marion took a sip of wine and made a face. 'I think the waiter put water in this.'

'What irritates me most of all,' Christine continued, 'is Henri's insistence that women believe in all kinds of foolish things. He'd be delighted to find out I believe in this sorcerer who's supposed to be hiding in the forest of Saint-Germain-en-Laye. That would prove he's right about women having no sense.'

Marion pushed her wine cup aside, stood up, and pulled Christine to her feet. 'Let's go! We have to figure out who murdered the nun. We have to show Henri that women are smarter than men!'

THIRTY-THREE

The good princess will follow the words of Chrysostom on the Gospel of Saint Matthew who says 'whoever wishes to enter the kingdom of Heaven must practice humility here on earth.'

Christine de Pizan, *Le Livre des Trois Vertus*, 1405

C hristine went to the prioress's quarters and found Mother Marie in her study, looking at the defaced manuscript with sisters Richarde, Geneviève, Thomasine, and Claude. They were all distressed, but Sister Claude most of all. She was beside herself with anger.

'This can't have happened here!' she cried.

'Why do you think bad things can't happen here, just like anywhere else, Claude?' the prioress asked.

'We are a royal priory. The king is supposed to protect us!'

'How could he have protected us from this? In fact, he's the one who needs protection now that he is ill. We must make sure he doesn't find out about this.'

'But everyone will know. What about the choir sisters? So far, I've been able to keep it a secret, but I know they're wondering what happened.'

Sister Richarde tried to smooth the pages of the manuscript. Some gold leaf fell away from one of the illuminations, and she drew back in horror.

'It is no use, Richarde,' the prioress said. 'It can't be saved.' She sat down at the desk, put her head in her hands, and said softly, 'I just hope we sisters can be saved.'

'Are you keeping something from us, Reverend Mother?' Sister Richarde asked.

The prioress and Sister Geneviève looked at each other. *They're the only ones who know what really happened to Sister Thérèse,* Christine thought. *I wonder how long they'll be able to keep it a secret.*

The prioress stood up. 'All will be well, Richarde. We must have faith.'

Supper that evening was a dish of eggs fried in butter and topped with a delicious red wine sauce, something Christine had not eaten before.

'I thought we should have something special tonight,' the prioress said.

'I must tell my mother about it,' Christine said.

Sister Claude hardly touched her food. 'I just can't believe it,' she muttered over and over. 'That beautiful antiphonary.' She started to cry, and her small body shook.

'This is not the only unfortunate occurrence at the priory,' Sister Thomasine said. 'You haven't said anything about the refectory table, Reverend Mother.'

'Who told you about that?' the prioress asked.

'Sister Dorian.'

The prioress shook her head. 'Dorian never could keep a secret.'

Sister Thomasine glared at her. 'If you told her not to talk about it, then she shouldn't have. No one should defy a prioress's orders. You are too lax.'

A disturbance at the door distracted them before the prioress could say anything. The princess ran in and climbed into her lap.

Sister Denise dashed after her. 'I'm so sorry. She insisted on seeing you.'

'She can come to me whenever she likes,' the prioress said.

Sister Claude turned to Christine and whispered, 'The princess has her own quarters. It's just as well. She would be frightened if she knew about all the terrible things going on here.'

The princess heard. 'I am not frightened by anything,' she said. 'I'm the king's daughter.'

'That does not mean you can be rude,' the prioress said.

The child shifted uneasily on the prioress's lap. 'I can be whatever I like. I'm a princess.'

'Even princesses have to learn to be humble,' the prioress said.

The little girl jumped up and ran around the room. Sister Denise caught her in her arms, but she wriggled away. Then she started to cry. At this, everyone gathered around and tried to comfort her. But she wouldn't stop wailing.

'You don't know what I saw! No one will believe me, anyway.'

'We have to find out what is troubling her,' the prioress said. 'Please, everyone, leave us.' She waited until the sisters had gone. Then she said, 'Come here, child.'

Sister Denise started to object. 'It's time for her to go to bed.'

'I will decide when it's time,' the prioress said.

The princess walked toward her slowly, dragging her feet.

'You said you saw someone with a knife,' the prioress said. 'Then you said you forgot about it. Tell us the truth.'

'I see lots of things.' The princess pointed her finger at Christine. 'Like that lady.'

'I told you before, Christine is the widow of *Maître* Étienne de Castel, who served as your father's secretary. You must treat her with respect. Now you will apologize to her.'

'I will not.'

Christine had seen this kind of behavior before. She had three children of her own. She said to the little girl, 'I often see things that aren't actually there, too. I'm sure you didn't really see a knife.'

The child looked at her, trying to decide what to do. 'If I said I saw a knife, then I did,' she finally admitted. The prioress started to say something, but Christine interrupted. 'What else have you seen?'

The child blanched and started to tremble.

'Something that frightened you?'

'Just shadows,' the child said, and she burst into tears again. 'And anyway, if I told you what I saw, you wouldn't believe me.'

'Why don't you tell me and let me decide?'

'It's time for her to go to bed,' Sister Denise insisted.

'Please be quiet,' the prioress said.

'I see all kinds of things,' the princess said. 'Men with dogs' heads, crows with human feet, dragons with red claws, angels with green wings, dwarfs standing on their heads.'

She's been looking at pictures, Christine thought. *The prioress must have a bestiary or two in her collection.* 'Do you really see those things? Or just remember seeing them in books?'

'I know they are in the books. But I see things in the shadows, too. They're scary.'

'And the knife?'

'I told you, I forgot.'

'You are not telling the truth,' Mother Marie said.

'I don't have to tell the truth. I'm the king's daughter, and I can say whatever I want, and you have to believe me.'

'You are no different from the rest of us. We have all learned humility, and you must, too.'

'I want to go to bed now,' the princess said. Sister Denise picked her up and had her out the door before the prioress could object.

THIRTY-FOUR

When women set out to do something, they are smarter and shrewder than men.

Christine de Pizan, *Le Livre de la Cité des Dames*,
1404–1405

Christine knew the princess was afraid. But of what? She left the prioress's quarters and went to hear the choir chant vespers, hoping the music would calm her thoughts. The church was growing dark, and it was hard to see the grille that concealed the presence of the sisters. For a moment, she imagined that nothing separated her from the singers, that she was part of the all-encompassing sound, even though she couldn't see who was producing it. *I'll never be able to see them*, she mused. *One of them may be a killer. How will I find her?*

'Puzzled?' said a voice beside her.

She jumped. 'Why did you sneak up on me, Henri?'

'I wouldn't want to disturb the music.'

'The music doesn't interest you. What do you want?'

'Your friend Marion has been snooping around, asking questions.'

'Why shouldn't she?'

'Because there's something dangerous going on around here, and you women shouldn't be involved in it.'

Christine opened her mouth to speak, but Henri interrupted. 'I know you're going to tell me the prioress asked you to come here and that gives you a perfect excuse to be sticking your nose into things. The prioress is just as foolish as you are – as all women are.'

Christine bristled. She'd never met a more competent woman than the prioress, and she couldn't understand why Henri didn't see that. Michel had told her that Henri had been brought up in a monastery. Perhaps he'd never known his mother, had known only men as a child. No matter what the reason, she despised him for his attitude.

Henri stood there laughing at her. She told herself to be calm. 'Do you know why Marion is here?' she asked.

'Tell me.'

'The queen's dwarf told her that when the Duke and Duchess of Burgundy heard I was here, they sent one of the queen's ladies after me. Marion came because she thinks I'm in danger.'

'Do you know who this woman is?'

'Her name is Symonne du Mesnil. Do you know anything about her?'

'A lot more than you. Tell your friend Marion to stay away from her.'

'Why?'

'There are things going on at the court that you know nothing about. Nor should you. Just take my word for it: this woman is dangerous.'

Why is he not telling me anything? she asked herself. She suppressed her desire to strike the man and asked, 'Won't you at least give me a hint as to why we should be afraid of Symonne du Mesnil?'

Henri looked at her for a long time. Then he said, 'I suppose I should confide in you a little. After all, you were the one who found the person tormenting the Duchess of Orléans several years ago. You seemed to have saved her life.'

'*Seemed* to?' Christine was livid. She'd been working for the Duke of Orléans's wife, Valentina Visconti, at a time when all of Paris was trying to prove that Valentina was a sorceress. She'd discovered that someone was actually trying to kill the duchess, and she'd identified the would-be murderer. And now Henri said she *seemed* to have saved the duchess's life. She clasped her hands behind her back to keep from slapping him and took a deep breath.

'That's right, Henri. I did save her,' she said calmly. 'And since I was able to do that, perhaps you could have a little respect for my intelligence and let me in on the secret about Symonne du Mesnil.'

Henri smiled, pleased to see that he'd irritated her. 'You are more intelligent than most women, I'll grant you that. But what are you going to do with any information I give you about Symonne du Mesnil?'

'Does it have to do with the murder of one of the nuns here?'

'To tell you the truth, I don't know.'

'You admit you don't know something?'

'That is so.' He cocked his head and stared at her. 'I suppose you might as well know this, anyway. But don't spread it around. Not even to your friend Marion.'

Of course I'll tell Marion.

'Haven't you ever wondered why the person who wanted the Duchess of Orléans to die was never punished?'

'I have wondered about it, of course. But Pierre de Craon had been murdering and robbing and lying all his life, and he'd never been punished for any of it. So I assumed he would get away with that, too.' As she said this, she remembered the one time she had met the villain, when he'd accosted her the day Valentina Visconti left Paris. Pierre de Craon had looked her in the eye and said, 'You succeeded in saving the duchess, but don't think that's the end of it.' She felt a shiver go down her spine.

'Is Pierre de Craon here in Poissy?' she asked Henri.

'It's possible.'

'What has he to do with Symonne du Mesnil?'

'Before I answer that question, let me tell you why Pierre is never punished, no matter what horrible crime he commits. It's because the Duchess of Burgundy protects him. He's related to her. He is her father's third cousin.'

'That seems a rather distant relationship.'

'It's enough to ensure that Pierre has gotten away with murder and theft. The duchess looks out for him.'

'And Symonne du Mesnil is the duchess's protégé.'

'*Brava!* Christine.'

'Oh, you don't have to congratulate me. I'm just a woman.'

'So you are. That's why I want you to keep out of what may be an extremely dangerous situation.'

'You know very well I won't keep out of it. So you'd better tell me what this is all about before I learn in some other, perhaps more dangerous, way. Who exactly is Symonne du Mesnil, and why is she here in Poissy?'

Henri shook his head. 'I'll tell you all about her in good time. But I don't have all the answers yet.'

Christine laughed. 'I never thought you'd admit that you don't have all the answers, Henri.'

'Don't worry. I'll get them.'

Perhaps I'll get them first, Christine said to herself.

THIRTY-FIVE

They sang in sweet harmony, and their voices filled the air like the sound of many waters.

Hildegard of Bingen (1098–1179), *Liber Vitae Meritorum*

She turned away, and after a while she heard Henri leave. She breathed a sigh of relief: now she could concentrate on the chant. But even the beautiful singing couldn't take her mind off the problem she was determined to solve. She returned to the prioress's quarters, ate a light supper the prioress's cook had prepared for her, and went to bed.

She woke before the sun was up to find the prioress standing over her. 'I'm sorry to disturb you so early in the morning,' Mother Marie said. 'But I thought you might like to come to the nuns' choir for prime. You won't be able to go in, but you can stand at the door. I've been reluctant to admit that one of the sisters might have killed Thérèse, but I have to consider the possibility. Perhaps if you observe them, you will see something that will give you a clue.'

She dressed quickly and went to the church. The prioress was waiting for her, and she took her to the private entrance to the nuns' choir. The sisters were not there yet, and the space was dark and so silent that when the nuns started to glide in, the sound of their feet moving softly over the stone floor seemed to rend the air.

The first ones to appear were the youngest, some of them yawning. After them came the older women, their faces set in unreadable expressions. One of them turned, looked at Christine, and smiled. Christine, astonished, smiled back.

The sisters took their places in stalls that faced each other across the great expanse of their choir. Then the prioress and Sister Thomasine came in, and after them, Sister Claude.

Sister Claude intoned the first words of the liturgy. The sisters on the right followed, and those on the left, led by Sister Thomasine, responded. Sister Claude, who seemed to grow in stature as she moved about the choir, gestured with her hands and mouthed the words, encouraging the sisters to sing out. Sister Thomasine did the same, and between them they brought the voices of more than a hundred nuns together in a sound that seemed to come directly from heaven. It was so overwhelming, Christine nearly forgot that one of the sisters producing this glorious music might be a murderess.

Morning light started to shine through the colored glass windows, and the nuns in their white habits no longer looked like ghosts. Individual characteristics began to stand out. There were a few wrinkled faces and toothless mouths, but most of them were middle-aged or young like her daughter. She concentrated on Marie for a while. She looked happy, and Christine tried to be happy for her, too.

When it was over and the sisters had filed out, the prioress came to her side. 'Were you able to see anything that might help you solve this mystery?' she asked.

'Unfortunately, no. I do want to ask you about one of the sisters, though.'

'I know who it is. The other sisters keep their names when they enter here, but Sister Blanche was allowed to change hers. I'm sure you will keep her secret.'

'Does Brother Michel know?'

'He does.'

She went out to the priory entrance to ask whether the *portier* had seen Michel that morning. 'He's over there,' Jacques cried, pointing to the inn across the street.

Christine found the monk sitting at a table by himself, so lost in thought that he didn't see her come in. She touched his shoulder.

'I've seen Alix de Clairy, Michel! She was in the choir.'

Michel's round eyes blinked furiously. 'Did she say anything to you?'

'No. But she saw me.'

'Then leave well enough alone, Christine.'

'I always assumed that once it became clear that she hadn't poisoned her husband, she'd gone back to her father's home near Amiens. You told me the king would make sure she inherited all of her father's wealth and estates. Didn't he do that?'

'Of course he did. The king is a compassionate man, Christine, in spite of his illness.'

'Then why is she here?'

'After all she'd been through, it took more than wealth and property to make her happy. Here, she is finally at peace.'

Christine sat at the table. 'I understand. I just hope the serenity lasts. We have to find out who murdered Sister Thérèse, Michel. Otherwise, the peace is shattered forever.'

'I'm afraid that is true. Have you discovered anything that will help?

'No. But I have something else to tell you. One of the queen's ladies-in-waiting, Symonne du Mesnil, is here in Poissy. Marion has seen her several times.'

'Is that the lady the Duchess of Burgundy brought to the queen?'

'Yes. No one seems to know anything about her except that she's a favorite of the duchess's. She's the only one the duchess treats kindly.'

'I've seen her. She's different from the queen's other ladies.'

'Henri says he doesn't know why she's here. I'm sure it has something to do with the murder. Have you talked to the friars, Michel?'

'They all believe Sister Thérèse died a natural death. I have great respect for Mother Marie. She's been able to keep the secret well.' He sat back and tucked his hands into the sleeves of his black habit. 'What about the sisters, Christine?'

'Mother Marie has introduced me to some of the more important ones. They all seem to know you. So far, I've met only two of the others – Juliana and Adelie, who has visions and thinks she hears King Philip's heart beating under the choir.'

'His heart really *is* buried somewhere in the church, you know. People think it's in a chapel under the king's tomb. Someone must have seen it at one time because everyone seems to be able to describe the urn it's in.'

'I know. Mother Marie told me about it. She took me down to the chapel. It's completely empty, except for an altar. It's dark and damp. She hides the key so no one else will go there.'

'Is there anything that might make the noise Adelie hears?'

'Nothing. Adelie just has a vivid imagination. She's driving the other sisters to distraction.'

'You've talked to Juliana. What do you think of her?'

'She'd do almost anything to get away from the priory. The more I get to know her, the angrier I become with Henri for putting her here. How could he have done such a cruel thing?'

Before Michel could answer, there was a disturbance, and they looked out of the open door to see Tassin of Archères, his wife, and his son Guy ride up to the inn. Tassin was so drunk, even at that hour of the morning, that when he dismounted, he fell to the ground. He picked himself up, brushed off his shabby tunic, and swaggered into the inn. Guy, imitating his swagger, followed him, leaving his mother waiting for someone to help her down from her palfrey.

Michel bounded out, offered the baroness his assistance, and escorted her into the inn. Tassin and Guy had disappeared into another room, where Tassin was loudly calling for wine, so Christine rose and asked Madame Marguerite to join them.

The baroness sighed and sat down. 'It is good to see you again.'

'And I am delighted to see you. This is Brother Michel from the Abbey of Saint-Denis.'

'I have heard of you,' the baroness said to Michel. 'I know you are writing a chronicle of the reign of our present king.'

Michel looked surprised. She caught the look. 'Do not think that because we live somewhat removed from the court, we don't know what is going on there. It is good that you are recording everything that happens in these difficult times.'

Christine reflected, as she had the first time she'd met the baroness, that this was a woman she admired and who merited the respect of even Henri Le Picart. Not only did the baroness bear the death of her daughters bravely, but she had a son who'd gone to Nicopolis and not returned, and she had a husband who mistreated her. Her sorrows were great, but she did not show it.

Christine sensed there was something behind the woman's words about the court. She realized what it was when the baroness said, 'Brother Michel, I must ask you something. Has the Duke of Burgundy paid the ransom for every one of the French troops that survived the massacre at Nicopolis?'

'Why do you ask, Madame?'

'Because I have a son who went to that battle. A knight came to Paris on Christmas Day three years ago to tell the king about the terrible defeat the French had suffered. The knight was a friend of mine, and he told me my son was not dead. You can imagine my joy when I heard this. And yet, after all these years, my son has not returned to me. It seems the duke has not paid ransom for him. Are there others in the same situation? And if there are, do you know why?'

Michel looked away. Christine could see that he was struggling to decide how to answer the question. He looked relieved when Tassin of Archères approached. His relief turned to alarm as Tassin shouted at his wife, 'Why are you not in your proper place with your husband?'

Christine opened her mouth to object, but Michel put his hand on her arm to stop her. 'Don't get involved in a dispute between a husband and wife,' he whispered.

The baroness brushed her husband's arm away and rose from her seat. 'Forgive my husband's rude behavior,' she said.

'Rude behavior, indeed,' Tassin shouted. He grabbed her arm, pulled her into the street, and flung her on to her horse. He shouted goodbye to Guy, who stood by the door to the inn watching them, and spurred his horse to a trot.

Michel watched Tassin and his wife ride away with a look of sadness on his face.

'Do you know the answer to her question?' Christine asked.

'I'm afraid I do. But I didn't want to be the one to add to her distress.'

'What could be worse than not knowing what has happened to your child?'

'This is worse,' Michel said. 'There are several men who will not be ransomed by the duke. There can be only one reason. They are traitors who betrayed their country.'

THIRTY-SIX

The Duchess of Burgundy, who was a cruel lady, had the queen under her control, and no one could speak with the queen unless she approved.

Froissart, *Chroniques*, Livre IV, 1389–1400

C hristine felt a great sadness. Surely the baroness had no idea her son was a traitor; otherwise, she would not have asked Michel the question. She longed to ride after her and comfort her. A woman who bore herself so graciously in the face of all her troubles deserved sympathy. The men in her life would not give it to her, that was for sure.

Marion bustled in. 'Did you see her?'

'Who?' Christine asked.

'Symonne du Mesnil.'

'Why didn't you follow her?'

'I'm tired of following her. She always gets away.'

Henri and Thomas appeared. 'You're talking about Symonne du Mesnil, I'm sure,' Henri said.

'Have you seen her?'

'Of course. She's over at the cattle market.'

Christine looked at Henri. 'Yesterday you said you know all about Symonne du Mesnil. I don't believe you. I think you're bluffing.'

'I said I'd tell you in good time.'

Even Michel looked vexed. 'You must tell us now, Henri.'

Henri settled himself on a bench at the table, signaled to the skinny waiter, and ordered wine. The waiter pretended to have a hard time hearing. He leaned over the table, and the peacock feather brushed Henri's cheek. Christine wished it had wiped the self-satisfied look off his face.

'All right,' Henri said. He looked so smug that Christine had to resist the temptation to slap him. 'You all remember when Pierre de Craon tried to kill the king's constable, I'm sure,' he began.

'Who could forget?' Michel said. 'It was seven years ago, but it seems like yesterday.'

'Then you must remember the details. Pierre laid his plot carefully. He had a house in Paris, and he hid his accomplices there for several days before they attacked the constable. Pierre had a steward, and this man, who knew nothing about what Pierre was planning, had a wife and a daughter living in the house with him.'

Henri took a swig of wine and crossed his legs. He removed his black cape and seemed to become another person, for underneath it he wore a red velvet jacket with ermine trim around the neck and a great number of gold chains.

The waiter reappeared. He plunked cups of wine on the table and stood at Henri's side. Henri waved him away. He took a few steps back but didn't leave. Marion got up and gave him a push. '*Tire-toi!*' He looked her up and down. '*Putain,*' he said, and he scurried off before she could push him again.

'Get on with the story,' Marion said as she sat down.

'Impatient, just like all women,' Henri said. 'That's the trouble with women. Impatience and the inability to keep their mouths shut. Pierre knew that, and he was careful to warn the steward not to let his women out of the house because he knew they would tell someone about the men hiding there.'

'*Pour l'amour des dieux!* Tell us what this has to do with Symonne du Mesnil!' Marion cried.

'After the assassination attempt failed, Pierre and his accomplices fled. Those that were caught were brought back to Paris and brutally executed. Their hands were cut off, and their heads and their bodies were hung on gibbets.'

'I saw them,' Thomas said.

'You were only nine at the time!' Christine said.

'Well, I *think* I saw them.'

'You have a great imagination, Thomas,' Henri said. 'But it really was horrible. And one of the most distressing things about it was that Pierre's steward got the same treatment as the conspirators because it was assumed he'd been in on the plot.'

'Poor man,' Marion said.

'The steward's wife and daughter were nearly executed, too. But the Duchess of Burgundy saw an opportunity. She told the steward's wife that her daughter would be spared if she would submit to her wishes. Of course, the unhappy woman agreed.'

'Was the mother spared too?' Marion asked.

'That's another story.'

'Why are you telling us this, Henri?' Christine asked.

'Because the daughter is Symonne du Mesnil.'

'Impossible! One of the queen's ladies-in-waiting!' Marion cried.

'That's not her real name. The duchess gave her a name that would make the queen think she was a noblewoman, noble enough to be admitted into her entourage. Haven't you noticed that Symonne doesn't act like the queen's other ladies?'

'I always wondered about her,' Christine said.

'The duchess wanted to have the queen under her control,' Henri said. 'In this young woman, she had the perfect means of obtaining that goal.'

'You mean Symonne is a spy for the duchess?'

'Exactly.'

'But what's she doing here?'

'As I told you yesterday, I don't know,' Henri said.

THIRTY-SEVEN

A brother sees a ladder coming down from heaven to carry the dying Father up.

Office of Saint Dominic, third antiphon of lauds

Christine went back to the priory, puzzling over what Henri had told them. She couldn't see any connection between Symonne du Mesnil, the Duchess of Burgundy, and the murder of a nun at the priory. Surely Symonne had not been inside the priory walls. *But then*, she thought, *perhaps she had. After all, Marion got in disguised as a beggar. Symonne could have done the same thing. Or perhaps she'd disguised herself as a nun.*

She went to the prioress's quarters, picked up the *Life of Saint Dominic*, took it to her room, opened it on her desk, and started on the copying as a way to calm herself. After she'd worked for a while, the princess rushed in.

'Where's my aunt?'

'I'm sure she'll be here in a while.'

'What are you doing?'

'I'm copying this manuscript. Do you want to see what it is?'

The princess stepped close to the desk. 'Start at the beginning.' She reached out to turn the pages.

Christine stopped her hand and turned the pages herself. 'Here's Saint Dominic,' she said when she came to a picture of the saint in his white habit and black cape.

'There's a dog at his feet!' the princess exclaimed. 'Why does the dog have a torch in his mouth?'

'Because before Saint Dominic was born, his mother dreamed she had in her stomach a little dog with a lighted torch in its mouth. She believed she would give birth to a dog that would set the whole world on fire.'

'That's silly.'

'Not really. You have to think of it as a story with a deeper meaning. It means Saint Dominic set the world on fire with his teaching. Doesn't Sister Petra teach you that?'

'I'm too little to go to the novice mistress's classes.'

'It's never too early to learn something about the order Saint Dominic founded.'

'Then show me more pictures of him.'

Christine turned the page. 'Here he is with a star on his forehead because when he was baptized, his grandmother said his star would shine its light on the whole world.'

The princess yawned and put out her hand to turn more pages. Christine gently pushed it away. They came to a picture of the saint sitting on a seat between two ladders. The little girl giggled. 'Why would a saint be sitting like that? And why does he have his hood over his face?'

'He has his hood over his face because he's dying and that's how he will be buried. He's going to get to heaven on those ladders. See at the top? Jesus and his Mother are holding the ladders and they are going to use them to lift him up.'

The princess studied the picture. 'I like the angels best,' she said, pointing to a group of excited angels who seemed to be running up and down the ladders.

The prioress came in. 'Where is Sister Denise?' she asked the princess.

'I don't know.'

'I see you have been looking at the pictures in the manuscript. Did you learn anything?'

'Saint Dominic went up to heaven on a ladder. He took some angels with him.'

'Let's look at more pictures,' the prioress said.

'I want to turn the pages,' the princess said.

'If you are very careful. Find a picture you like.'

The princess turned a page and let out a little cry. 'His books are going to get all wet!'

'That's because one day when Saint Dominic was crossing a river, all his books fell into the water.'

'How could a saint be so careless?'

'I don't know. But it didn't matter because three days later a fisherman found the books attached to his fishhook, and when he pulled them up, he discovered that they were all perfectly dry.'

'I don't believe it,' the princess said. She kept turning the pages until she came to a picture of the saint holding a knife.

'Saint Dominic used a knife to cut open a sick man's body and take out the things that were making him ill,' the prioress said.

'That must have hurt,' the princess said, holding her stomach.

'It didn't hurt at all,' the prioress said. 'Remember, Dominic was a saint. He could cut the man open and there would be no pain.'

The child looked intently at the picture and seemed to be about to say something. But before she could, Sister Denise raced into the room. 'I've been looking everywhere for you,' she cried. 'I apologize,' she said to the prioress as she carried the child away.

Christine and the prioress looked at each other. 'I think the picture reminded her of the knife she saw. She was going to tell us about it,' Christine said.

'I think you're right,' the prioress said.

THIRTY-EIGHT

Any woman who has a mind is capable of accomplishing any task.

Christine de Pizan, *Le Livre de la Cité des Dames*,
1404–1405

The prioress sat at the desk and put her head in her hands. 'I just don't know what to do about Denise.'

'Has she been here long?'

'Only a few years. She came after her husband died at the Battle of Nicopolis. She had no children and his death left her alone and distraught. She's a highly educated woman and a fine singer. I thought it would be a helpful distraction to have her take care of the princess while Catherine, the child's real guardian, is away. It's not turning out well. She just can't seem to control the child. Perhaps it's because she never had children of her own.'

'Are there many widows here?'

'After the disaster at Nicopolis, many widowed women decided to go into monastic orders. Several of them came here. None of the others bemoan their fate as much as Denise.'

The prioress stood up and went to the window. A driving rain beat against the colored panes. 'Will this never stop?' she asked. 'The gardeners are complaining. The sun comes out for a few days, they plant their seeds, and then more rain comes and washes everything away.'

Christine smiled, remembering that her mother was having the same problem back in Paris.

The prioress turned and said, 'There's been another incident with Adelie. Now she says she sees fantastic animals. She's causing so much disruption that some of the sisters have come to me and demanded that I send her away.'

'Do you think it's possible she's using her visions to make herself special? To make it look as though she's some kind of saint?'

'Heaven forbid! If we had a saint here, everyone would want to visit. But no, I don't believe Adelie is doing that. I'll start to worry about it when she claims to have seen Christ or the Blessed Mother.'

'Where is she now?'

'I think she's with Juliana, in the room by the laundry Juliana thinks I don't know about. I have no idea what to do about those two.' She put her ear to the window. 'At least the rain has stopped. I don't hear it now.'

'I'll go and talk to them.'

'It might do Adelie some good. While you're at it, could you try to get Juliana to behave, too? She caused a stir this morning. She wouldn't get out of bed, and Sister Thomasine had to hit her with her nightstick. I know she only tapped her; I've seen Thomasine do that in the past. But Juliana claims she beat her. She told some of the other sisters about it as they were filing into the choir, and she almost started a rebellion. Fortunately, Sister Claude was able to get them to calm down and begin the chant. You wouldn't think a woman of such small stature would be able to keep all those women in order, but she does. She amazes me.'

'Wouldn't it be best to let Juliana leave the priory?'

'She's better off here.'

Why don't you talk to her father about it? Christine wanted to ask. But she could tell from the look on Mother Marie's face that the subject was closed.

She left and went to the room by the laundry, where she found Juliana sitting on a pile of discarded houppelandes, lace collars, and jeweled belts.

'The prioress told me Adelie was with you.'

'How did she know I was here?'

'You don't give her enough credit, Juliana. Mother Marie is a clever woman.'

'If she's so clever, why doesn't she see how much I hate it here?'

'She knows. Where is Adelie?'

'She was here a while ago. She was very excited about something, but she wouldn't tell me what it was.'

'Did you go to sext today?'

'No. And I'm not going to nones or vespers, either. Maybe I'll go to compline. That office makes me drowsy, and when I go to bed after, I fall asleep right away.'

'And then you don't want to get up for matins. The prioress told me.'

'Who cares whether I go to matins or not.' She got up and paced around the room, trailing a long blue silk scarf behind her. She wound the scarf around her neck and pretended to choke herself with it. 'Have you discovered who murdered Thérèse?'

'I was hoping you could tell me something about the other sisters.'

Juliana sat down on the pile of clothes again. 'Claude didn't like her. Thérèse didn't sing well. The chant is everything to Claude. I believe she'd commit murder to make sure it goes the way she wants it to.' She picked up one of the jeweled belts and waved it around. 'Petra hit her with a switch.'

'Sister Petra says she doesn't really have a switch. She says she just pretends to scare you all.'

'I know. She tells Mother Marie that. If Mother Marie believes her, she's not as clever as you think.'

'What about Sister Geneviève?'

'She didn't like Thérèse. I saw her frowning at her as though she knew something really bad about her.'

The door opened, and Adelie came in. When she saw Christine, she turned and started to leave. Christine grabbed her arm. 'Wait, Adelie! I want to talk to you.'

'Why?' She pulled her arm away and smoothed the bandage on her hand.

'You should let the infirmaress look at that,' Christine said.

Adelie tucked her hand under her scapular.

'Will you at least let *me* look at it?'

Adelie shook her head violently and ran out the door.

'There is nothing to be done when she's like that,' Juliana said.

'What do you know about Adelie's family, Juliana?'

'She says they put her here because she's ugly. I think they just wanted to get rid of her because there were a lot of children, and they didn't want any more girls.'

'Where do you get ideas like that?'

'I've heard that people say women are not fit for anything but having children and doing housework.'

'That's not true. A woman can do anything she sets her mind to. Think of Mother Marie and Sister Richarde. They handle the priory business better than any man could.'

'I'm sure everyone outside the priory assumes there's a man somewhere who takes care of everything.'

'Not everyone is that stupid. You must not believe all the terrible things people, especially men, say about women.'

'How will I ever know what to believe when I'm locked up here?'

'Tell me, Juliana, what would you like to do if you could leave?'

'I'd do anything you suggest.'

Juliana was sorting through the pile of discarded clothes. She held up a blue velvet houppelande with fur-lined sleeves. 'This is too big,' she said. She threw it down, dove into the pile again, and found a red silk cotte with a pattern of silver flowers. 'How's this?' she asked.

'Don't you dare take off your habit and put those clothes on,' Christine said. 'This time I really will tell Mother Marie.'

'I can look, can't I?' She dug into the pile and came up with a gold-trimmed surcoat and a small embroidered purse. She held the purse up. 'Put some coins in here, and I'll be ready to go out into the world.'

Christine couldn't help admiring the purse, which was embroidered with flowers and birds, all worked in gold and silver threads.

'We do better than that here,' Juliana said.

'Really? What do you make?'

'We're allowed to make only purses and belts and collars. I'd like to make an altar cloth, or a cope for a priest. But no one ever asks me to do anything like that.'

'You have grand ideas, Juliana.'

'Why not? At least I'd be doing something worthwhile. The things we make are useless. We're supposed to give them away to friends or relatives. I don't have any friends or relatives.'

Christine looked down, to hide her tears, and examined the purse.

'If I show you something, will you promise not to tell the prioress?' Juliana asked.

'That depends.'

'I'll show you anyway.' Juliana reached under her scapular, brought out an embroidered purse she'd attached to her black belt, and handed it to Christine. 'We're supposed to do saints. I prefer this.'

Christine took the purse to the room's one small window and held it up to the light. 'This is extraordinary,' she exclaimed as she looked at a scene of lovers under a rose arbor exchanging golden rings.

'Did I get it right? I saw the Blessed Mother sitting under an arbor like that in a book, and I decided I'd rather have lovers.'

'Exactly right. What about the pink cupids?'

'I made them up.'

Christine laughed. 'The unicorn might be a little out of place, but the birds and butterflies are perfect.' The purse shimmered in the light. 'Where did you get the gold and silver thread?'

'They make us wear habits of coarse wool, but for this they give us expensive thread. And fine linen on which to stitch the designs.'

Christine handed the purse back to Juliana. 'You'd better keep this hidden.'

'You won't tell anyone?'

'Of course not.' *Although I might tell Marion*, Christine thought. *She'd really like to see this.*

Juliana sat down on the pile of clothes again. 'You said you came to talk to Adelie.'

'I did. Do you know where she went?'

'She might be in the cloister. Sometimes she sits there for hours.'

'Just thinking?'

'I suppose so. Making up things to put in her visions. Although I sometimes believe she really does see things.'

'Has she always been this way?'

'No. She's been difficult before, but not like this.'

'She's been getting worse?'

'Yes. She's beginning to frighten me.'

THIRTY-NINE

The demons attempt to strike fear, changing their shapes, taking the forms of women, wild beasts, creeping things, gigantic bodies, and troops of soldiers.

Saint Athanasius of Alexandria (296–373),
Life of Saint Anthony

Christine found Adelie sitting on a bench in the cloister. The girl seemed to be in a trance. Suddenly, she came out of it. 'See the big snake!' she cried. She pointed to the lawn. 'There, in the grass.'

'There isn't any snake.'

Adelie curled up on the bench, her head in her hands. 'No one ever sees what I see.'

'Tell me what you see.'

'I told you. A big snake. It has wings.'

'Can you see anything else?'

'Lions with men's heads and scorpions' tails. A horse with a big horn in the middle of its head.'

What a charlatan, Christine thought. *Where did she learn about those things?*

'Do you know how to read, Adelie?'

'Of course I do. No one can become a nun here unless she can read.'

'Where did you learn?'

'When I was a child. My parents taught me. We had lots of books.'

Perhaps one of those books was a bestiary.

Adelie became very quiet. Christine didn't want to frighten her with too many questions, so she stopped talking, too, and looked around the cloister. A light rain was falling, and the lawn was an intense emerald green. In contrast, the shadowy vaulted walkway where they sat seemed gloomy – until she looked at the floor and saw that it was paved with tiny yellow and red tiles that glittered even in the shade. She looked up to see if the vault had similar colored stones and suddenly she knew the source of Adelie's visions. The capital at the top of one of the columns that supported the vault was decorated with fantastic sculpted beasts – basilisks, manticores, and unicorns.

'Are those the animals you see, Adelie?' she asked, pointing to the capital.

Adelie put her hands over her ears. 'Now I hear the king's heart.'

'Don't change the subject.'

'It's beating so loud. It wants to go back into the king's body.'

'I thought you had to be in the choir to hear it.'

'No. It follows me everywhere.'

'Why doesn't anyone else hear it?'

'They don't have the powers I do.'

'Do you really think I believe what you're telling me, Adelie? Look up at those capitals. That's where you got the idea for the things you see, isn't it?'

'You're just like everyone else. You think I'm making it up.'

'I know you are, Adelie. You are a liar.'

'I'm not a liar. I really see them. You're just jealous because I hear and see things you can't. I see demons, too. And the demons are going to get you, you evil woman.'

Sisters Richarde and Thomasine came down the walkway. Sister Richarde's long nose twitched, and Sister Thomasine's pale face was grim.

'This is outrageous!' Thomasine cried. 'I don't understand why Mother Marie doesn't expel this girl immediately. We have no discipline here. Things have to change.'

'Calm yourself,' Sister Richarde said. 'I know who can take care of this.' The two nuns hurried off.

Adelie cringed. 'They're going to get Petra. I hate them.'

When Sister Petra came into the cloister, she made straight for Adelie.

'What are you doing out here?'

Adelie curled up on the bench again. 'Don't hit me!'

Sister Petra looked at Christine. 'She thinks I have a switch. I like to keep them guessing.'

Adelie clutched Christine's arm. 'She does have a switch. She hit me, and she hit Thérèse with it.'

'You know that's a lie, Adelie,' Sister Petra said. 'You must go in right now.'

'I'm afraid I was keeping her here,' Christine said. 'I wanted to talk to her.'

'A lot of good that will do,' Petra said. 'No one here has ever been able to talk any sense into her head.'

Adelie jumped up from the bench. 'You're all jealous. If you could see what I see, you'd be special, like me.'

'What do you see today, Adelie?' Petra asked.

Adelie looked up. 'I see an angel. He's coming to tell you to stop persecuting me.'

'There aren't any angels,' Petra said.

'Actually, there are,' Christine said. She pointed to the capital of the column next to the one with the mythical beasts. Petra looked up and started to laugh. A sculpted angel stood blowing a trumpet right over their heads.

'Is this what you see, Adelie?'

Adelie shook her head. 'My angel is not like that. My angel is bringing the Blessed Mother here. She will tell you I am a special person. Then everyone will know it, and all kinds of people will come here because you have a saint in your priory.'

'I've been fearing this,' Sister Petra said. 'So far she's claimed to see only insignificant things. But now this.' She grabbed Adelie's arm and lifted her off the bench. 'Enough! You must come inside. You are not well.'

Adelie screamed as Petra dragged her away.

FORTY

[The church] was so well made, one could tell it was built by a noble king who had spared no expense.

Christine de Pizan, *Le Livre du Dit de Poissy*, 1400

C hristine hadn't seen her daughter for a while, so she was surprised to wake up very early the next morning and find Marie standing in the shadows beside her bed.

'It's still dark,' she said.

'I know. I'm on my way to prime.'

She remembered when Marie was a child, always the first to jump out of bed, ready to wake the other children.

'Are you the one who goes around the dormitory waking everyone up?' she asked her daughter.

'Sometimes Sister Claude lets me do it. How did you know?'

Christine laughed. 'I'm glad to see you, Marie, even in that uncomfortable-looking habit.'

'I know you didn't want me to become a nun.'

'I was just worried about you.'

'You never have to worry about me, Mama. I know exactly what I want to do. I always have.'

Christine had to admit to herself that this was true. Her sons, Jean and Thomas, had not always been so sure. Especially Thomas.

'You never have any doubts?'

'None at all.'

'Then you'll never be unhappy like your friend Juliana.'

'Do you think you can help her? She wants so much to leave.'

'She says the sisters are mean to her.'

'Juliana likes to exaggerate. She claims Claude hits us in the choir, or when she wakes us up for matins, but it's not true. Claude merely wants us to sing well, and she praises us when we do.'

'What about Sister Petra? Does she really have a switch?'

Marie laughed. 'She says she does, just to scare us. And some of the novices believe it because she looks so stern. She's really very kind, once you get to know her. Whenever one of the novices gets homesick, she goes out of her way to comfort her. She reassures her that in no time at all she will consider *this* her home.'

'Haven't you ever been the least bit homesick?'

'In the beginning, I did miss you all. Even Thomas and his foolish jokes.'

'I'm sorry Thomas can't come into the priory to see you,' Christine said.

'I am, too. But think how disruptive he would be. I'm sure he would do something to upset the other sisters.'

'You always were hard on Thomas. He's grown into a fine young man.'

'I'd like to see him. Can you think of any way that might be possible?'

'I'm sure you wouldn't want to do anything that would go against the rule of your order, or the rules here at the priory.'

'Of course not.' Marie went to the colored glass window. A faint red light tinted her white habit pink. 'On the other hand . . .'

'Perhaps the prioress would give you permission to meet your brother in her parlor.'

'I don't think so. But I have an idea. We mustn't tell the prioress.'

'I'm surprised at you.'

'I go into the orchard sometimes. Thomas could go there; no one would know he wasn't one of the cooks' boys or a carpenter's helper.'

Christine smiled. Perhaps her daughter wasn't so prim after all.

'I have some free time between prime and terce,' Marie said. 'We don't have Chapter today. And for a change, it's not raining.'

'Meet me in the orchard, then. I'll see if I can find Thomas.'

Marie went away, humming to herself, and Christine got out of bed, dressed, and went to the church to hear the nuns sing the chants for prime. *They don't sound the least bit sleepy*, she mused. *I'll have to get up for matins sometime and see how they sound at that hour of the morning.*

She went to the priory entrance and was glad to see Thomas there, talking to the *portier* and his grandson.

'Do you want to see your sister?' Christine asked him.

'How can I? They won't let me in there.'

'Will you let my son come with me into the orchard?' Christine asked the *portier*.

The *portier* thought for a moment. Then he nodded.

'Come on, Thomas,' Christine said. She led him into the walled courtyard with the laundry.

Thomas stopped to look at the walls of the church. 'I haven't seen it from this side before. It looks bigger than ever. As big as our cathedral in Paris.'

Christine didn't say anything; she was remembering how Henri had warned Mother Marie that the priory was not safe from intruders. *Lots of people come in this way*, she thought. *Does anyone really know who they all are?*

'These nuns must have pots of money,' Thomas said.

Certainly one of the nuns could have murdered Sister Thérèse. But it could just as well have been someone from outside. How would anyone have been able to bring in a dog? The portier *would have seen it. Unless it was a dog small enough to be hidden under a coat or a jacket.*

Thomas stopped and stared at her. 'You aren't listening to me!'

'It was built for them by a king, long before our time,' Christine said.

Thomas looked at the wall of the nuns' choir. 'Why don't we go in there?'

'Only the nuns go in there. That's where they sing.'

'I'd like to see them.'

'You never will. The nuns' choir and all of that part of the priory – the cloister, the refectory, the nuns' dormitory, the chapter house – are restricted; no man will ever enter.'

They continued through a wide passageway and out into the orchard. Beyond the orchard were many other buildings. 'Who lives there?' Thomas asked.

'The friars who say mass and hear confessions, and people who work for the nuns.'

'There must be masons and carpenters to care for the church,' Thomas said, looking back at the huge building. 'They're men, and they'd have to go in.'

'I suppose so,' Christine said.

'I'd like to be one of those masons.'

'To see the church or the nuns?'

'The church, of course. The nuns all look alike.'

'That's not true, Thomas,' said a voice from under the trees.

Thomas stared at his sister. He hadn't seen her since she'd become a nun, and at first he didn't recognize her. She held out her arms to him. 'Am I allowed to touch her?' he asked his mother.

Christine and Marie burst out laughing. 'Of course,' Christine said. But Thomas was embarrassed.

'You'll just have to get used to me,' his sister said.

'You always did act like a nun,' Thomas said. 'Now you really are one.'

'Stupid boy,' Marie said. Christine breathed a sigh of relief. They were right back where they used to be, trading barbs.

'Why aren't you in there?' Thomas asked, pointing to the church.

'I came out here to see you. Do you want me to go back?'

'Not really.'

'Then let's not argue. I probably won't see you again after today.'

Thomas looked at the ground.

'Let's sit over there for a while,' Christine said, pointing to the bench by the wall.

The gardeners were still pruning the apple trees. They looked at Marie, but they didn't seem surprised.

'Do you sisters come out here often?' Thomas asked.

'We do, when we have permission.'

'Do you have permission now?'

Marie got up and wandered over to the wall. It was covered with ivy, and at its base were some early daffodils, their bright yellow petals contrasting with the shiny green leaves of the ivy. Marie stooped to pick a flower. *Someone could have climbed over the wall,* Christine thought. *But carrying a dog?*

'Look at this!' Marie cried. She was pointing to the lower part of the wall. Behind the ivy leaves there was a small door.

Thomas ran over and pulled some of the ivy away. The door had obviously been there for a long time; the wood was weathered and covered with mold.

'This door has no latch,' Thomas said. 'It must be boarded up on the outside. Otherwise, anyone could get in here.'

Christine looked closely. 'It was nailed shut on this side at one time, too,' she said. 'See, there are holes where the boards have fallen away.'

Thomas rummaged behind some tall bushes and emerged with two decaying boards in his hands. 'Here they are. I wonder whether there are any more on the outside. I'm going around to look.' He ran back the way they'd come.

Christine and Marie sat on the bench by the wall. 'I know what he's going to tell us,' Christine said.

Marie smiled. 'I'm sure you do, Mama.'

After a while, they heard the door creaking as it slowly opened and Thomas walked through. 'There was a lot ivy, but I found it,' he said. 'At one time someone nailed a board over it to keep it shut, but the board has fallen away. I have it here.' He held up a warped plank with rusty nails sticking through it.

'Go out and put the board back. Those old nails should hold it for a while,' Christine said. 'Try to hide it with the ivy. I'll have the prioress send a carpenter to nail the door shut on both sides so no one will be able to open it again.'

Thomas stepped out and shut the door behind him. Christine and Marie could hear him setting the board into place and pushing the nails through it.

'So, Mama. Tell me what you're thinking,' Marie said.

'I'm sure you know. Whoever killed Sister Thérèse could have come in through that door. There is no way anyone could have gotten past the *portier* at night with a dog.'

Thomas came back through the passageway. 'We have to cover it up with ivy on this side, too,' he said as he gathered the ivy they'd pulled away and placed it over the door.

They heard someone behind them. It was Jacques.

'Do you know about the door?' Thomas asked him.

'Of course. And I know who uses it.'

'Who?'

'The sorcerer.'

'You let your imagination get away with you, Jacques,' Christine admonished the boy. But she couldn't help thinking about what he'd said. She realized that she had to consider a number of possibilities – the murderer could be one of the sisters, someone who worked at the priory, someone who sneaked in through the door in the wall, or perhaps, even, farfetched though it seemed, the mysterious sorcerer everyone talked about.

FORTY-ONE

O Pride, root of all evil, I know that from you come all the other vices.

Christine de Pizan, *Le Livre des Trois Vertus*, 1405

The prioress stood by the window in her study. Shafts of light coming through the colored glass sent rainbow colors flickering over her white habit. When Christine told her about the door in the wall, she sent a message to the carpenters asking them to board it up on both sides.

Sister Richarde stormed in. 'That man again! He's been asking around the town about last year's crops, trying to find out whether we received sufficient revenues. How much for the wheat? How much for the hay? What business is it of his?'

The prioress smiled. 'I don't think anyone will ever be able to convince Henri Le Picart that we can take care of ourselves.' A cloud passed over the sun, and her habit turned pure white.

'When he goes around the town asking questions like that, it makes us look weak,' Sister Richarde said.

If I am not able to discover who murdered Sister Thérèse, things will be even worse, Christine thought. *I have to talk to Michel. Perhaps he can do something to make Henri stop trying to prove that the sisters are incompetent.* She left the two nuns going over some accounts Sister Richarde had brought, and went to the priory entrance to ask the *portier* if he'd seen the monk that day.

'I have,' Jacques said. 'He went into the inn across the street.'

Michel was sitting with Henri, who jumped up when he saw Christine and made a mock bow. 'Have you solved the problem yet?'

Christine tried to ignore him, but he stood close to her and said,

'Do you see that man over there?' She looked where he was pointing. A burly man with a club sat at a table in the corner, watching everyone who came into the inn.

'That's the provost of Paris's lieutenant,' Henri whispered.

'Why are you telling me this?'

'Don't you know? The king protects the priory. His provost watches over it. Just say the word, and his lieutenant will step in and keep the nuns safe.'

'And then the king and all of France will think the prioress is not able to care for her nuns. No, thank you, Henri.'

Henri sat down. 'Very well. But as soon as you admit that you can't solve this yourself, I'll get him to do it. He'll make short order of it and have the murderer in custody in no time.'

Christine turned to Michel, who was looking into a cup of wine and pretending not to hear what Henri was saying. 'Please come with me,' she said to him.

Henri sprang up again.

'This doesn't concern you,' Christine said.

Henri stood like a puffed-up rooster, daring her to leave him out. Christine just took Michel's arm and led him out the door.

'What makes him so arrogant?' she asked the monk.

'I really don't know. I used to think I did because I know of his past life. I told you how he was forced into a monastery as a child, and how much he hated it. I always thought he had good reason to be proud, because he overcame an unhappy childhood and became a rich man, friends with the king and his brother, and much respected at the court. But now his pride seems to have gotten the better of him.'

'If he hated being in a monastery, why can't he understand that his daughter might feel the same way?'

'I don't know that either. Quite frankly, he's become insufferable.'

'I'm glad you see it, too, Michel. Sometimes I think it's just me.'

'No, it isn't just you. I can see how he is irritating the prioress and her treasuress. I wish I could do something about it.'

They went into the priory, and Christine led him into the orchard. A carpenter was already there, examining the door.

'This is what I wanted to show you,' Christine said. 'The murderer could have come in through this.'

Michel asked the carpenter, 'How long do you think this door has been here?'

'It had to have been put there when the priory was built. Someone left a way to sneak in.'

The carpenter reached into a sack he was carrying. 'I have something to show you, Brother.' He opened his hand. In it was a hare's foot. 'Boys carry these things. It must belong to one of the boys who come to work for the sisters.'

Christine said, 'I hate to ask you this, Michel, but do you think it could have been one of the friars?'

Michel waved his hands in her face. '*Deus avertat!* Absolutely not! And anyway, the friars don't have to sneak in. They live here.'

'It was only a suggestion, Michel.'

'Don't make any more suggestions like that. People go around spreading all kinds of evil rumors about monks. Don't add to the slander!'

'Do you know all the friars?'

'Of course I do. Why do you think the king sent me here with you? If I didn't know everyone, I wouldn't be much help, would I?'

Christine couldn't help thinking that he hadn't been much help, anyway. But she said nothing.

The carpenter hammered nails into boards.

'He's doing a good job,' Michel said. 'No one will be able to get in that way again.'

'No one will be able to get out that way either,' Christine said.

FORTY-TWO

The seventh virtue is concord or benevolence. You must have this among yourselves, so love it and hold it dear in your convent . . . whoever removes benevolence from a group of people might as well take away the sun.

Christine de Pizan, *Le Livre des Trois Vertus*, 1405

The next day Christine found the prioress with sisters Claude, Richarde, Petra, Thomasine, Geneviève, and Dorian, all talking angrily.

'We have to get her out of here!' Geneviève exclaimed, jabbing her finger in the air. Her cheeks quivered. 'I can't keep her in the infirmary: she upsets all the other patients so much they don't get well.'

'Adelie again,' Mother Marie said to Christine. 'Now she claims she sees angels. Geneviève is keeping her in the infirmary to calm her down.'

'Besides the angels, she keeps talking about the beating heart she hears in the choir,' Sister Geneviève said.

'Does anyone else hear strange sounds there?' Christine asked.

'Of course not! It's all her imagination, and it disrupts the chant. I won't have it!' Sister Claude stamped her foot. 'I don't care how much money her family gives the priory. She has to go!'

'We can't abide it any longer,' Sister Petra said. 'She upsets everything.'

'Even our meals,' Sister Dorian said. 'She can't sit still at the table, and she talks during the reading.'

'You had her as a novice,' Sister Richarde said to Sister Petra. 'Why didn't you straighten her out then?'

'I can't work miracles,' Sister Petra said. She turned to the others. 'No one has done anything about her. You, Claude, could have made it clear that there is no beating heart in the choir. You could have humiliated her in front of the others. That might have induced her to stop talking about it.'

Sister Richarde chimed in. 'People like to say we nuns can't manage our own affairs. What if Henri Le Picart finds out about this? Then everyone will believe we really are inept.'

'It's your fault, Mother,' Sister Thomasine said to the prioress. 'You're supposed to be in charge here.'

The colored rays of light streaming through the window were suddenly extinguished. The room became dark, and raindrops splattered against the glass.

Mother Marie stood gazing at the others, smiling sadly. Then she began to sing, softly at first, then louder, her voice rising above the angry words. Sister Richarde stopped talking, Sister Geneviève hummed softly, and Sister Petra began to cry. Sister Claude gestured as though she were leading the choir, and they sang together, just as they did when they were in the church. Only Sister Thomasine was silent. She stood apart from the others, her pale face contorted into a scowl.

Christine watched them for a while, then left and went to look for Marion.

She didn't have to go far, because Marion had come into the priory courtyard to find her. The rain was coming down heavily now, so they dashed across the street to the inn. The skinny waiter looked at Marion and said, 'I don't serve prostitutes.'

'A pox on you, donkey pizzle!' Marion said.

'*Putain*,' the waiter said.

Christine put her hand on Marion's arm. She turned to the waiter. 'What makes you think she's a prostitute?'

'I saw her in Paris.'

'I'm sure you did,' Marion said. 'I saw *you* there, too. I saw you in a shop on the Grand Pont stealing that big ring you're wearing.'

The waiter stared at her open-mouthed. He started to say something but thought better of it and walked away.

'Did you really see him steal the ring?' Christine asked.

'Of course not. It was just a wild guess.'

'It certainly worked. I don't think he'll be coming to wait on us anymore.'

'I didn't want wine, anyway,' Marion said. 'We can talk freely now that that donkey turd is gone.'

'Don't lapse back into your old ways, Marion,' Christine said, laughing. 'Remember, you have to go back to Paris and sell your embroidery to the queen.'

'I almost forgot.'

'I want to tell you what my daughter and I discovered.'

Marion sat forward on the bench.

'There's a door in the wall that surrounds the priory. Somebody has been using it to get in.'

'The person who killed the nun?'

'It could be.'

'Saint Justina's wrinkled knees!'

'The prioress had it boarded up on both sides. That's a problem, because if the murderer is hiding somewhere in the priory, now there's no way to sneak out. We've got to do something before someone else gets killed.'

'Do you think Symonne has something to do with this?'

'If she does, at least she can't get in through that door again.'

'But it's not hard to get into the priory through the courtyard. You saw how easy it was for me in a beggar's costume.' Marion thought for a moment. 'Of course, the *portier* knew who I was. He'd certainly keep strangers out.'

'He's supposed to keep strangers out, but I don't think he can catch everyone.'

'What if it's Symonne? She's dangerous,' Marion said. She jumped up. 'I'm going to go and look for her.' She started out the door.

'If you're going to follow her, you must be careful!' Christine called out.

'I will,' Marion called back.

Christine went across the street to the priory gate. There she found the *portier* talking to Thomas. The *portier* was very upset.

'He's been gone for several hours. That's not like him. Oh, please help me find him,' he pleaded with Thomas.

'Who is gone?' Christine asked.

'My grandson.'

'Perhaps he's in the orchard,' Thomas said. 'I'll go and look for him.'

Christine stood talking with the *portier*, trying to calm his fears, until Thomas came back.

'He's not there.'

The *portier* let out a cry of anguish.

'I think I know where he's gone,' Thomas said.

FORTY-THREE

In the dense forest, which was turning green again, many great oaks, tall, large, and beautiful, stood so close together that the sun could not reach the ground.

Christine de Pizan, *Le Livre du Dit de Poissy*, 1400

Thomas hurried through the streets of Poissy. The rain made walking treacherous, but it was a cattle market day, and, in spite of the weather, everyone was out. He wove his way through clusters of bellowing steers, shouting herdsmen, and butchers crying their wares, ignoring the imprecations of angry people on whose feet he stepped, until he came to the town wall. He slipped through one of the gates, slid down an embankment, and ran across a wide meadow, ignoring the wet grass that soaked his shoes and hose. He climbed a hill and stopped to catch his breath. In the distance, the town seemed to be a mirage, a cluster of tiny houses with glistening roofs sheltering around the huge priory church and its tall spire.

Thomas had always been fascinated by the stories he'd heard about sorcerers. He knew a lot about Jean of Bar and the prohibited practices in which he'd indulged because Henri had told him. Henri seemed to believe Jacques when he talked about a sorcerer hiding in the forest of Saint-Germain-en-Laye, a sorcerer who had been Jean of Bar's assistant. Henri said someone should go and find him. Thomas was convinced that Jacques had decided to do it. *He's a little boy*, he said to himself. *I can't let him go in there all by himself.*

But now, as Thomas, who'd lived all his life in a city, contemplated entering the forest, he wondered whether it was such a good idea. The great mass of trees looked forbidding, and he could see no way in except for a narrow path covered with damp, moldy leaves. He started on the path tentatively, walking on tiptoe at first, then gathering his courage and plodding on with firm steps. The unfamiliar odor of moldering leaves stung his nostrils, and the soggy, slimy earth sucked at his boots, holding them so firmly that it was a struggle to lift his feet. Drops of rain plopped on to his head, sometimes into his eyes, momentarily blinding him. High above, a lone bird called wistfully.

He slogged on for a while, then turned to look back, knowing full well he would no longer be able to see the town. By this time, he had no idea where he was, not even in which direction he was going. Branches creaked in sudden gusts of wind, and somewhere in the distance a second bird let out a weak chirp. Other than that, all he heard was the incessant patter of rain on leaves and the sound of his water-laden boots squishing through the mud.

When he came upon a narrow trail, he remembered Henri telling him that kings and noblemen had been coming to this forest for centuries to hunt deer and wild boar, and he told himself that it was just a hunting track. He wondered whether wild boar were dangerous. He'd heard that the king who founded the Poissy priory had died because a wild boar had charged his horse, causing him to fall. Had that been here or in some other forest? He couldn't recall.

He looked around and saw nothing but trees, their leaves shaking as the rain battered them. He was cold and wet and beginning to be frightened. Then he saw a hut in the distance. He ran toward it, stumbling over tree roots hidden under sodden leaves and letting out whoops of joy, hoping someone would hear and come out to welcome him. But no one appeared, and as he got closer, he realized that what he'd thought was a hut was nothing more than a heap of old boards.

A track led away from the non-existent hut, and he followed it, getting deeper and deeper into the forest. *This can't go on forever*, he thought. *And I can't afford to be afraid.* He tried not to think about the sorcerer, but he had to ask himself, *What will I do if I find him?* He mused about this for a while. *Henri said Jean of Bar had demon friends. Perhaps his assistant is trying to summon them. Perhaps if I offer to help he won't hurt me.*

Henri had told him something about polishing a fingernail until it shone like a mirror so you could see demons in it. He looked at his fingernails. They were caked with mud. He spat on one and rubbed it. Then he laughed. *I haven't even found him yet.*

A frightened deer dashed out of the woods and disappeared. The rain stopped for a moment and everything became very quiet. In the distance, he could hear someone talking. *I think I've found him*, he whispered to himself.

Thomas crept toward the voices. The rain started hammering the earth again. A heavy mist rose, and he could hardly see his hand in front of his face. Tree branches slapped his cheeks like whips, and a bush he couldn't see wrapped itself around his legs so tightly that he nearly fell. He swore, tore the bush away, and thrust it aside, cursing the day he'd left the city streets, where the main impediments were piles of horse dung and old women with market baskets.

He stumbled blindly on until he came up against a wall. He crept along it until he reached a door. He heard a voice inside. *Should I call out and let him know I'm here?* he asked himself. *No, I'd better not.*

He inched his way farther along and came to a window. Some of the oiled paper that covered it had fallen away and he could see into a large room. A tall figure in a white robe decorated with strange black symbols stood in front of a table covered with a cloth. *That must be the sorcerer*, he thought. *Is Jacques there, too?* The sorcerer went to a pile of blankets in a corner and lifted one of them. Jacques lay there, seemingly asleep. The sorcerer picked the boy up, carried him to the table, and laid him on it.

Then the sorcerer turned around.

Thomas put his hand over his mouth to keep from crying out. The sorcerer was a woman.

FORTY-FOUR

I, Jehan de Bar, have many times during the past eighteen years, and especially during the past two years, invoked devils by evil arts that are prohibited by God and the Church.

Confession of Jehan de Bar,
condemned and convicted of sorcery in 1398

Thomas closed his eyes. He'd seen Jean of Bar on his way to be executed – a tall man, thin as a spike, who'd kept his head down and his face hidden from the crowd. He'd tried to imagine that face and had decided it was lined and gaunt, with flaming eyes. He shuddered, took a deep breath, and looked again at the figure in the room. Except for the fact that she was a woman, she was as he'd imagined – tall, thin as a spike, with a lined and gaunt face, and large shining eyes.

'Wake up now,' she said to the boy on the table.

Slowly, Jacques sat up.

The woman giggled. 'You bothered to come all the way through the forest and knock on my door. But as soon as I let you in, you fell asleep. How can you help me if you go to sleep?'

Jacques jumped down from the makeshift altar. 'I'm wide awake now. I was just tired after my long walk.'

The woman chuckled. 'Good.'

I'm imagining things, Thomas thought. *This is an old woman, not a sorcerer. She's just playing with Jacques.* He decided to walk straight into the room, take the boy in his arms, and carry him home. He went to the door and lifted the latch. But before he could open it, he heard the woman coming toward it. 'Is someone there?' she called out.

He crept to the window again and watched her go back to the altar. She whispered something to the boy. Then she grabbed his hand and examined his fingernails. She smiled. 'If we clean them, they will do.'

'Do what?' Jacques asked.

'I'll tell you in a moment.'

Thomas surveyed the room. There was a lot more there than he'd first realized. And what he saw was worse than anything Henri had told him about the practices of Jean of Bar.

Most frightening were the wolves. Two of them. They sat in the shadows at a far corner, their unblinking eyes glistening in the light of the flames in a small fireplace. The strangest thing about them was that they didn't move. They just sat there, staring.

Thomas had never seen a wolf before, but he'd seen pictures of them in manuscripts his mother brought home to copy, and he'd heard a great deal about them from his grandmother, who said she'd seen one creeping through the streets of Paris one night. His mother had scoffed, claiming that all Francesca had seen was a dog, perhaps even a large cat, and Thomas had believed her, until now.

He noticed that the altar had spiked protrusions that looked like horns on the corners. He also saw what appeared to be thuribles, just like the ones in church, and he thought he could smell burning incense. On another table, all jumbled together, were scrolls and books and, in the midst of them, a crystal stone.

'You'd like to see more, wouldn't you?' the woman asked. Thomas jumped. She was standing close to the window now, and he thought she was talking to him. But she was talking to Jacques. She picked up a little box, lifted the lid, and held it in front of the boy's eyes.

He cried out in surprise. 'Those are nail clippings!'

'That's right. Here's something else.' She opened another box. 'Look at these pretty rings. And here's a nail from a horseshoe.'

'I know about that!' Jacques said. 'My grandfather told me. A horseshoe nail will prevent bad luck.'

'That's right, my dear boy. Since you know so much, tell me what this is.' She opened a small box that contained a small furry animal that looked half dead.

'It's a mole. What are you going to do with it?'

'Eat its heart, of course. If I swallow it before it stops beating, I'll be able to see everything.'

Jacques laughed. 'No one can see everything.'

'I can.' She picked up a glass vial with red liquid inside. 'Can you guess what this is?'

Thomas was nauseated, but Jacques was fascinated. 'Is it blood?

'It is. The blood of a hoopoe. Have you ever seen a hoopoe?'

'No. What is it? Do you have one?'

The woman got up and opened a large coffer. She was close enough to the window that Thomas could see that inside the coffer was a dead bird. It was pinkish-brown, with black-and-white striped wings and a large crest like a crown on its head. 'This is a hoopoe,' she said.

'What are you going to do with it?' Jacques asked.

'This is where I got the blood.'

'I know!' Jacques cried. 'My grandfather told me. You're going to write with it.'

'That's right. But the blood of a hoopoe is useful for other things, too. Did your grandfather tell you that if you mix it with the hair of a man who's been hanged, you can use it to make yourself invisible?'

'No. Now I can tell *him* something.'

The woman laughed. She went to the table with the scrolls and books, and picked up a piece of parchment and a quill pen. She stuck the quill into the red liquid, then scratched some words on to the parchment. 'I'm writing to a demon.'

She's doing all the things sorcerers are supposed to do, Thomas thought. *But she can't be a sorcerer. Sorcerers are men.* Then he thought of what his mother would say. 'You of all people should know that a woman can do anything a man can.'

He wished his mother were with him now.

'What are you telling him?' Jacques asked.

'I'm asking him to come to us. Here, look. I've signed my name. Can you read?'

'No.'

'I'll tell you then. My name is Péronnette. You can call me that.'

'Péronnette,' Jacques repeated. 'That's a nice name. The demon will like it.'

'But it's not enough. We have to do something else.' She reached behind the altar and brought out what appeared to be a figure of a man. She laid it on the altar. 'Come, look closely.'

Jacques leaned over the figure. Thomas desperately wanted to see it, but it was too far away. Then, as if in answer to his prayers, the woman picked up the figure and began to dance around the room with it. When she brought it close to the window, he felt cold needles pierce his spine. It was a copper image of a bearded man with a battered face and a missing arm, the figure the traveling players had used in the demonstration of the sin of Wrath. The figure Symonne du Mesnil had stolen.

But it was different now. It was wearing a crown.

FORTY-FIVE

When I was a boy, I was taught the psalms by a priest who practiced the art of crystal gazing, and he used me and another, somewhat older, boy for his sacrilegious art. He moistened our fingernails with sacred oil or chrism . . . in order to see through us the information he sought.

John of Salisbury (1120–1180), *Policraticus* (1159)

'Now the demon is almost ready to come,' Péronnette said. 'He knows I have the king here. He is going to cure him.' Jacques stood by her side, quivering with excitement. 'First we have to baptize the king.'

Thomas looked on in horror as she dipped her fingers into a cup of water and sprinkled it over the copper figure, all the while whispering words he couldn't understand. It was all he could do to keep from crying out, 'That's sacrilege!' He stopped himself just in time and watched as she reached out for Jacques, drew him to her side, took a cloth, and proceeded to rub one of his fingernails vigorously.

'Why are you doing that?' the boy asked.

'Your soul is pure. When your fingernail is clean, the demon will come, and you will be the only one who will be able to see him.'

Thomas heard hooves splashing through the mud, and he flattened himself against the wall of the hut. The horse came to a stop.

Someone jumped to the ground and ran to the door of the hut. Leaning in so close to the window that he hit his head on the frame, he watched Symonne du Mesnil rush into the room. 'That's enough, Mother,' she shouted as she tried to wrench Jacques away. The boy, who was staring at his fingernail, resisted. He seemed to have fallen into a trance.

'Do you see the demon?' Péronnette asked.

'Yes, yes, I do!' he cried.

'He doesn't!' Thomas almost screamed. He put his hand over his mouth.

Péronnette stroked the boy's hair. 'Tell the demon to come to us.'

'That's enough, I said!' Symonne shrieked. 'Someone's coming, but it's not a demon. It's the overseer of the forest. Put everything away!'

'Just when the demon was almost here!' Péronnette wailed. She let go of Jacques and began stuffing the scrolls and books into a big box, along with the robe decorated with strange black symbols, the crystal ball, the thuribles, and the horns from the makeshift altar. Then she pulled up several floorboards. Under them was a deep hole, and she threw into it the big box, the coffer with the hoopoe, and the smaller boxes with the mole and the fingernails. Then she put the boards back. Symonne grabbed the copper figure and took it and the wolves outside through a door on the other side of the room. 'I'll put these in the kennel. He never looks there,' she said.

'Who's coming?' Jacques asked Péronnette.

'The man who's in charge of the forest. You mustn't tell him anything. You're just visiting me, do you understand? Tell him I'm your grandmother.'

'But I want to see the demon!'

'Later.'

Symonne came back and sat in a chair in front of the fireplace. 'Just a normal day at home, with your daughter and grandson visiting. How pleasant.' She began to hum, a mournful tune that sounded to Thomas like a lament for the dead. The tune broke off, and Symonne began to giggle. He remembered that Péronnette had giggled, too. *This really is her daughter*, he thought.

Thomas heard another horse approaching, and he pressed against the wall of the hut again. It was growing dark, but the rider had a torch, and in its light Thomas was able to watch him dismount and stride to the door. Inside, Péronnette put her arms around

Jacques, nearly smothering him, and Symonne went to the door and opened it. A large man in a brown leather jacket and huge boots swaggered in. He strode to the table that had served as an altar, lifted the cloth, and peered under it. Then he sauntered around the room, eyeing everything. When he came close to the window, Thomas heard him mutter to himself, 'One of these days I'll catch them at it!' He looked at Jacques. 'Aren't you the grandson of the *portier* at the priory?'

Jacques, terrified, nodded.

'What are you doing here?'

'The poor boy got lost in the forest,' Péronnette said.

'Is that right?' the man asked Jacques. The boy swallowed and nodded again.

'Your grandfather will be worried about you.' He grabbed the boy's arm and pulled him to the door. He turned to Péronnette. 'You haven't seen the last of me.'

The man lifted Jacques on to his horse and galloped away. Thomas looked through the window and saw the two women sitting by the fire, the old one staring into the flames and the younger one holding her head in her hands. 'He's going to get you someday, Mother,' Symonne moaned.

'I'm too clever for him.'

'You're not. Besides, as I told you before, the Duke of Burgundy sent me here to tell you not to continue with this for a while.'

'But I want to go on trying to call the demons who will cure the king!'

'Not at the moment. There's a woman from the court here, sticking her nose into what's going on at the priory. The situation there has to be settled first.'

'That should be taken care of soon,' Péronnette said.

'How can you possibly know that?'

'Because I'm helping.'

'I don't understand what you're saying, Mother. Who are you helping?'

'Do you know Tassin of Archères?'

'I've never heard of him.'

'His son Bernart went off to fight the infidels at Nicopolis, and he didn't come back. He's being held hostage, and the duke won't pay ransom for him.'

'Why not?'

'I don't know. He's paid ransom for everyone else who was captured.'

'I can think of a reason. He was a traitor.'

Péronnette gasped. 'I never thought of that.'

'What has this to do with the priory?'

'Tassin and his other son, Guy, want to get Bernart back.'

'I don't see what this has to do with you.'

'Guy's been coming to me, learning about the demons and how I call them. At first, he thought he could use the demons to get even with his cruel father because he tried to kill his dog. But then he told me about his brother and how he thought he could get into his father's good graces if he helped him get his brother back. I gave him a plan. The king's little daughter is at the priory. I told him that if they abducted her, the king would pay them a lot of money in exchange for her release. They could use the money to pay the ransom.'

'How could they possibly abduct her?'

'I told him he could use sorcery, or at least people's belief in it.'

Symonne stood up and stamped her foot. 'For God's sake, Mother.'

'It's simple. Nuns are just as superstitious as anyone else. He puts signs of sorcery around the priory, and then he abducts the princess, and they think she was taken by a phantom, not an actual person.'

'No men are allowed there.'

'I told him where to hide.'

'Where is that?'

Péronnette said something Thomas couldn't hear, no matter how he strained. He could, however, hear Symonne ask angrily, 'Does this have anything to do with the fact that one of the nuns at the priory died?'

'Of course it does. That nun was Guy's sister.' Péronnette's voice became so low again that Thomas couldn't hear what she said next. But he heard clearly when Symonne shouted, 'You foolish woman! Don't you know you could be executed? Now that that nosy woman is here, you will surely be found out.'

'Be calm, daughter. The demons will know what to do with her.'

'As far as I can see, you haven't succeeded in producing any demons. I don't believe Jean of Bar succeeded either, in spite of the images of the king he made.'

'Surely the image you brought me will work,' Péronnette said.

'I told you before, it is just something the players had. Unless you can get one specially made to represent the king, there's no use trying.'

'We'll see about that,' Péronnette said.

'Do you mean you intend to go on with this?'

'Of course.'

Thomas heard Symonne curse her mother, run outside, and climb on to her horse. Night had fallen, and he could barely see, but he followed her as she rode away, realizing he'd never be able to find his way out of the forest on his own. It was so dark that Symonne couldn't spur the horse to a gallop, or even a trot, without risking a bad fall, so she had to ride slowly, and he was able to keep her shadowy figure in sight. He took no notice of the rain that soaked his clothes and nearly blinded him when it fell into his eyes. He had only one thought: to get back to Poissy and protect his mother.

FORTY-SIX

There was a great cloister, a spacious, beautiful, uncluttered green space in the middle of which stood a very tall pine tree, as full and straight as a fir.

Christine de Pizan, *Le Livre du Dit de Poissy*, 1400

Christine spent the rest of the day in the prioress's quarters with the *Life of Saint Dominic* open on her desk, her quills, knives, parchment, and inkhorn scattered around, unused. If any of the sisters came in, they would think she was at work on her copying. What she was really doing was thinking.

She had no idea where Thomas had gone. *He's old enough to take care of himself*, she reasoned. Her problem was to discover who had murdered Sister Thérèse and who was causing all the mischief at the priory. She hoped the culprit was someone from the outside, one of Thérèse's acquaintances, for example, someone who had a grudge against her. She also had to consider Symonne du Mesnil – the woman could be in Poissy for no good reason – and the sorcerer in the forest.

Finally, although it pained her to do so, she had to think about
the sisters. A kitchen boy had told Marion that he'd seen one of
them steal a knife. He said that she was shorter than the other sisters
he'd seen. Could it have been Claude? She was tiny, and she was
angry at Thérèse for not leaping joyfully out of bed for matins and
for making mistakes in her singing. Thomasine was exasperated
with Thérèse for the same reasons; but she was not short. And there
was Geneviève – small and squat. She'd convinced the prioress to
keep the cause of Thérèse's death a secret. Was it because she knew
Thérèse was pregnant, and she wanted to keep the priory from being
disgraced?

All the other sisters she'd met had reasons for disliking Thérèse.
She'd angered Sister Dorian by disrupting order in the refectory.
But Dorian limped, and the kitchen boy would surely have noticed
that. Thérèse had argued with Sister Petra over the seriousness of
her lessons, but Petra was not short, just very thin. How about Sister
Louise? She was short and fat, and Thérèse had frightened her
chickens so they failed to lay their eggs. Or Sister Richarde? Thérèse
had mocked her mannerisms. But Richarde was tall.

She wondered about Juliana, who was not particularly tall. Could
she trust her?

She hadn't seen the prioress all day, but that was not unusual.
When a lay sister came in, bringing her a supper of soup and bread,
she realized she'd missed vespers. *I'll go to compline*, she thought.
The music will help me think.

No one was around as she went down the stairs, along some
passageways, and out into the cloister. A storm was on the way, and
a fierce wind scattered clouds that raced across the moon. She
walked around the vaulted passageway, her feet tapping on the
colored tiles, which glittered whenever the moon appeared, and
stepped out on to the lawn. Her feet struck something and she nearly
fell. A nun, her habit askew, lay in the grass. Christine knelt beside
her. It was Sister Denise.

The woman sat up and cried, 'Where is the princess?' She
struggled to her feet and ran through the cloister arcade, calling
loudly for the little girl. Stunned, Christine stood immobile for a
moment, watching her. In the center of the cloister, the huge pine
tree swayed, making a moaning sound as the wind tossed its
branches up and down in an unvarying rhythm, like the waves of
the sea. On one of the upward swings, a white shape emerged

from its depths. It was the princess. Christine ran to her and caught her in her arms.

'He didn't get me!' the little girl exclaimed.

'Who didn't get you?' Christine cried.

The princess wriggled away and did a little dance around the tree.

'He pushed Sister down, but I hid in the tree. He ran away when you came out.'

'Who?' Christine asked again.

'A man. Wasn't it clever of me to hide in the tree?' She patted one of the branches. 'The needles are scratchy.'

Sister Denise ran up and grabbed the child. 'Why did you run away from me?'

'The man who pushed you down was after me.'

'There was no man.'

'There was. He pushed you down.'

'I fell.'

'Did you see the man's face?' Christine asked the princess.

'Only a little. It was dark.'

'Can you tell me anything about him?'

'He was big. But not strong enough to hold me.' The princess pointed her finger at Sister Denise. 'You didn't protect me.'

It began to rain. Christine carried the princess into the cloister arcade and set her on a bench. The little girl jumped up and ran around the walkway, repeating over and over again, 'He didn't get me!'

'We should take her to the prioress,' Christine said. Sister Denise agreed, and between them they managed to calm the child and make her walk to the prioress's quarters.

Mother Marie was sitting at her desk, and when she saw them, she jumped up and took the princess in her arms. 'What has happened?'

'A big man tried to catch me in the cloister, but I ran away and hid in the pine tree,' the princess said.

'Is this true?' the prioress asked Sister Denise, who was weeping.

'I fell. There wasn't any man.'

'There was. He pushed you down,' the princess insisted.

'Are you hurt? Shall I call the infirmaress?'

'No. I'm all right.' Sister Denise brushed at her habit, which was covered with mud. 'Let me go to the dormitory and rest for a while.'

'But the attacker could still be out there somewhere. Let me get someone to go with you,' the prioress said.

'There is no attacker. I simply fell. I want to be alone. I don't want anyone to know what happened.' Sister Denise sank on to the bench by the fireplace and buried her head in her hands.

The prioress, holding the child close, sat on the bench beside her. 'I'm sure you did the best you could.'

Sister Denise wiped her eyes and stood up. 'Please let me go now.'

'Then take a candle from one of the sconces,' the prioress said. 'Just be careful.'

Sister Denise took a candle and left without saying anything further.

'Compline is over, so the other sisters are around,' the prioress said. 'Otherwise, I wouldn't have let her go alone.'

'She isn't telling the truth,' the princess said. 'There was a man.'

'Do you know who the man was?'

'I don't know who he was, but I've seen him before.'

FORTY-SEVEN

Before Saint Dominic was born, his mother dreamed she had in her womb a little dog with a lighted torch in its mouth.

Jacobus de Voragine, *The Golden Legend*, thirteenth century

Christine and the prioress stared at the child. 'Where did you see him?' the prioress asked.

'In the cloister.'

'When?'

'One night, about two weeks ago.'

'What were you doing in the cloister at night?'

'Sister Denise said she couldn't sleep. I know why, because I've sat on her bed. It's hard. Not like mine. Mine's nice and soft.'

'So Sister Denise couldn't sleep and she went out into the cloister. Why did she take you? You were supposed to be asleep.'

'I was wide awake, because of all her tossing and turning. I was in my nightdress, and I was cold. She went to get me a cape. Then the man came. He was big and he had a funny eye.'

'Did he see you?' the prioress asked.

'His eye scared me, so I hid in the big pine tree, just like I did tonight.'

The prioress tightened her hold on the child. 'That was a clever thing to do.'

'I'm a princess. Princesses are clever. He didn't see me, but I saw him. He had a little dog. It didn't bark like dogs are supposed to. He had a big taper, too. He took the dog and the taper into the dormitory where all the sisters sleep. I thought men weren't supposed to go in there.'

'Of course they aren't,' the prioress said.

'Then he was a bad man. I knew that, anyway, because he looked bad. I think he would have hurt me if he'd found me in the tree.' She started to cry.

'But he didn't find you,' the prioress said.

The princess wiped her eyes. 'I know. I'm too clever.'

'Did the man come back?' Christine asked.

'He came back, and one of the sisters was following him. He was holding the light up so she could see. The dog ran around his feet. I don't like dogs.'

'Were you afraid the dog would bite you?' the prioress asked.

'Not me. He was going to bite another sister who came out.'

'*Another* sister?'

'Yes. She had a knife. The dog jumped at her, and she tried to stab him with the knife. But the dog didn't get hurt because the first sister grabbed him. She was the one who got hurt. I know because she fell down.'

'What happened then?'

'The man with the funny eye picked up the dog and ran away. The sister with the knife ran away, too. The other sister just lay on the ground and didn't move.'

Christine and the prioress looked at each other.

'What did you do then?' Christine asked.

'I ran back to my room. Sister Denise was just coming out. I didn't tell her what I'd seen. I was too scared to tell anyone.'

'Did you recognize either of the sisters?'

'No. I don't live with the sisters, so I don't know them.'

The prioress sat for a moment, deep in thought, holding the princess close and smoothing her hair. The princess squirmed in her arms.

'I think you should go to bed now,' Mother Marie said.

'I don't want to go to bed. That man may come, and if I'm asleep, I won't see him and he'll get me.'

'No one will get you because you're going to sleep here with Christine. We'll keep watch over you.' She carried her into Christine's room.

Christine sat thinking. When the prioress came back, she asked her, 'Do you remember what Thérèse said the night she returned home from her sister's funeral?'

'She said she had something she wanted to tell me. She was almost ill with fatigue, so I told her it could wait until the next day.'

'So she went to bed, and then she got up and went into the cloister with a man with an eye patch.'

'It's incomprehensible,' the prioress said. 'How could a man have gotten in?'

'He must have come through the door I found in the wall.'

'Of course! The *portier* would never have let a stranger with a dog in.'

'I think it was her brother, Guy. I saw him when I went to Archères. He's in his teens, but he's so big he must have seemed like a man to the princess. He had a black patch over one eye. That's why the princess said his eye was funny.' She thought before she asked, 'Did you know Thérèse was pregnant?'

'Yes. Sister Geneviève thinks I don't, but how could I not when the poor girl was often sick in the morning, and she was always holding her stomach.'

'Do you have any idea who the father of her child could have been?'

'I hate to say this, but I believe it was her brother. She talked about him sometimes, and she told me she was afraid of him. She didn't say why, but I could guess.'

'The boy's a brute. He looks like someone who wouldn't hesitate to force himself on a woman, even his own sister. I think it's possible he did that on one of Thérèse's visits to a sick relative. Her mother told me that the last time she was home, she was very anxious to get back to the priory. She must have been terrified of him.'

'Perhaps she was going to tell me she was pregnant. Perhaps she was finally going to ask for help. The poor child.' Tears ran down Mother Marie's face.

'Possibly. Perhaps Guy suspected that, and he came here to make sure she wouldn't have a chance to tell anyone.'

'Do you think he meant to kill her? The princess said it was one of the sisters who stabbed Thérèse.' The prioress went to the fireplace and added some logs. They sputtered and spat as the flames caught them. She sat down on the bench and stared at them. Her face, illuminated in the flickering light, had become almost as white as Sister Thomasine's. 'I wonder whether the princess really understood what she saw.'

'The princess is just a child,' Christine said. 'She could very well have been mistaken. It's quite possible that Guy was the one who stabbed his sister. After all, he was the one who led her out into the cloister.'

'If Thérèse was afraid of him, why would she follow him?'

'There was someone she would have followed anywhere,' Christine said. She left the study, tiptoed into her room and lifted the *Life of Saint Dominic* from the desk. The princess lay on her bed, watching her. 'What are you doing with that book?'

'You should be asleep,' Christine said.

'I'll sleep when I want to. I have to make sure that big man doesn't come in here.'

'He won't,' Christine said. She pulled the covers up over the child and went back to the prioress's study. She laid the book on the desk and opened it.

'Saint Dominic had a dog,' she said. 'Here's a picture. It has a torch in its mouth.'

The prioress gasped. 'I think I begin to see.'

'Guy is not as stupid as he looks,' Christine continued. 'He knew his sister would follow Saint Dominic anywhere.'

The prioress finished the thought. 'It was dark. Thérèse saw a dog and a light. She followed because she thought it was Saint Dominic. But it was really her brother, who may or may not have killed her. The question is why did he come back again after she was dead?'

'He was after the princess,' Christine said.

'And thanks to you, he ran away before he could get her. But why would he want her?' The prioress rose and paced around the room.

'We have to find him,' Christine said.

'He can't have gone far. The door in the wall has been boarded up. That means—'

'That means he's still somewhere in here with us.'

The prioress picked up a taper and lit it in the flames of the fireplace. 'He may try again tonight to abduct the child, but he can't get into my quarters if the doors are securely locked. I don't like to leave you and the child alone, but I must find Brother Michel and ask him what he thinks we should do. I don't want the whole world to find out about this. Compline is over now, and everyone is in bed. Lock the door after me and you'll be safe.' She hurried from the room.

Christine turned the key in the lock and walked around the room, trying to calm herself. A strong wind had come up, and it howled around the building, shaking the big glass window. She sat down at the prioress's desk and idly turned the pages of the *Life of Saint Domi*nic. She heard a noise behind her and turned to find the princess watching her.

'Are you sitting like that because you're afraid that man is going to come in here?' the princess asked. 'If he does, I'll protect us.'

'You are a brave little girl!'

'A brave little *princess*.'

'That's right,' Christine said.

The princess climbed on to Christine's lap and looked at the open book. 'Let me turn the pages.'

'If you do it carefully.'

'I don't want to see the dog with a torch in his mouth again.' The princess turned the pages until she came to a scene of Saint Dominic preaching to a group of men.

'Who are all those people?'

'Those are people who don't believe what the priests tell them.'

'Will Saint Dominic make them believe it?'

'He will.'

'Could Saint Dominic make people believe I saw a man in the cloister?'

'No one doubts you.'

The princess laid her head on Christine's chest. 'Sister Denise doesn't believe me.'

'The prioress and I believe you. That's all that matters.'

They came to a scene of Saint Dominic standing with a man who had little horned demons coming out of his body. 'The saint is driving the demons away,' Christine said.

'Sister Denise told me about demons,' the princess said. 'She said there's a sorcerer in the forest who talks to them.'

'You mustn't believe Sister Denise.'

'Sister Denise says my father has demons in his head.'

Christine turned the child around so she was facing her. 'Don't listen to Sister Denise. There are no demons in your father's head. He is ill, and he has many doctors caring for him.'

The princess turned another page and came to a picture of Saint Dominic admonishing some monks. 'Why is he doing that?' she asked.

'They behaved badly,' Christine said.

'Naughty monks,' the princess said. 'Nuns don't do bad things.'

Perhaps they do, Christine said to herself.

It had started to rain, and huge drops drummed against the glass window.

'The window is shaking,' the princess said. 'It's demons, trying to get in.'

'I told you, there are no such things as demons. I think you should go back to bed now.'

'If you'll stay here.'

'I'll be right here.'

The princess fell asleep quickly, and Christine sat looking at the *Life of Saint Dominic*, wishing she had his courage, until the fire in the fireplace died down and the room became very dark. She got up and added more logs, then stood there, staring into the flames. She seemed to see little figures, little men leaping toward her. *I'm just as bad as the princess*, she thought.

The princess came running out. 'I heard something!'

'It's probably Sister Denise at the door, coming to take you to your own bed,' Christine said. 'Is that you, Sister Denise?' she called out. There was no answer.

The princess began to cry. 'I don't want to go with her. She's not nice to me. I wish Sister Catherine would come back.'

'I'm sure she'll be back soon.' She called out again. 'Let me know if it's you, Sister Denise.'

Still no answer.

'There's nobody there,' she told the princess. You can go back to bed.'

'No! I want to stay with you. Let's look at the book some more.'

Christine sighed, picked the child up, and sat at the desk with her. By now she was so sleepy herself that she had a hard time keeping her eyes open as she watched the little girl turn the pages of the manuscript.

'Why don't you tell me what these pictures mean?' the princess complained as she came to images of the saint.

'You must go to bed now. Everything is all right here.'

'It's not all right. Someone is at the window.'

Christine listened. There really was someone at the window. Someone was pushing on the panes. She took the princess in her arms, grabbed a candle from a sconce on the wall, turned the key to open the door, and dashed from the room.

FORTY-EIGHT

In front of the roof over the side-aisles there must be a passageway over the entablature. There must be another passageway at the top in front of the windows . . . Before the great roof, there must also be passageways and crenelated tablements, to allow circulation in case of fire.

Villard de Honnecourt (thirteenth-century architect),
description of a cathedral

Thomas followed Symonne back through the forest, stumbling and nearly crying with fear and fatigue. Several times, he almost lost her as the path widened and the horse was able to trot. But he persevered and was always able to catch up. When they finally came out of the woods, Symonne spurred the horse to a gallop across the open meadow, but by that time Thomas knew where they were and he didn't need to follow her anymore. He could see the lights of the town in the distance, and he headed for them.

He stumbled through the town gate just as the night watchmen were about to close it. 'You're lucky, my boy,' a big man with a club said. 'You wouldn't want to stay out there all night.'

'I wouldn't be afraid,' Thomas said, thinking he'd never be afraid of anything again, now that he had survived the forest and the sorceress. He hurried through the streets to the inn.

Henri was sitting at a table, nodding over a cup of wine. Thomas clapped him on the shoulder. 'Wake up, Henri. I've found the sorcerer. My mother is in danger. I need your help.'

'Calm down,' Henri said. 'I've been waiting for you. Where have you been?'

Thomas grabbed Henri's arm and pulled him up from his seat.

Henri wrenched his arm away, took Thomas by the shoulders, and made him sit down. 'Now, tell me about it calmly. Then we'll decide what to do.'

'I told you. I found the sorcerer.'

Henri laughed. 'I knew you could do it.'

'I went to find Jacques. There's a hut in the forest, and he was there with the sorcerer. But he's a she. Her name is Péronnette and she really is a sorcerer.'

'Sorceress.'

'Right. The sorceress was trying to get Jacques to see demons in his fingernails. She didn't succeed, though. A man who seemed to know all about the woman came and took Jacques home.'

'That must have been the superintendent of the forest. Why didn't he arrest the sorceress?'

'She hid everything when her daughter warned her that he was coming.'

'Wait a minute, Thomas. You didn't say anything about a daughter.'

'She wasn't there at first. Then she came in and told her mother the forest man was coming. It was Symonne du Mesnil. I recognized her because I saw her steal a copper figure of a man from the players. She'd brought it to her mother. Her mother put a crown on its head and used it to summon demons.'

'Where were you when all this happened?'

'I stood outside and peered in through a window. I saw and heard everything. That's what I've come to tell you. Péronnette is helping someone named Guy with a plot. He and his father have a plan to get the money they need to ransom another son who's being held hostage at Nicopolis. They're going to abduct the princess.'

Henri took a drink of wine and set the cup down with a bang.

'Péronnette and her mother are very upset that my mother is here because they think she's going to find out what they're doing. My mother is in danger. We have to help her!'

'How did you get back?'

'I followed Symonne on her horse. She had to go slowly because it was so dark.'

'Where did she go?'

'I don't know. Péronnette said she told Guy to hide in the priory. I don't know where. You have to help me catch him!'

'I think I know where he is,' Henri said. He grabbed two candles from the table, gave one to Thomas, and dashed across the street. Thomas ran after him. At the priory entrance, Jacques was regaling his grandfather with an account of his visit to the sorceress, and the *portier*, looking very angry, didn't notice as they raced past and hurried to the entrance to the church.

'There's a door here in the wall of the transept,' Henri said. 'I'll wager you never noticed it before.' He opened the door. Inside there was a narrow spiral staircase. He started up, and Thomas followed.

It was pitch-black, and the only light came from their flickering candles. They climbed for a long time. When they finally reached the top, Henri took Thomas's hand and steered him through a small opening that led to the outside. The rain came down heavily, but the sky was permeated by an eerie green light, and Thomas could see that they were on an exterior passageway that went around the roof. He looked down and marveled. He'd never been up so high. Henri took his arm and pulled him back through the opening, and they stood in a gallery that looked down on the public space of the church below.

Henri had a sack that Thomas hadn't noticed before. He reached into it and pulled out a torch, which he lit from his candle. 'This will give us more light.'

Thomas shivered. He could hardly see anything.

'Where are we going?'

'The upper parts of the church are riddled with passageways. Otherwise, how could workmen repair the masonry or replace broken windows? This is where we'll find Guy.'

They could hear scuffling noises in the distance. 'He's ahead of us somewhere,' Henri said. 'Follow me.'

The shadowy passageways were connected by steep, narrow steps, and Thomas nearly fell several times as he stumbled after Henri.

There were dark recesses in the walls, too, and Henri held his torch high over each one to make sure Guy wasn't hiding there.

'How do you know your way around here?' Thomas asked when they came out on to a wide gallery where they could stand next to each other.

'The windows,' Henri said. 'I'm sorry it's so dark you can't see them.'

'I have seen them, during the day, down below.'

'But you haven't seen them up close.' He put his hand on the dark surface of one. 'When the sun shines, they seem to be made of jewels. This one – I know you can't see it, but I know it well – is a scene of the birth of Christ. The blues and reds are the most vibrant I've ever seen. I intend to learn the secret of achieving those colors.'

'How are you going to do that?'

'Alchemy.'

Thomas remembered what his mother said about alchemy, that it was practiced by fools who claimed they could make gold of anything. He knew Henri had drawn his grandfather into this delusion, and that it had nearly ruined him.

'I know what your mother thinks about alchemy,' Henri said, as though he could read Thomas's thoughts. 'We won't tell her.' He started off again, taking them through the gallery until they came to another spiral staircase.

'Do you know where we are now?' he asked.

Thomas had no idea.

'I'll show you.' He started down the steep steps, holding the torch high so Thomas could see to follow. When they got to the bottom, he opened a small door and stepped out. The rain beat down, the wind howled, and it was nearly pitch-black, but Thomas could see just enough to know that they were in a courtyard.

'We'll find him,' Henri said. He charged through the rain to the orchard. The trees were just dark shapes, swaying in the wind, water flying from their leaves. Thomas swore as his feet sank into the muddy ground. Henri seemed not to notice.

Thomas began to be afraid. He was even more afraid when he saw Henri approach a dark shape by the wall. Henri and the dark figure struggled for a moment. Then the figure was still. Henri beckoned to Thomas to come and look.

Guy lay on the ground holding his head. 'Someone boarded up the door,' he wailed.

FORTY-NINE

From the fourth week of March until the middle of April this year [1399], the Seine, swollen by its tributaries, flooded its banks and caused great devastation to the countryside along its banks.

The Monk of Saint-Denis, *Chronique du Religieux de Saint-Denis, contenant le règne de Charles VI de 1380 à 1422*

Christine raced out of the prioress's residence and down a corridor, holding the princess tight and resisting the temptation to turn and look back. After a while, the princess became too heavy for her to carry, and she set her on the ground.

'You have to run now,' she cried, barely able to get the words out, she was so winded. 'Take my hand and hold on tight.'

The child grabbed her hand so hard it hurt, and Christine practically dragged her along. The princess was crying and coughing, but she didn't stop. Through the labored breathing, Christine could hear her saying to herself, 'I won't let him get me.'

She could hear footsteps behind her as she raced along deserted passageways and into the cloister. The storm that had threatened earlier now raged: rain battered the grass, and a savage wind buffeted the pine tree. She dashed into the church and turned to see if they were being followed, but she could see nothing but flickering shadows created by candles in sconces on the walls. She stopped at the entrance to the nuns' choir, trying to think what to do. Her eye fell on the figures of Saint Louis's children on the far wall and the door to the underground chapel. She ran to the statue of Isabelle and drew the key to the chapel out from the cold stone folds of her gown. Her candle started to go out, so she threw it down and took another one from a sconce and held it high as she inserted the key into the lock and pulled the door open. She picked up the child and went through, pulling the door shut behind her.

The candle in her hand showed the top of the long flight of stairs;

below that, all was in darkness. She felt around with her foot until she came to the first step and lowered herself on to it. Then she helped the little girl down, standing in front of her in case she fell. How many steps there were, she didn't know, but they seemed endless as they inched their way through the darkness to the bottom. Finally, her foot touched the ground.

'This place smells bad,' the princess said. 'Where are we?'

'In a chapel under the nuns' choir.'

The princess sniffled. 'My aunt wouldn't let me come into such a moldy place.'

'There was no alternative. We had to get away from that bad man.'

'He's looking for me. What are we going to do?'

'He'll never find us here. We'll wait a while and he'll go away.' She imagined Guy searching around in the church, swearing because he hadn't caught them.

'But it's wet and cold.'

'It can't be helped. We'll leave once it is safe.'

There was a sound at the top of the stairs. Christine knew immediately what it was. She broke out in a cold sweat and cursed herself: in her haste, she'd left the key in the lock. Someone had turned it. They were locked in.

The princess heard it, too. She reached out for Christine's hand, and Christine could feel that she was trembling.

'What's he going to do?'

Christine couldn't imagine – unless Guy had torture as well as kidnapping in mind. She didn't think he was imaginative enough for that. She was sure the lock would turn again, and they would hear him creeping down the stairs.

There were several inches of water on the floor, and her feet were soaked. She tried to remember the rest of the room. She knew there were thick columns in the center and on one side several arches open to the priory grounds. The prioress had told her that when it rained, the water seeped in through the grilles that covered the arches. She could hear the water now. It was not seeping in – it was *rushing* in. The rain had been pouring down for days; the river was overflowing its banks and flooding their underground prison.

She remembered the altar, and she hoisted the princess up on to it. There was a window above it, and she could hear the rain hammering against it like a drum.

'You come up here, too,' the child said.

'It's too high for me. But you'll be safe there.' She remembered the statue of the Virgin, and she reached up and touched the hem of the figure's gown, hoping it would bring her luck. The candle flickered and went out.

'Something's falling on me,' the princess cried. Christine felt along the top of the altar and her hand struck a pile of stones and pebbles. Another stone fell. 'Keep your head down,' she said to the princess. She picked up a stone thinking she might use it as a weapon.

But why isn't Guy coming down after us? she asked herself. *If he wants to get the princess, this is his opportunity.*

The water was already up to her knees. She thought of the stairs. If they could get to the top, they'd be safe for a while longer. That wouldn't protect them if Guy came through the door, but it was either that or stay at the bottom and drown. She dropped the stone and lifted the child. 'We have to get to the stairs,' she said.

'Are we going to drown?' the princess asked.

'Not if I can help it.' She held the child high and slogged blindly through the water until her foot touched the bottom step. Still holding the princess, she started to climb, weighed down by the child and her waterlogged gown. Finally, she came up against the wooden door. Exhausted, she slumped down in front of it. She knew there was no use trying to open it. All they could do was wait for Guy to turn the key in the lock and charge in after them. She crouched as far to the side as she could, thinking that as soon as he came in, she'd push him down the stairs. She held the little girl against her chest and moaned in despair. She was supposed to protect her, and she'd failed.

'Don't be sad,' the princess said. 'God will save us.'

I wish I could believe that, Christine thought as she listened to the water rushing in below. She tried to sit up so she'd be ready for Guy, but it was no use. She was too exhausted. She clutched the child. Suddenly, the door swung open, nearly knocking her down the stairs. Someone grabbed her, pulled her through, and laid her gently on the floor.

Christine's first thought was, *Where is the princess?* As if she'd heard, the child, who was lying right beside her, grasped her hand. Someone was holding a taper over them. It was Symonne du Mesnil. Then the prioress appeared. She knelt down and reached for the child. Christine tried to hold on to the princess, but she didn't have any strength. Mother Marie lifted her from her arms.

Christine sat up and looked at the prioress and Symonne. She was cold and wet and terrified. *They've been plotting with Guy to abduct the princess!* she thought. *How could I have been so blind!*

Michel stepped out of the shadows.

Her head reeled. *Michel was in on the plot too! He's supposed to be my friend.*

Michel reached down, took her hand, and helped her up. 'I can imagine what you're thinking, but that's not it at all,' he said. 'You can thank Symonne for saving you.'

'I don't understand.'

'Of course you don't,' the prioress said. 'How could you?' She hugged the princess, who looked up at her and said, 'I told her God would protect us.'

'And He did,' the prioress said.

'Who locked us in the chapel?' Christine asked, her voice shaking.

The princess struggled in the prioress's arms and cried out, 'It was Sister Denise.'

'Hush, child,' the prioress said. 'You know that's not true.'

'It *is* true. Denise did it. She always said she'd lock me in there if I wasn't good.'

'She didn't mean it. Now be quiet.'

'It must have been Guy,' Symonne said.

'How did you know we were there?'

The prioress answered. 'Symonne came to tell me you were in danger. I already knew that, after Michel and I went to my rooms and found the window in my study broken, and you and the princess gone. We looked everywhere for you, and then Michel thought of the chapel. Thank goodness he was right.'

'But how did Symonne know we were in danger?'

'I'll let her tell you. But not here. We have to go to my quarters so you and the princess can put on dry clothes.'

Christine felt unsteady on her feet. When she tried to walk, she stumbled and fell against the door to the chapel, which had swung shut behind her. As she reached back to steady herself, her hand hit something. It was the key. Cursing herself for having left it in the keyhole when she'd fled down the stairs, she withdrew it. Then she felt something else. She couldn't see clearly, but she knew it was a piece of cloth. She pulled it away from the key and stuffed it into her sleeve.

The prioress took her arm and led her to the public entrance to the church. Just as they got there, Marion rushed in and nearly knocked them down. She had a torch, and she held it up to Christine's face. 'It's you. Thank goodness,' she said.

'What are you doing here?' Christine cried.

'I followed them,' Marion said as she stepped aside so Thomas and Henri could drag Guy in.

FIFTY

They do not wear nightdresses, and there are no feather beds; they pass the night on coarse wool blankets and hard mattresses filled with flocking.

Christine de Pizan, *Le Livre du Dit de Poissy*, 1400

Juliana lay awake wondering where Adelie was. Usually, she heard her friend tossing and turning in the bed next to hers, but not that night. She thought about the hard mattresses they had to sleep on, and how much she hated the dormitory and the horrible beds. Adelie had never complained about her mattress before, but perhaps she'd finally had enough. She closed her eyes and tried to sleep, but it was impossible. She got up and wandered out into the cloister.

The wind almost pushed her back into the dormitory, and she had to clutch one of the columns of the arcaded walkway to keep from falling. She sat on a bench, not minding the wind and the rain; they took her mind off her misery. In the center of the cloister, the branches of the big pine swayed and shook, and the rain pounded down on the grass, swamping it under pools of muddy water.

As she sat there, a specter appeared. It was Adelie, crouching and creeping through the arcade, her white habit moving through the darkness like a ghost. She was sure Adelie would turn back, but she didn't; she stepped out into the muddy courtyard and started across it. Juliana picked up the skirt of her habit and followed.

Adelie tripped and nearly fell, but she managed to right herself and slog through pools of mud that shimmered in a strange, ghostly light. Juliana took a big breath and plunged after her, cursing the waterlogged wool of her habit. Adelie came to the door to the room next to the laundry and opened it, but the wind pushed it shut again. Juliana caught up with her and the two of them managed to push it open just long enough to squeeze through.

Inside, Adelie turned on Juliana. 'Why are you here? I don't want you.' She tried to shove her back out the door. But Juliana was stronger, and she was able to thrust her aside. Adelie's small body shook with anger. 'Go away!'

'I won't go away until you tell me what's wrong. Why did you come out here in the middle of the night? Just look at yourself!'

'You look at *yourself*,' Adelie said. 'You're as wet as a duck.'

'Wetter,' Juliana said. She picked up the skirt of her habit and tried to wring out the water. 'This doesn't help. Why am I bothering when there are perfectly good clothes right here.' She ran to the pile of discarded finery and picked up a red houppelande. 'This is too big, but it will have to do.' She took off her veil, pulled her habit over her head, and stood shivering in her chemise. 'Quick. Help me.'

Adelie helped her put on the houppelande. She reached into the pile of clothes, drew out a leather belt, and tied it around Juliana's waist. Then Juliana dove into the clothes and seized a brocaded green houppelande. 'Get out of that wet habit, Adelie. Here's a gown for you.'

Adelie did as she said, and soon both of them were dressed like disheveled noblewomen in gowns that didn't fit. 'Let's put our veils back on,' Juliana said. 'My head is cold.'

Adelie had forgotten her worries in the excitement of getting into the fancy gown, but now she started to cry.

Juliana made her sit down on the pile of clothes. 'Tell me what's wrong, Adelie.'

'I can't tell anyone. Not even you. No one will ever understand. Why should they? I'm an evil person.'

With a sudden movement that took Juliana off guard, Adelie reached under the clothes and drew out the knife that was hidden there. She turned the tip of the knife against her chest and would have driven it in had not Juliana seized it.

'What are you thinking, Adelie!'

Adelie crumpled on to the floor, heaving and moaning with deep sobs that shook her body. Frightened at the sight of such suffering, Juliana tried to take her in her arms, but Adelie pushed her away violently. Juliana fell to the floor beside her. A streak of lightning, accompanied by a tremendous clap of thunder, lit up the room. Adelie clapped her hands. 'God is going to kill me. I won't have to do it myself.'

'That's crazy, Adelie. God won't kill you. He'll protect you and forgive you, no matter what you've done.'

'*You* say that.'

'I know you claim to see and hear things the rest of us don't. Do you really?'

Adelie laughed through her sobs. 'Of course not.'

'Then why do you say you do?'

Juliana was holding the knife loosely in her hand, and Adelie reached for it. Juliana pulled her hand back. 'You can't kill yourself, Adelie. You will go to Hell.'

'I'm in Hell already. I have been ever since I was born. Just look at me. No one could ever want to be with anyone who looks like this.'

'It's ridiculous to carry on like that. Not everyone is born a beauty. Even Mother Marie is not beautiful.'

'Don't talk to me about her. She hates me.'

'She doesn't hate you. She doesn't hate anyone. She'd help you if you'd let her.'

'Perhaps she would have at one time.'

'Why? Have you done something worse than claim to see and hear things?'

Another flash of lightning illuminated the room. For a split second, Juliana saw Adelie's grief-stricken face, and it terrified her. The lightning was followed by a deafening crash of thunder that sent Adelie diving into the pile of clothes. 'You'll smother yourself,' Juliana said, trying to sound calm.

'God is sending the storm to take vengeance on me. You must leave because the next bolt is going to strike me dead. It will set this room on fire. Leave now!'

Juliana pulled houppelandes and kirtles and headdresses off the pile, uncovering the weeping girl. 'That's not going to happen, Adelie. You've admitted that you lie about your visions. Now stop lying and tell me what else you've done. If you tell the truth, God will forgive you.'

'You're not my confessor.'

'No, I'm not. But tell me anyway, and God will hear.'

Suddenly, Adelie stood up and threw her arms around her. 'You're my only friend.' Then she fell to the ground.

She's pretending to be in a trance, Juliana thought. She tried to pull her up, but she was dead weight. She stood in a daze, not knowing what to do. Then she put her arms around the girl and tried to drag her out the door. Adelie moaned and started to move her feet. 'Walk, Adelie,' Juliana said. 'You can do it. We're going to get help.'

'Where are you taking me?'

Juliana thought for a moment. 'King Philip is waiting for you in Reverend Mother's parlor,' she said.

Adelie smiled. 'Let's go.'

FIFTY-ONE

I marvel yet, that anie can be so bewitched, as to be made to believe, that by virtue of their words, anie earthlie creature can be made invisible.

Reginald Scot (c. 1538–1599),
The Discoverie of Witchcraft, 1584

I n the church, Thomas gave Guy a kick. 'Here's the murderer,' he announced.

Guy struggled to get up. 'I didn't kill anyone!'

The prioress held her torch high and looked at him. 'Is this Thérèse's brother?' she asked Christine.

'He's pretty disheveled, but I recognize him because of the eye patch.'

'Where did you find him?' the prioress asked Henri.

'He was hiding in the passageways under the roof of the church.'

'He must have gone there after he locked Christine and the princess in the underground chapel,' the prioress said.

'What are you talking about?' Guy screamed. 'I didn't lock anyone in a chapel! And I didn't kill anyone!'

'Then you'd better explain what you were doing here,' the prioress said. 'But we can't stay here while you do it. We'll all go to my quarters.' She started toward the public entrance to the church. 'Unfortunately, we'll have to go outside and through the courtyard. No men are allowed in the cloister.'

'I thought for a moment this was my chance,' Henri said.

The prioress glowered at him, picked up the princess, and carried her out of the church and into the courtyard, where she was met with driving rain and ferocious wind. Thomas and Henri followed, dragging Guy with them. Marion and Symonne lifted their skirts and tried to step around the puddles, but Christine was already so wet she didn't even bother. Michel swore under his breath as his sandals once again became waterlogged. They sloshed through mud and water, pushed along by wind that seemed to grow stronger with each blast. Lightning forked around them, and claps of thunder shook the ground. Thomas slipped and fell, taking Guy down with him into a pool of water. He struggled to his feet, pulled Guy up, then pushed him down again with his foot.

'Have some compassion, Thomas,' the prioress said.

A flash of lightning lit up the sky. In the sudden illumination, the rain-soaked faces became momentarily visible.

'That's the man I saw in the cloister!' the princess cried, pointing to Guy.

'Are you sure?' the prioress asked.

'Yes. Don't let him get me!'

'Come inside quickly,' the prioress said as she entered her residence. She led them up the stairs to her parlor, where she set the princess down on a chair, hurried to the fireplace, and built up the fire. 'I have no clothes for you,' she said to Thomas and Henri. 'You'll have to stand by the fire until you get dry.' She looked at Michel. 'You can go to the friars' residence and change.'

'Absolutely not,' Michel said. 'I don't want to miss anything.' His wet sandals squished as he stationed himself in front of the fire.

Guy had slumped to the floor. 'Make sure this fellow gets dry, too,' the prioress said. She took Christine, Marion, and Symonne into another room where she went to a trunk and drew out some gowns. 'These are clothes some of my visitors have left. I hope something will fit you.'

Christine started to go to her room to get an extra gown she'd brought from home. The prioress, who was holding the princess in her arms again, caught up with her, took her into her study, and shut the door against strong gusts of wind blowing through an opening in the window. Pieces of glass lay on the floor.

'At first, I thought it was just the wind, but then I realized someone was pressing on the glass,' Christine said. 'That's why I took the princess and fled.'

'That's what we thought,' the prioress said. 'The opening is large enough for someone as small as Adelie to squeeze through.'

The prioress touched a piece of glass gently with the tip of her shoe. 'Fortunately, these pieces fit into a large panel. None of them are broken, and the panel can easily be put together again. It has been loose for some time. All that was needed was a good push. Don't say anything about this to the others. I took them to the parlor so they wouldn't see it.'

'*I* see it,' the princess said.

'You don't have to worry,' the prioress said. 'You're safe now. We're going to change your clothes, and then you will go to bed.'

Christine went to her room and dressed in dry clothes. Then she went to the room where Marion and Symonne were changing. Marion was wearing a bright red houppelande.

'That doesn't suit you,' Christine said.

'Why not?'

'It clashes with your red hair.' She went to the pile of clothes the prioress had left on a chair and picked up a dark-green gown with ermine-lined sleeves and a wide gold belt. 'Here, try this.'

Marion did as she was told, and then stood before Christine looking more like a noblewoman than a reformed prostitute.

'Much better,' Christine said. 'Now, tell me. What made you decide to go into the church in the middle of the night?'

'I was worried about you. I decided to find the prioress and ask her if you were all right.'

'The *portier* let you in?'

'Of course.' Marion looked over at a corner of the room where Symonne was putting on a bright blue kirtle, and lowered her voice to a whisper. 'I was going to tell the prioress about Symonne, too. What's she been up to? What happened here tonight?'

'The princess and I were locked in an underground chapel. A few minutes more and we would have drowned.'

'Saint John's severed head! I knew she was up to no good.'

'It wasn't Symonne. She'd come to warn the prioress that I was in danger.'

'She was worried about *you*?' Marion cried. 'I don't believe it, after what Alips told me about her and the Duke and Duchess of Burgundy. You'd better not let her out of your sight. You can't trust her.'

'Don't worry. I'm not going anywhere,' said Symonne, who'd come over to where they stood. 'Where would I go now, anyway?'

'What does she mean?' Marion asked Christine.

The prioress, who had changed into a dry habit, came in, still holding the princess in her arms. She said to Marion, 'Symonne has told me everything about herself. I'm not surprised she worries that she won't be able to go back to her old life.'

Symonne stood with her hands on her hips. 'I know none of you trust me. But my mother and I were merely pawns in the Duke and Duchess of Burgundy's schemes.'

'I already know part of your story,' Christine said.

'How could you know anything about me?'

'The man who told me is out there in the parlor. We'll go and ask him.'

Henri, Thomas, and Michel stood with their backs to the fire. Guy lay face down on the floor, and Thomas had his foot on his back. Symonne looked at Henri, sighed, and turned away.

'That's the man I mean,' Christine said. 'Do you know him?'

'Of course I do. He's the reason I became one of the queen's ladies.' She turned and faced Henri. 'I should thank you for saving me, all those years ago, but don't think it's been a pleasant life.'

'I don't understand,' Christine said. 'Henri told me it was the Duchess of Burgundy who saved you.'

'Who do you think put the idea in the duchess's head?'

'I'd better explain,' Henri said. 'Women never get the facts straight.'

'We're aware of your contempt for women,' Christine said. 'Just tell us what happened.'

'After Pierre of Craon's unsuccessful attempt to assassinate the king's constable, Symonne and her mother, who'd known nothing of the plot, were about to be executed. I decided to save them. I convinced the Duchess of Burgundy that Symonne would be useful as a spy if she could place her in the queen's entourage.'

'You told us that before. What about Symonne's mother? How did you save her?'

'As you know, there are many magicians and sorcerers at the court, all claiming they can cure the king's madness. Jean of Bar was one of those sorcerers. He was working for the Duke of Burgundy, making figures of the king that could be used to call up demons to help make the king well. I knew that Symonne's mother practiced sorcery, so I convinced the duke to have Jean of Bar take her on as an assistant. After Jean was executed, Péronnette ran away. Now we know she has continued to practice sorcery in the forest here.'

'So you can understand why my mother and I have been beholden to the Duke and Duchess of Burgundy for all these years,' Symonne said.

'That still doesn't explain why you came here,' Christine said.

'When the Duke of Burgundy found out you'd come to Poissy, he assumed you'd been sent to find my mother and expose her for practicing sorcery. He doesn't care if my mother burns, but he does care about his reputation. He doesn't want anyone to know he really believes someone might be able to call up demons to cure the king of his madness.'

Christine looked at Guy, who was writhing on the floor under Thomas's foot. 'Do you know who this is?' she asked Symonne.

'I've not seen him before, but it must be Tassin of Archères' son, Guy, who visited my mother in the forest. My mother told me she'd thought of a plan he and his father could use to get ransom money for his brother who'd been captured at the Battle of Nicopolis. She told Guy that if he abducted the king's daughter, the king would pay a lot to get her back.'

Everyone turned to look at Guy, who was struggling to get free of Thomas's foot. Henri went to him, pushed Thomas's foot away, and lifted him to his feet. 'Did you really think you could get away with it?'

Guy was weeping uncontrollably. 'It's not fair that the duke won't pay the ransom for my brother.' He looked at the princess, who was clinging to the prioress. 'My father and I wouldn't have hurt her.'

The princess turned her face away.

'How did you know about the door in the wall?'

'I found it one day when I was out hunting. My dog was trying to dig out a rabbit that had burrowed under it. The sorceress told me she could make me invisible, and I could sneak into the priory through the door and get the princess.'

'How was she going to make you invisible?'

'With the blood of a hoopoe.'

'You believed that?'

'Of course. She also told me to carve a figure of a hoopoe on something in the priory. The sisters would know it was a magical bird, and then when the princess disappeared, they would think she'd been taken away by the same magic.'

'Did you tell you to destroy the manuscript in the choir, too?' Christine asked.

'No. She asked me to get her a book to use in the ceremonies where she calls up the demons. I saw a big book on a stand, and I grabbed it. I heard someone coming, and I dropped it.'

'Was it necessary to walk on it too?' Christine asked, her voice rising in anger.

'It was only a book.'

Christine turned away from him in disgust.

'How many times have you snuck into the priory?' Henri asked.

'Several times. I don't know for sure.'

'Tell us about the night your sister died,' the prioress said. 'The princess said she saw you in the cloister.'

'I didn't hurt her! Someone else did.'

'Did you know that she was pregnant?' Christine asked.

Guy stared her open-mouthed. He began to shake uncontrollably. 'God forgive me! I had no idea.' He hid his face in his hands. 'Do you think I was there because of that?' he wailed.

'Why *were* you there?'

'When she was home for my sister's funeral, Thérèse found out about our plan to abduct the princess, and I suspected she was going to tell the prioress about it. So I came to take her away so she wouldn't be able to do that.'

'You lured her out of the dormitory by making her think Saint Dominic had come for her,' Christine said.

'She was always talking about Saint Dominic. She told me a story about how when his mother was pregnant with him she saw a little dog with a lighted torch in its mouth. She thought the dog represented the saint, and she said she'd follow him anywhere. So I brought my dog and a torch.' Guy was weeping so hard he couldn't go on.

'Poor Thérèse, half asleep and dead tired, believed Saint Dominic was signaling for her to follow him. You didn't think she'd see you because the sorceress had convinced you that you were invisible. But how did you keep the dog quiet?'

'The sorceress gave me a hare's foot. The right foot of a hare will keep a dog from barking. I lost it.'

'We know,' Michel said. 'It was found by the door in the wall.'

Guy buried his head in his hands. 'I was just going to take my sister home. I didn't hurt her. There was someone else there.'

'Did you know she'd been stabbed? What did you do when you saw her fall?'

'I ran away.'

'Coward,' Christine said under her breath.

'When did you come back?' the prioress asked.

Guy started to say something but changed his mind.

'It's no use lying,' Henri said. 'You've been here since yesterday, hiding in the passageways of the church. You came back to get the princess, didn't you?'

Guy nodded dumbly.

'You followed the princess and the nun who cares for her into the cloister,' Christine said. 'You knocked the nun down, but the princess ran away. You didn't have time to look for her because I came along.'

'Sister Denise was helping him!' the princess cried. 'She didn't try to save me at all.'

'I don't know anything about the nun. She just fell.'

'She said she would lock me in the underground chapel,' the princess said.

'Be quiet,' the prioress said. 'I'm sure she wasn't the one who did it.'

'How did you know about the passageways where you've been hiding?' Christine asked.

'The sorceress told me.'

'I'm not sure this boy didn't kill his sister, in spite of what the princess thinks she saw,' the prioress said. 'Nevertheless, he tried to abduct the princess. He's a criminal. Will you please go and get the provost's lieutenant, Henri?

'He must be the murderer!' Marion cried.

'No,' Christine said. 'It wasn't Guy. And it wasn't Guy who locked us in the underground chapel, either.'

'I told you I didn't,' Guy screamed.

'I told you it was Sister Denise,' the princess said.

'It wasn't Sister Denise,' Christine said to the princess. 'Guy tried to abduct you, and he pushed Sister Denise down in the process. But someone else murdered Sister Thérèse. That person broke a window in the prioress's quarters, chased us, and locked us in the underground chapel. And I know who it was.'

'Then it's about time you told us!' Marion said.

'If you really know,' Henri sneered.

'I do know. Because of this,' Christine said as she drew out of her sleeve the piece of cloth she'd found on the key to the underground chapel and held it up. 'This is linen. It was caught on the key to the chapel. If it had come from a nun's habit, it would be wool – according to the rules of the Dominican order, habits must be made of unfinished wool. But someone was wearing this piece of linen in another way.'

Before she could continue, there was a disturbance at the door. Everyone turned to see Juliana and Adelie, wearing long, wet houppelandes, stagger in. Juliana cradled Adelie in her arms and took her to the prioress

'What happened to your habits?' the prioress asked.

'They were all wet.'

'So you left them in the laundry room.'

'How did you know?'

The princess had hidden her face in the prioress's bosom. She started to cry and shake. 'That's the sister I saw with the knife,' she wailed.

Adelie's face was contorted with fear. In the flickering light of candles and the flames in the fireplace, she looked like a wizened old woman. Juliana set her gently on the ground and stood holding her hand. 'I'm your friend, Adelie,' she said. 'Don't be afraid. I'm right here and I'll stay with you.'

Adelie leaned against her. 'Everyone hates me,' she said.

'Nobody hates you,' Christine said. 'You hate yourself.' She reached for Adelie's bandaged hand. 'Why won't you let anyone see how you hurt yourself?'

Adelie pulled her hand away and hid it under her scapular.

'That won't save you,' Christine said. 'You've done something very wrong, and you can't hide it any longer.'

'Whatever it is, Adelie, God will forgive you,' the prioress said.

'There is no God!' Adelie cried. 'If there were a God, he wouldn't have let me be born.'

Christine held up the cloth she'd taken from the key. 'The person who locked us in the chapel left this.' She drew Adelie's hand out from under her scapular, unwrapped the makeshift bandage, and held it up next to the first piece of cloth. 'These are both linen. Juliana told me that linen is used as the ground for the embroidery the sisters do in their free time. Someone has been using a piece of that linen for another purpose.'

The prioress took a candle and held it close to Adelie's hand. 'What have you done, Adelie?' she cried. 'Your hand is infected. Why didn't you let Sister Geneviève take care of it?'

Adelie tried to draw her hand away, but the prioress held it tightly. 'What are these marks?' she asked.

'They are the marks of a dog's teeth,' Christine said.

'How could she have been bitten by a dog?'

'Because she was there when Guy used his dog to lure Thérèse out into the cloister. The dog attacked her.'

'Is that true, Adelie?' the prioress asked.

'I didn't mean to kill her!' Adelie cried. 'I saw her get out of bed, and I followed her. I just wanted to see what she was doing.'

'Then why were you carrying a knife?' Christine asked.

'I have to protect myself. Everyone hates me. I didn't mean for it to kill Thérèse. I was going for the dog. He attacked me! I lashed out with the knife and got Thérèse instead.'

'Why did you say you found the knife under Sister Petra's pillow?'

'To make it look as if she was the one who killed Thérèse.'

FIFTY-TWO

I admonish and bid you, abbesses and prioresses, don't let any threats or arguments or flattery weaken your spirit so much that you moderate any part of this holy Rule.

Saint Caesarius of Arles (502–542), *Regula virginum*, the first Western Rule written specifically for nuns

Adelie lay on the floor, weeping, and Juliana sat beside her, trying to comfort her. Sister Thomasine barged into the room. 'I've been looking everywhere for you two. Where are your habits? Why are you in those clothes?' she shrieked.

'Calm yourself, Thomasine,' the prioress said. 'Their habits were wet, so they changed them.'

'And where did they get those outlandish gowns?'

'In the room with the discarded clothes left by you noble ladies,' Juliana said. 'Perhaps you'll see something of yours here, Thomasine.'

'How dare you speak to me like that?' Thomasine's face was so white she looked like a phantom. She said to the prioress, 'It's your fault. You must get rid of these two immediately. If word of this gets out, we will be disgraced. And the king will be disgraced.' She looked around the room. 'What are these men doing in here? This is scandalous, Marie. You are not fit to rule this priory.'

'It is time for the night office now. You will be just as disgraced if you fail to observe it,' the prioress said. She went to Adelie, picked her up, and took her in her arms.

Sister Thomasine started to protest, but the prioress held up her hand and said, 'Have some compassion for this poor girl.'

'She must be sent away!'

'That is not your decision to make,' the prioress said.

'It is. When I tell the others, they will decide it is time to elect a new prioress.'

The prioress stood calmly, her hands folded. 'If there is a dispute here, it must be dealt with in Chapter.'

'It will be. I know they will elect me prioress when I inform them of what I've seen here tonight. You haven't even tried to explain it. Who will respect a priory where the prioress allows such people into her apartments? And what about all the mischief that has gone on? Carvings in the refectory table. A valuable manuscript destroyed.'

And she doesn't even know that the princess was nearly abducted, or that Sister Thérèse was murdered, Christine thought.

Sister Thomasine moved toward the prioress, looking as though she would physically remove her from the room.

The prioress stood like a statue.

Thomasine looked at Christine. 'Why did you bring this woman here? Who knows, she may have added to our misery with all her snooping around. And who is this other woman standing there like a harpy with red hair? Have we come to the point where just anyone can barge in here and disrupt our lives?'

Marion stepped up to Sister Thomasine and held a taper in front of her face. 'Your sister sends greetings,' she said.

Thomasine put her hand in front of her eyes to shield them from the light. 'How do you know who I am?'

'Your skin is almost as white as your sister's.'

The prioress handed Adelie to Juliana and put her arms around Thomasine, who looked as though she would faint. 'She's ill. We must make her lie down,' she said.

Christine and the prioress supported Thomasine between them and helped her to the bed in Christine's room. Marion followed, and Thomasine glared at her.

'Did Mahaut send you to humiliate me?'

'Your sister merely asked me to give you her greetings.'

'Why are you so upset about that, Thomasine?' the prioress asked.

'My sister wants to ruin me.'

'I understand,' Marion said. 'Her sister used to be a prostitute.'

Thomasine let out a howl of anguish.

'You're ashamed of your sister, aren't you?' Christine asked. 'You think that if the others find out about her, they will despise you.'

Thomasine began to cry. 'I am disgraced.'

The prioress put her arms around her. 'This is not a disgrace, Thomasine.'

'It is. No one will ever respect me again.'

'Then we won't tell them,' Christine said. 'We won't tell them on the condition that you stop trying to provoke rebellion here.'

Sister Thomasine nodded, her eyes full of tears.

'By the way,' Marion said, 'Mahaut is not a prostitute anymore. She has a shop where she sells herbs and seeds.'

'Just herbs?' Christine asked.

'Well, other things, too,' Marion said. She looked at Thomasine. 'I won't tell her,' she whispered. 'It might upset her too much.'

The prioress went to a cupboard, took out a cup of wine, and mixed it with dried valerian. 'This will calm you and make you sleep,' she said as she held it to Thomasine's mouth.

Thomasine sighed and drank.

'We'll leave you now,' the prioress said. As they went out the door, they heard the woman muttering, 'A prostitute. No one will respect me.'

Marion went back to her. 'What's so wrong with prostitutes, anyway?'

Thomasine moaned. 'Go away,' she said.

They went into the parlor. Thomas stood with his foot on Guy's back, but Henri had disappeared. Then there was a commotion at the door, and Henri came in, bringing the man he'd pointed out to Christine at the inn, the provost's lieutenant. The man strode to Guy and pulled him to his feet.

'Treat him gently,' the prioress pleaded.

The lieutenant scoffed and dragged Guy away.

'What did you tell the lieutenant?' the prioress asked Henri.

'I didn't tell him Guy was planning to abduct the princess. I'm sure you wouldn't want anyone else to know about that. It would be bad for the reputation of the priory.'

'But he and his father will try again!' Christine exclaimed.

'I don't think they will. Tassin of Archères and his son are cowards.'

Just like the son who's being held in Nicopolis, Christine thought. She turned to Marion. 'Do you think the townspeople know what's been going on here?'

'I haven't heard a murmur about it. I would know if they suspected something. People talk.'

'They won't find out from the lieutenant,' Henri said. 'All I told him was that Guy was a sneak who wanted to spy on the nuns.'

FIFTY-THREE

Then it was time to go, and when I kissed the one most dear to me, I became so sad, my eyes filled with tears.

Christine de Pizan, *Le Livre du Dit de Poissy*, 1400

Christine, Marion, Henri, and Thomas stood listening to the sisters chant prime. It was still dark in the church, but candles cast flickering shadows over their faces. Marion took Christine's arm and tried to get her to go outside. 'I want to know what's going to happen now,' she said. 'Then I'm going to bed. We've been up all night.'

'Later. Just listen. We need to hear the music.'

Everyone was quiet for a while, letting the chant wash over them. Even Henri seemed to be affected by it.

When it was over, they all trooped to the inn across from the priory. The skinny waiter was nowhere to be seen. 'He's probably still in bed,' Marion said.

'It doesn't matter,' Christine said. 'We just need to sit here and talk.'

'What do you want to talk about?' Henri asked. 'We've accomplished what we came for. It's time to leave now.'

'There are a lot of unanswered questions,' Christine said. 'For example, how could you have let the Duke and Duchess of Burgundy get Symonne and her mother into their clutches?'

'I told you. They were about to be executed.'

'But if you wanted to save them, couldn't you have thought of something better?'

'Not at that moment. Things were moving at a furious pace in Paris after Pierre de Craon tried to kill the king's constable. Anyone connected with Pierre was caught and put to death immediately, no questions asked. When I saw those two innocent women dragged before the provost's men, I knew I had to do something. I thought the daughter would make a good spy, and I knew the mother practiced sorcery, so I made the suggestions to the duke and duchess.'

'Does your interest in sorcery have anything to do with your interest in alchemy?' Christine asked.

Henri laughed. 'I'm interested in everything. Not like women, who are interested only in housekeeping and babies.'

Christine clenched her fists. She was tempted to get up and leave. But she wanted to learn more about the Duke of Burgundy. She asked Henri politely, 'Since you know about the duke's involvement with sorcery, can you tell me whether he intended to use the image he had Jean of Bar make to help or harm the king?'

'I'm surprised at you. The king is his nephew, you know.'

'Does that mean he wouldn't hurt him if it meant he could gain more power?'

Henri clapped his hands. 'We could use some wine.'

'You don't really know, do you, Henri?'

Henri looked around the room. 'There must be a waiter here somewhere.'

'What will happen to Symonne and her mother now?' Christine asked.

'Nothing. The mother will continue to live in the forest, hiding the sorcerer's paraphernalia when the superintendent is around, and Symonne will go back to Paris and tell the duke and duchess there is nothing to worry about. And you, Christine, will go to the queen and tell her it was all a misunderstanding – the prioress simply wanted you to copy a manuscript. No one will ever know what happened here. I have discussed this with the prioress, and she agrees.'

Michel came in and sat down. 'I heard what you said, Henri, and it is so. Mother Marie has told me everything. She wanted to know whether any of the friars know about what has been happening here, and I was able to assure her that none of them did. All they know is that one of the sisters claims she has visions. I told them the prioress and the infirmaress are taking care of her.'

'Do you think they will be able to control Adelie?' Christine asked.

'Sister Geneviève has some powerful herbs in her storeroom,' the monk said. 'I believe they will keep her calm for a long time. Perhaps, with proper care, Adelie will come to her senses. Mother Marie of Bourbon is a very capable woman.'

'Just as capable as any man,' Christine said, looking at Henri.

'Let's hope she's a miracle worker,' Henri said.

Marion suddenly stood up. 'There he goes!' she said, pointing to the door. They all turned just in time to see the skinny waiter's peacock feather bobbing down the street.

'He won't have to worry about you anymore, Marion, because we'll be leaving for Paris tomorrow morning,' Christine said. She turned to Henri. 'You told me the other day that it's possible Pierre de Craon is around here somewhere. Do you still think so?'

Henri pulled on his black beard. 'I've been wondering how Symonne's mother was able to think up such an elaborate plot for Guy to follow. And who told her about the passageways where he could hide in the church? Yes, I do suspect Pierre may be around, working his evil.'

Christine shivered. 'I hope you're wrong, Henri.'

'Well, I can't prove it, so put it out of your mind.'

Christine said, 'There's something else we have to talk about, Henri.'

Michel put his hand up to stop her, but she hurried to say, 'I just don't understand how you could do such a thing to the girl.'

'Do what to which girl?'

'Your daughter. How could you have put her here? Don't you have a heart?'

Henri got up and started to leave. Marion grabbed his arm and pulled him back.

Henri sat down. 'No one was ever supposed to know this, but I expect I'll have to tell you since you're so insistent. Just like all women.'

'Being a woman has nothing to do with it,' Christine said. 'Or perhaps it has everything to do with it since your daughter is a woman.' She stamped her foot. 'Would you have done such a thing with an illegitimate son? Would you have put him in a monastery?'

Michel put his finger to his lips, and she knew he was cautioning her not to say she knew about Henri's unhappy childhood.

Henri was for once very subdued. 'Juliana is not my daughter,' he said. 'She's the illegitimate child of a friend who died when Juliana was just a small girl. My friend asked me to take care of her. I couldn't do that myself. I thought the best solution would be to put her here. I told the king she was my child. I've been useful to the king in the past, and he makes allowances for me.'

Henri sat back and crossed his legs, obviously thinking he'd explained the situation to everyone's satisfaction. 'Isn't she happy here?'

'Happy!' Christine cried. 'The poor girl is miserable. She has no business being here. And you have no feelings at all. Like most men, you assume that women have no minds of their own and will accept whatever fate men decide they should have. You are a monster.'

Henri sat looking down at the table. 'You are mistaken, Christine,' he said quietly. He got up and strode out of the inn.

'Good riddance,' Christine said.

'Have you talked to the prioress about Juliana?' Michel asked.

'I tried. But there was no discussion. All she would say is that the girl is better off here.'

She stood up. 'I'm going to get ready for the trip back to Paris. We'll meet at the priory entrance tomorrow morning. I suppose Henri has to accompany us, so I'll leave it to you, Thomas, to make sure he's ready.'

Christine found the prioress in her study with men who'd come to repair the broken window. 'They think it was struck by lightning,' the prioress said, with a sly look at Christine.

'Luckily, it's the frame, not the glass, that was damaged,' one of the men said. 'We'll take everything to the workshop and put it back together as good as new. In the meantime, you won't be bothered by the wind or the rain,' he said, pointing to boards they'd placed over the broken area.

The prioress didn't seem tired, but Christine was exhausted. She excused herself, went to her room, and fell into a deep sleep from which she awoke in time to go to the church and hear the nuns chant sext. She went back again for nones and vespers: she wanted to hear as much of the beautiful singing as she could because she knew it would be a long time before she'd have another opportunity. She didn't see the prioress again until suppertime.

'There is no way I can thank you for what you've done here,' Mother Marie said. 'I hope you will visit us another time, under better circumstances.'

The princess came in and climbed on to Christine's lap. 'I told Sister Denise I don't need her anymore.'

The prioress said, 'Sister Catherine has returned. Now she has a proper companion.'

'I think you should apologize to Sister Denise for accusing her of locking us in the chapel,' Christine said.

The prioress laughed. 'I made sure she did that. And I gave her a lecture on humility.'

'I didn't listen,' the princess said.

'Has Sister Denise recovered from her fright?'

'She seems to be all right,' the prioress said. 'She doesn't understand what happened, and I will not tell her. She committed no crime.'

'And Adelie?'

'Only Sister Geneviève and I know what she did. Geneviève and I are determined to help the other sisters understand why Adelie says she has visions and pretends she hears the king's heart. We truly believe that if we can get the others to treat her with the kindness and love she needs, she will change.'

'I certainly hope you're right.'

The prioress smiled. 'I know you have doubts, but you are wrong. You have seen the worst of us here, but in reality things are very different. Sister Claude complains about the choir sisters, but that is only to make them do their best. And you have heard what their best is. Claude is very proud of them, and they know it. Petra and Dorian are hard taskmasters, but they are also capable of great compassion. The same is true of Richarde: she looks stern, but she has a big heart.'

'What about Sister Thomasine?'

The prioress shook her head. 'She's ambitious, and I'm sure that will not change. But I know she will keep her knowledge of what she saw last night to herself, thanks to your friend Marion. She's terrified of losing her reputation for righteousness.'

'There is one other person I would like to ask you about,' Christine said. 'I'm concerned about Madame Marguerite, Tassin of Archères's wife. Is there anything you can do for her?'

'I have been thinking of her, too. She has written to tell me that her other daughter, Suzanne, would like to enter the priory. That would be a good thing, and I will approach the king about it. It would take some of the burden off the baroness's shoulders.'

Christine nodded. *But she will still have to deal with her husband and her son*, she reflected. *No woman should have to suffer that.*

Early the next morning, Marie came to the prioress's quarters to say goodbye.

'Before you go, Mama, tell me what happened. All I know is that Adelie has been confined to the infirmary.'

'It's complicated. But you should understand this: no one was murdered. It was an accident.'

'Does it have to do with Adelie?'

'It does.'

'Then it's better you don't tell me. None of the other sisters know anything about what has been happening here, and I don't want to be tempted to tell them.'

'That's a wise decision, Marie. Things will return to normal at the priory, and all this will be forgotten. I am leaving today, and you can go back to your peaceful life.'

'You sound as though you think I'll be glad to be rid of you!'

Christine smiled sadly. 'Won't you?'

'Of course not! But you must understand, Mama: I'm happy here.'

'I know you are, but we miss you at home, especially your grandmother.'

'*Grand-maman* has you and Thomas and Georgette. And soon Georgette's baby.' She laughed. 'I can't imagine Georgette with a baby.'

Christine said, 'I had hoped to see Juliana before I left. I wanted to tell how sorry I am that I haven't been able to think of a way she could leave the priory.'

Marie smiled. 'She understands.'

'Please tell her goodbye for me.'

'I will.' Marie kissed her mother and left quickly. Christine hid her face so she wouldn't see her tears.

Just as she had gathered up her belongings and was about to leave, Sister Geneviève came in. 'I wanted to thank you for all you've done. It's distressing to think that Adelie has caused so much trouble, but at least we know now that Thérèse's death was an accident, not premeditated murder.'

'All should be well now if you and Mother Marie can help Adelie get well.'

'I think we will.' Sister Geneviève reached into a large sack she was carrying and brought out two small jars wrapped in heavy cloth. 'I thought your mother might like to have some of my headache medicine,' she said as she unwrapped one of the jars. 'It's clearly labeled for that use.' She unwrapped the other jar and held it up. 'This is for aching joints. Older women often suffer that way. It is clearly labeled, too. Tell her to be careful with it. It's a mixture of henbane and hemlock, and it's not meant to be drunk. She should only apply it to troublesome spots.'

'That is most kind of you. I know my mother will be grateful.'

Sister Geneviève put the bottles, carefully rewrapped in the heavy cloth, back in the sack and handed the sack to Christine. 'I'll say goodbye now. Thank you again for all you've done.' The squat little woman wiped her eyes as she went out the door.

Christine went out, too, and found Thomas and Michel waiting for her at the priory entrance.

'Where's Marion?' she asked.

Thomas sniggered. 'She went back to the inn. She said she had something to say to the waiter with the peacock feather in his cap.' He looked across the street. 'I guess she's said it.' The waiter was running down the street, and Marion was watching him, doubled over with laughter.

Jacques was holding the horses and Michel's mule. 'I'd rather ride a horse than a mule,' he said. 'Horses are better-looking.' The mule bared his teeth and brayed.

'You mustn't insult him,' Michel said. 'He can go as fast as the horses.'

'When are you coming back?' Jacques asked Thomas. 'I found the sorcerer in the wood. I'll take you there.'

The *portier* gave his grandson a slap. 'No, you will not take him to the sorcerer. You will not go into the forest again.'

Christine put her hand on Thomas's arm and whispered, 'He doesn't know you followed him. You must never tell him or anyone else what you saw.'

'I know,' Thomas said. 'I can keep a secret. Not like—'

'Were you going to say, "Not like a woman"?'

'Actually, I was. I'm sorry. I've been around Henri too long.'

'Where *is* Henri?' Christine asked.

'I couldn't find him,' Thomas said.

Sister Louise appeared carrying a basket covered with a white cloth. 'Please take this to your mother,' she said as she lifted the cloth to reveal a large cheese. 'It is the finest *angelot*, made for us here at the priory.'

'I know my mother will be overjoyed,' Christine said. Thomas took the basket and held it while she mounted her palfrey. 'You'd better carry it, Thomas,' Christine said. 'I already have all my belongings and a sack with something the infirmaress gave me.'

Sister Louise waved goodbye and hurried away. Then the prioress came out holding the princess by the hand. She said, 'Henri left last night. I'm sure that will please you, Christine.'

Christine tried not to look pleased.

'I don't want you to go,' the princess said. She looked up at the prioress. 'Can't you make her stay and take care of me?'

'Sister Catherine is here now. She'll keep you safe.'

The princess looked at Christine. 'It was clever of me to hide in the tree, wasn't it?'

'Yes, you are a very clever little girl.'

'Clever little *princess*. I don't need anyone to keep me safe. I'll keep you safe, too, if you'll come back.'

FIFTY-FOUR

Farewell to nunhood and the convent. You will not see me here anymore.

Eustache Deschamps (c. 1340–1404), *Virelai* 752

Rain was falling as they rode away from Poissy, and when they reached the forest, they were glad to be under the cover of the trees. Thomas looked around to see if he could find the path he'd followed when he'd been looking for the sorcerer, but the trees were so dense he couldn't spot it.

'Surely you don't want to go back there,' Christine said.

'No. I don't. I don't want to go into *any* forest ever again. I prefer city streets.'

Marion bounced along on her palfrey, and Michel kept up on his mule. He seemed to be enjoying himself. Every so often he chuckled. 'What's so amusing about riding on a mule?' Marion asked Christine.

'I suppose he's just happy to be going back to Paris,' Christine said.

They came out of the forest and crossed the Seine. The water had risen to the bottom of the bridge. It swirled and eddied, grey and threatening. Christine thought of the underground chapel and the water rising to her knees. She shivered.

'That bridge will wash out soon,' Michel said. 'I'm glad we've made it safely across.' He chuckled to himself again.

They crossed the river three more times before they reached the city wall, and each time it looked more menacing. Christine thought of her mother and Lisabetta and Georgette, and she hoped the Seine in Paris would not overflow its banks and flood the streets before they got home.

As they spurred their mounts through the nearly deserted streets of the city, they encountered torrents of water. The horses slipped, but Michel's mule was unfazed. At Christine's house, Thomas tied the horses and the mule to a post, and they slogged through deep puddles to the door.

'*Grand-maman* will be surprised,' Thomas said.

'*She's not the only one*,' Michel said under his breath.

In the hallway, they stopped to take off their wet cloaks. They heard talking coming from the kitchen. Christine dropped her cloak to the floor and rushed in.

Her mother sat at the table holding a baby. Georgette and Lisabetta sat beside her making cooing noises, and behind them stood a young woman wearing a ruffled veil and an emerald-green houppelande with a wide lace collar, long sleeves trimmed with pure white miniver, and big purple flowers embroidered down the front. Christine opened her mouth to say something, but no sound came out. Francesca, Georgette, and Lisabetta looked up and started to laugh. 'I have not seen my daughter speechless before,' Francesca said.

Juliana jumped up, startling Goblin and Berith, who lay under the table. The dogs raced around her feet as she ran to Christine and threw her arms around her. 'I knew you'd think of something!'

'I didn't think of anything,' Christine breathed.

'You must have! Otherwise, why would the prioress have let me go?'

Marion and Thomas bumped into each other as they ran into the room to see what was going on. Michel kept back, rubbing his hands together and chuckling.

Francesca stood up and handed the baby to Georgette so she could hug her daughter. 'I knew you would be home today. My right ear itched this morning.'

Christine held her mother tight. 'I'm happy to see you, too, Mama. But how did Juliana get here?'

Juliana bounced up and down. 'We left yesterday. It was rather late. It was exciting to ride when it was getting dark.' She ran around the room and skidded to a stop in front of Christine. '*Everything* is so exciting!'

'Who's "we"?'

'Me and Henri Le Picart, of course. I'm sorry I ever thought he looked like a sorcerer. He's not like that at all.'

Christine couldn't agree. *He must be playing some kind of game*, she thought. She turned to her mother. 'Henri brought her here? Last night? What did you think?'

'I did not know what to think. I wanted to tell them to go away because as far as I am concerned, anything to do with Henri Le Picart is suspicious. But after he explained how unhappy Juliana was at the priory, I could not refuse to take her in.'

There was a loud squawk from the corner and Marion rushed to Babil, who sat in his cage, shaking his head from side to side and emitting sounds she had never heard before.

'Did you feed him well?' she asked Francesca.

'He ate all the food you brought, and then he ate all the violets I had been trying to save from the rain.'

Marion opened the cage, and Babil climbed on to her arm and rubbed his beak against her shoulder. Francesca came over and scratched his head.

Christine whispered to her mother, 'What did Henri tell Juliana? Who does she think he is?'

'She thinks he is just a nice man who helped her get away from the priory.'

Juliana heard, and she pranced up to them. 'Mother Marie was very nice, too. She told me to choose something to wear from the pile of clothes in the room by the laundry. I decided on these because you told me I looked like a princess in them.'

Christine remembered how scandalized she'd been the day Juliana had thrown off her habit and put on the discarded garments she was parading around in now. She said to Francesca, 'We'll have to get her some other clothes. She can't go around dressed like that all the time.'

'Surely she can wear some of your old gowns. If they are the wrong size, I can alter them.'

'I suppose that's the least of our problems. What on earth are we going to do with her?'

'I do not know, *Cristina*. Can we not just let her stay here for a while and enjoy her freedom?'

Marion said, 'She learned to do embroidery at the priory, didn't she?'

'She did. I've seen one of her purses, and it's extraordinary.'

'The queen and her ladies give me a lot of work. I could use a helper.'

Christine looked at her mother, waiting for her to object.

'Are you sure you are not a prostitute anymore?' Francesca asked Marion.

Marion laughed. 'Even if I were, I'd never put anyone else up to such a profession. Surely you know that, Francesca.'

'I did not mean to insult you.'

'What *did* you mean?'

'I do not know.' Francesca fiddled with her apron strings. 'If Juliana is good at embroidery, she would be a good helper for you.'

Georgette came over with the baby. 'I didn't get a chance to tell you what we've decided to name her,' she said to Francesca.

'So tell us now, before we faint with anticipation,' Marion said.

'At first we thought of Francesca, but that's an Italian name. So we settled on Françoise. That's close.' She handed the baby to Francesca. 'You can hold her whenever you like.'

Francesca hugged the baby and wiped tears from her eyes. Then she reached into her sleeve and took out a letter. 'Henri left this for you, Christine.'

Christine took the letter to the window so she could see it clearly. *My dear Christine*, it began.

My dear Christine indeed! What is the despicable little man up to?

'"Since you believe so strongly that Juliana does not belong at the priory, I'm giving her to you,"' she read aloud. 'Signed, "Henri Le Picart."'

After that, he'd added: *I'm sure you don't believe that Juliana is not my daughter. She really isn't. But if I ever do have a daughter, I hope she will be just like her.*

'What else does he say?' Francesca asked.

'He mocks me, as usual. He seems to have grown fond of Juliana, though.'

'Why do you suppose he wanted to help her?'

'I don't know, Mama.'

Christine watched Juliana grab Lisabetta's hands and lead her in a wild dance around the room. Goblin and Berith scampered along beside them, and the little girl's eyes sparkled.

'I have never seen Lisabetta look so happy,' Francesca said.

'Perhaps Henri isn't such a monster after all,' Christine said.

ACKNOWLEDGMENTS

Thanks to R. C. Famiglietti for invaluable advice regarding the court of Charles VI; Sara Porter, my editor at Severn House, for insightful comments and skillful editing; Josh Getzler, my agent, for constant encouragement; and my husband, Robert M. Cammarota, for his indispensable knowledge of liturgical and editorial matters, and enthusiastic support.